ACCOUNTABILITY

JESSICA AIKEN-HALL

MOONLIT MADNESS
PRESS

ACCOUNTABILITY

ALSO BY JESSICA AIKEN-HALL

The Monster That Ate My Mommy- A Memoir

Boundaries: Scope of Practice Book One

Confidentiality: Scope of Practice Book Two

For Heather, my soul sister.

CHAPTER ONE

The ringing of the phone pierced the stillness of the night. My nights have been sleepless since the evening at Earl's cabin. I stared at the ceiling as I counted the rings, paralyzed by what would meet me at the other end. Tim knocked the glass of water off his nightstand as he felt around for his lamp. Still unable to move, the pounding of my heart became louder than the phone.

With his eyes squinting to meet the light, Tim cleared his throat. "Hello."

Silence filled the empty spaces as he listened. My imagination fed me every possible scenario... well, almost every one. It had spared me for what was about to come.

"Val...are you awake?" Tim set the phone down on the bed as he looked over at me.

"Mhmm." I stretched as I waited.

"Val, it's your gram...she ah..."

The pain from his unfinished sentence took the wind out of my lungs. "No...please no."

"I'm so sorry, Val. They said she went in her sleep." He pulled me into a hug and stroked my hair. "I'm so sorry."

Gabe stood by the door. "Guys, is everything okay?"

"Come on in." Tim patted the side of the bed for him to take a seat. "Val's gram passed away."

"I'm sorry." Gabe's hand rubbed my back. "Is there anything I can do?"

I shook my head. The three of us sat together, huddled in a hug on the bed. I knew it was coming, but I thought I had more time. I wanted to see her once more. I wanted to hear her voice, get one more hug. But my time had run out. All the years I had lost with her came rushing back and landed with a thud in my lap. I wasted so much time.

"They said we could go see her if you want to." Tim pushed the hair out of my face. "They're going to wait to call the funeral home until morning if you want to go."

"I... I just want to see her." The words left me with an emptiness.

"Of course. Let's get dressed. Gabe, do you want to come?"

"Yeah, if you want me to." Gabe rubbed my back before he stood up. "I love you."

Gabe left to get dressed. I sat on the bed, unable to move as Tim pulled on his jeans. The phone rang again, this time it was Tim's. He picked the phone up off of his nightstand and looked down at the display. "Jesus... not today." He blew out a sigh. "Hello." He paused before he continued. "I really can't... not now. We're in the middle of a family emergency."

From the tone of his voice, I knew this was the call I had been expecting earlier. Of course, it would happen on one of the worst days of my life. It couldn't be any other way. He wouldn't be pulled away if it wasn't for me. I did this, and now I had to suffer the consequences.

Tim threw the phone on the bed and pulled his shirt over his head. "That was my boss. There's been another murder. Looks like the serial killer is at it again. He wants me to get to the scene as soon as I can, but I told him..."

"Go. You should go."

"I can't. You can't go alone."

"It's okay. I'll be fine."

"You're more important than this job. You need me, and I need to be there for you." Tim paced the room.

"Gabe would want to go. I'll call Norma, I'm sure she'll go with me."

"I don't know." Tim scratched his head. "I really want to be there for you. I know how important she was to you."

"I know you do. It's fine. This is important, too. I understand."

Tim made the call to Norma for me as I got dressed. She was at the house in ten minutes. Tim and Gabe waited for her to arrive before they left. I was kind of glad I would have some time alone with Norma. We hadn't had a chance to talk alone since the night at Earl's, and I had a lot of questions to ask. It was the perfect thing to take my mind off what was happening.

Tim and Gabe waved us off as Norma turned out of the driveway. Silence circled around us as the pavement hummed under the tires of Norma's Honda Accord. As I waited for her to speak, tears fell down my cheeks. My heart pattered against my chest, intensifying the grief that was to come. With her eyes still on the road, she reached her hand over to take mine.

"Oh, honey, I don't know what to say to make this better." Norma gave my hand a squeeze.

I sucked in the emotion and closed my eyes tight. "Can we talk about... the other night?"

Norma's shoulders lifted and fell with a heavy sigh. "I suppose we should. What do you want to know?"

"Everything."

"You feel up to this now? There are more important things to worry about right now."

"Worry? Why should I be worried?" I turned to focus my attention on her expressionless face.

She let my hand fall and gripped the steering wheel. "I just mean you don't need to hear about my troubles when you have enough of your own."

"Are you sure?" I pulled my hands inside my sleeves. "I can't lose you, too. Please promise me you're not going to leave me."

"I love you, Val. I hope you know that. I can't make promises I can't keep. None of us know what the future holds."

"You're Martha, aren't you?" I felt my chest rapidly rise and fall as it all fell into place. "You do plan on leaving, don't you?" The grief of losing Gram multiplied as I imagined a life without Norma, too.

"Oh, honey, there is so much for me to share with you. I have no plans to leave, I still have work to do."

"I just want you to know your secret is safe with me. I'll never tell."

"I know. I trust you. Besides, how would you explain why you were there?"

"So, my secret is safe with you, too?"

"Of course. All of them." She nodded her head and smiled.

"Since we trust each other, there's no reason not to share with me. What's your real name?"

The smile faded from her face. "Right for the jugular." Her body stiffened as she adjusted herself in her seat. "Well, that's a long story." She turned to look at me as she sighed before returning her eyes to the road. "Rose, but no one has called me that for years."

"I've got time to listen to that long story."

She laughed. "Of course you do."

"How long has it been since you've been Norma?"

"Well, since I moved to Lawrenceville. So about two years."

"What do you want me to call you?"

"Norma is fine. That is who I am... right now."

"How many names have you used? How do you keep track?"

"I'd have to think about it. There's been a few."

"And Martha?"

"Yes, that was me."

"They think you're dead."

"I guess they just stopped looking. People don't really care about missing old ladies without any family. It was just easier to say I was dead than for them to keep looking. That's usually how it works."

"Why did you leave Maine?" I asked.

"I needed a change." She smiled.

"For the same reason? You killed those men, too?"

"I don't like to think they were men. Men wouldn't treat women and children the way those monsters did. I'm more like an exterminator. I get rid of varmint that are causing problems."

"How many varmints have you gotten rid of?"

"I don't know. I guess I lost count."

"What made you want to take care of these problems?"

Norma put the car in park as we arrived at the nursing home. "It's part of that long story. We can talk more after."

The reality of what was happening came crushing back down on top of me as I looked out the window. It was time to say goodbye to one of the most important people in my life. The desire to escape the pain overpowered me. Norma met me at my door and took my hand.

"Come on, honey. I won't leave your side."

I hung on to those words, hoping they would extend past today.

CHAPTER TWO

A short, round woman met us at the nurses' station. Her wide-brimmed glasses were tight against her face, magnifying the sweat rolling off her forehead. With the straw from her cup resting on her lips, she raised one eyebrow.

"We're here to see Marianne Cooper." Norma's hand was still tight around mine.

She looked up at the clock on the wall, and then down to the watch on her wrist. "Umm." She set her cup down and scratched her head. "One moment."

My body vibrated with adrenaline as I watched her walk down the hall. "What's going on?"

"She probably doesn't know what she's doing. The poor thing."

A tall skinny woman appeared in the hall, the short, round woman following behind. "Hi, there." The tall woman gave a condescending smile. "Millie told me you are here to see Mrs. Cooper." She shook her head and placed her hand on her heart. "I'm afraid we have some bad news."

"Ma'am, we are aware that she passed away. We're here to say our goodbyes." Norma matched her smile.

"Oh, okay then. Right this way." The tall, skinny woman held her arm out to point down the hall. "We moved her to our end of life room the other day, so the family could have some privacy."

"Excuse me? You moved her the other day? What's going on? Why wasn't I called?"

"I'm sorry, and you are?" She cocked her head as she stood in front of the closed door.

"I'm her granddaughter. My number is in her file. Why wasn't I called?"

"Her daughter informed us there was no other family to notify."

"If that's the case, how did you know to call Valerie this morning?" Norma stared her in the eyes.

"Well... we... ah... saw her number in the file when we called the funeral home." She ran her fingers through her thinning salt and pepper hair.

"So, you just listened to that bitch and took away any chance Valerie had to say goodbye to her grandmother?" Norma shook her head. The heat from her hand made mine sweat. "That's unacceptable. That's something you'll never be able to make right."

"I'm very sorry. Elaine was Mrs. Cooper's Power of Attorney, it was up to her who we called, and didn't call. The note in the file was from Mrs. Cooper. She wanted to make sure Valerie was notified in the event that anything happened to her. Elaine doesn't know we called you."

I closed my eyes tight and scrunched up my nose to push out the lingering migraine. With my teeth clenched, I tried to push out the anger brewing inside of me. My mother would not be happy until she destroyed me. I could not let her win. "Can I see her, please?" The words barely loud enough to be heard escaped my mouth.

"Yes, of course." She opened the door and let us enter. "Take all the time you need."

The light above Gram's bed was on, making it look like she had a halo. A little smirk on her face made me wonder what she was thinking about as she took her last breath. I could only hope she went as peaceful as she looked. I took small, calculated steps as I reached her bed. I let go of Norma's hand for the first time since getting out of her car and replaced it with Gram's. Norma stood behind me and placed her hand on my back.

"Oh, Gram." The tears hit her skin as I looked down at her body. "How am I going to make it without you?" I rubbed her frail skin under my thumb. "I'm so sorry I let you down." My head dropped to my chest.

"Oh, Val, you didn't let her down. She loved you very much and was so proud of you. She told me so, many times."

"She did?"

"Yes, she did. She told me how proud of you she was for the life you were able to make for yourself after what your mom and Chad did to you. She felt like she let you down. We talked a lot about things."

"How often did you come visit her?"

"A couple times a week since we met at your wedding. She was an exceptional lady." Norma put her finger on the corner of Gram's mouth. "You have her smile, Val."

"You think so?" A laugh pushed away some of the pain.

"I know so. She wouldn't want to see you being so hard on yourself. Try to remember all of the good times you had together and don't focus on the other stuff. She knows it wasn't your fault. She knows you love her."

I turned to hug Norma, the warmth from her embrace filled me with love. "Thank you for being such a good friend to her; and me."

She pulled me in tighter. "You're a good girl, Val. I love you."

The sound of the door opening made both of our heads turn. "What are you doing here?" A voice I hadn't heard in almost two decades penetrated my ears.

Norma stepped out of our hug to look at me before her eyes went to the door. She knew who it was without an introduction. "The question is, what are *you* doing here?"

"And you are?" My mother crossed her arms as Chad entered the room.

My heart sank to the pit of my stomach at the sight of them. It had been years since I had been this close to either of them, but the fear came rolling back in like it had never left. Norma stepped in front of me to place herself between us.

"I think you both owe Valerie the time to say goodbye to her grandmother. You both know damn well you've already stolen so much from her."

Chad took a step back and pulled on my mom's arm. She pushed him off of her and kept her stance, staring at Norma.

"I have no idea what she has told you, but I hope she's been taking her medications." She shook her head. "We all know what a sick, sick girl she is."

"I'm going to ask you one more time to get out of here before I call the police. I am sure they'd love to hear what Valerie has to say. Isn't that right, Chad?"

"Come on, Elaine, let's go get some coffee." Chad's voice trailed off as he pulled on her shoulder to get her to follow him.

Norma shut the door after they left and locked it. "Are you okay?"

My hands covered my eyes as the room began to spin. "Why are they here?"

"I don't know, honey. I'm so sorry you have to deal with this on top of everything else." The weight of her hand helped ground me, bringing me back into my body.

I spent a few more minutes with Gram before I couldn't take being in the same building as them any longer. I bent down, gave her a kiss, and took one last smell of her sweet skin before Norma unlocked the door and led me back to her car. She was on high alert as she looked around to make sure Chad and my mother were not in our path. I scanned the parking lot to see if I could tell which car was theirs, but there were too many to tell.

Before Norma left the parking lot, I saw my mom and Chad standing by the picnic table. "Can we stop for a minute?"

"Are you sure you want to?" Norma looked over to gauge my reaction before she put the car in park.

"I need to tell my mother something."

Norma followed behind me.

"Hey, Elaine." My mother turned around. "I just wanted to see if you had anything to say to me?" I inched closer to them.

She crossed her arms tight against her chest and shook her head. "Not a thing."

"Nothing? You don't want to apologize to me for letting your husband rape me? Or impregnate me?"

"I see you're just as crazy as ever." She turned to walk away from me. "Let's go, Chad."

I pulled her back to me by the strap of her purse. "No, I'm not done with you. You need to know that I didn't need you. You might have thought you destroyed me, but you didn't. I took care of myself; that's something you'll never be able to say. I didn't need you. I never did."

"Are you done?"

"You'll never change, but you know what, I did. So, you can go fuck yourself."

"The only thing you changed was your level of crazy."

I shook my head and walked back to Norma's car. "I hope you and your husband rot in hell."

"I guess you weren't kidding when you said your mother was a bitch." Norma looked over at me to check for my reaction.

"I can't believe they were here. I hadn't even prepared myself for the possibility."

"You handled it very well. Standing up to your mother took courage."

"Yeah, well, you did all the hard work." I laughed as I

thought about the look on Chad's face. "You were awesome in there."

"So were you. You know your mother is the one who is mentally ill?

"Yeah, I do now. It took me a while to figure that out. I thought I was the crazy one."

"Why wouldn't you? When your mom throws that around so much, why wouldn't you start to believe it? She's the one that was supposed to protect you and build you up. I can't stand people like her."

"Now that Gram's gone, I'd be just fine if something were to happen to her."

Norma winked at me. "Life has a mysterious way about it sometimes, doesn't it?"

"I guess you can say that." I looked out the window as my heart rate slowed down. I had wanted to tell my mother that for years. Now that it was off my chest, I could move on. She wasn't going to hold power over me any longer.

"Did you see the look on Chad's face?"

"Yeah, that was great. I hope it made him think."

"I'm sure it did. That was a look of guilt if I ever did see one."

"I wish I would have turned him in instead of running away."

"There's still time. I think it might be just what you need to put that fear behind you once and for all."

"I don't know. I have thought about it. When all those child molesters were found dead, I fantasized reading about Chad's death in the paper."

"You know I'd love to take care of him, but it's too risky. It would be easy to connect the dots to one of us if he turned up dead. If he lived in Lawrenceville, there'd be nothing that could stop me. But with him in a different town and connected to you, and the other guys from the group, I'm afraid Tim would catch on."

"You're right. I hadn't even thought of that." I focused my attention on the trees zipping by the window.

"But, you know what's better than death?"

I shook my head.

"Death of his career and his reputation. Think about it and talk it over with Tim. I think that would be the sweetest revenge."

I played out the possible scenarios in my head. If Chad lost his license, he would lose their only income. The lifestyle they are accustomed to would be ripped right out from under them. And his reputation; if that were tarnished, he'd never be able to make a living ever again. And without Gram's money going to Mom, she would suffer, too. I liked the sound of this better with each passing thought.

CHAPTER THREE

"The Executioner is at it again." Gabe threw his jacket on the back of the couch as he walked to the kitchen. He paused to look at me. "Ah, shit. I'm sorry, I forgot. How are you doing?"

I gave him a half-smile. "I'm alright. So, how was your first crime scene? Bloody or gross?"

His eyebrow shot up and he ran his hand through his hair. "You're sure? I mean... I know you got bad news today."

"Yeah, I'm fine. Death is a part of life. It's what I do, I'm practically an expert in it. So, tell me all about it."

"Well, Tim said I can't share too much. But I can tell you I know what the trademark is. I can also tell you it wasn't that gross, either. I mean, it looked like the killer cleaned up before he left."

"Hmm. That's interesting."

"You're not even going to ask me what it was? What the trademark was?"

"Nah. I know you can't tell me. I'll respect that. I know

this is an important case. Were there any other clues left behind?"

"No, not really. There wasn't any evidence left behind. The guy was just released from jail, but I don't think there was anything in the paper about it." Gabe covered his mouth. "I don't think I was supposed to tell you any of that."

I put my hand to my heart. "Your secret is safe with me. I won't ask any more questions. I don't want you to get in any trouble."

"I've really got to learn when to shut my mouth." He shook his head. "It's just so exciting to think I could be the one to crack it. It would put me on the map. I'd be able to get a job anywhere."

"I know. That would be something, wouldn't it?" I pushed up a smile.

"What are you guys talking about?" Tim opened the fridge and grabbed a beer.

"Oh, nothing." I winked at Gabe.

"For real? You're at it again?" Tim gave me a smile as he walked over to wrap me in a hug. "How are you doing? I've been thinking about you all day."

I looked over at Gabe, who was now sitting on the couch with Gabriel. The feeling of nausea washed over me as the image of Chad came back to me. "It was a hard day."

"Oh, Val, I'm sorry. I really should have been there for you."

"It's okay. I was glad to have Norma with me." I pulled out of his hug to look into his eyes. "My mom was there. And Chad." I tried to keep my voice low, so Gabe wouldn't hear me over the TV.

"Oh, my God. I'm such a dick. I should have been there for you."

"Tim, it's okay. I know you would have been there if you could have been, and I had no idea they'd be there. The thought didn't even cross my mind. Norma was awesome, though." I smiled as my thoughts took me back to the morning. "She told them to get out and let me say goodbye. My mom wasn't going to leave, but Norma mentioned something about knowing what Chad had done and that made him back out of the room. If I hadn't had been so afraid, I would have laughed my ass off at the sight."

Tim cocked his head. "Wow, I would have loved to see his face."

"You might get your chance."

"What do you mean?"

"Norma and I talked about the stuff he did to me and how he was never held accountable. She thinks I should turn him in."

"And what do you think? Are you up for that?"

I looked over at Gabe to make sure he wasn't listening. "I think I am. He needs to pay for what he did to me, and if he lost his job over it, then my mom would have to pay, too. I think it's a win-win situation."

"I understand he should pay for what he did to you, but I don't want to see you get hurt from it." Tim put the beer bottle to his lips and took a long sip before setting it on the counter. "I just worry about what this might do to you."

"You don't think I can handle it, do you?"

"That's not what I'm saying at all. I just don't want to see the woman I love being hurt by some scumbag. I know how much he's already hurt you. I don't want you to have to relive all of it all over again."

"Don't you think I do anyway? I mean, when I look at Gabe." I closed my eyes and shook my head. "I want to make him pay. I want to take his power away from him. Maybe it will give me some freedom."

"Okay. I'll stand beside you in whatever you choose to do. I'm not trying to be a jerk. I know you can handle it. I love you. I just don't want to see you hurt."

"Thanks. I know I want to do this. Maybe once it hits the news, the Exterminator will take care of him."

"Exterminator?"

My cheeks burned as I realized my mistake. "I meant Executioner. Same thing, though, isn't it?" I shrugged my shoulders, hoping he didn't notice the hue on my cheeks.

"I guess you're right." He laughed. "Stranger things have happened. You never know what might happen to a child molester once their secret is out."

"That's exactly the motivation behind finally reporting him. Norma said the death of his career and reputation would be better than his actual death. I'm looking forward to watching his life fall down around him like mine did. Payback's a bitch."

Tim's laugh returned. "I guess I didn't need to worry about you, you know what you're doing. I think that's the perfect motivation."

"Oh, I almost forgot to tell you the rest. As we were leaving, I saw Mom and Chad outside. I asked Norma to stop the car. We got out, and I had the chance to tell my mom all the stuff I'd wished I'd been able to tell her all these years. After all of these years, she's still calling me crazy. I guess she'll never be sorry for what she did to me, or let Chad do to me."

"Wow, Val, I'm glad you had the chance to get that off your chest. I hope you find some peace in it."

"I already have." Seeing Chad and my mom brought back the fear I had been running away from since moving to Lawrenceville. I knew it had never left, but the feeling it evoked was all I needed to move forward. He was going to pay for what he took from me, and he would never steal from me again. If he wasn't going to be killed, I at least wanted to make sure the rest of his life would be a living hell.

"How was your day? Gabe seemed to have a good time."

"It was stressful. Unsolved murder number six and we've got nothing." Tim threw his hands up in the air. "Whoever it is, they know what they are doing. Not one clue left behind... well, except for their calling card."

"That must be frustrating. Was this guy another piece of shit?"

"From the looks of things. He was just released from jail for assaulting his wife. We looked into it, and that piece of information hadn't been published in the paper. From all we can figure out, the guy either knew the victim or knew the wife."

"Well, she'd be a victim, too, if he assaulted her. I don't feel sympathy for the piece of shit."

"Fair enough. You're right. We do know the pattern is consistent with the victims... ah, I mean..." Tim scratched his head. "The dead guys have all been charged with crimes against either a child or a woman. Well, most of them had been charged. Either way, they all had a history of violence against women or children. It leads me to believe the killer is someone from the area. I mean, this is such a small town, it wouldn't be hard for a local to know about these guys. People talk. But that's all we have." He shook his head and took the last drink from the bottle before reaching for another one. "So, we pretty much have nothing. By this rate, if Chad's case hits the paper, you might get your wish."

"And that's the push I needed to make my decision. Goodbye, Earl."

"What did you just say?" Tim's head spun around.

My heart shot up into my throat as I heard the words I had just said. "Uh, goodbye, Chad."

Tim rubbed his eyes. "Huh. I guess I'm just tired."

Between the grief, fear, and exhaustion, I had to make sure I didn't say or do anything to jeopardize Norma's identity, or mine for that matter. That was too close for comfort. Luckily, Tim was just as tired and stressed out as I was.

CHAPTER FOUR

News of Earl's murder was on the front page of the *Village News*. I expected as much, but I wondered if this was how Lily was going to find out. Would the news be a relief to her, or would she be upset? I know Lily still had feelings for him, but it was unclear if they were out of fear. I could only hope his death would bring her the freedom and safety she was chasing.

I took the copy of the paper over to Norma's house. When I arrived in the driveway, it was filled with cars. It looks like I was late for the meeting I hadn't been invited to. Familiar feelings of being unwanted and unworthy brought back the bitter taste of rejection. With my foot on the brake, I pushed back the tears while I thought about driving away. *Why hadn't they called me?* As I exhaled to push the tears back, the door opened. The smile on Maggie's face took away all of the doubt that had been lingering.

She motioned for me to come in as she walked off the stairs. "Hey, Val, what are you doing here?"

Holding the paper, my eyes went to my feet to hide the embarrassment I wore on my cheeks. "I ah...wanted to check on Lily."

"Yeah, that's what we're doing, too. Norma didn't want to bother you with this. She knows you've got a lot on your mind with everything."

"Why would she think that? Of course, I want to be there for Lily. You ladies are everything to me. Besides, I could really use the distraction to get my mind off things."

Maggie covered me in a hug. "We love you, Val, and we didn't want to put any more stress on you. I'm glad you're here now. Everyone will be happy to see you."

Lily was at the table, a cup of tea sitting in front of her. Norma was beside her with her arm around her shoulders, and Sonya was passed out on the couch. "Hey guys, look who's here." Maggie pulled out a chair for me to sit. "Val heard the news and wanted to check on you." She pulled out a chair next to Lily and sat down. "That's sweet, don't you think?"

Lily nodded, her eyes stained with tears. "Hey."

"Hi, Lily. I saw the news, and I wanted to make sure you were okay."

"I'm fine. I guess I'm just in shock. Part of me loved him. I know how stupid that sounds." Lily dropped her head.

"It doesn't sound stupid, not at all. It's alright to be sad," I said.

She sucked air in through her nose. "I just can't get it out of my head. He must have been so scared. He was a jerk, but no one deserves to die like that."

Norma and I held eye contact before we focused our

attention back to Lily. "Maybe he wasn't scared. Maybe he didn't even see it coming. If it'd be helpful, I can ask Tim if it looked like there was a struggle."

"I don't think I want to know. I just don't understand why anyone would have wanted to kill him. He wasn't that bad."

Sonya sat up. "Lily, don't make him out to be something he wasn't. He was a piece of shit. You know it, I know it, we all know it... and we didn't even know him. Don't be sad he's dead. This is something to celebrate. I'm sure Norma can whip up a cake or something."

I shook my head in disbelief. "Wow, Sonya, nice to know you're still your sweet self."

"What? Someone had to say it." Her shoulders rose up.

"It's normal to remember the good in people after they're gone. But, Sonya has a point, too. He tried to kill you. You're safe now. It's okay to be sad, and it's okay to feel relieved." The pep talk was as much for me as it was for Lily. Seeing the aftermath of my attempted handiwork was almost too much to bear. If Norma hadn't killed Earl, I would be the one who was dead. It would have been my picture plastered on the front page of the *Village News*. And worse, Tim would have thought I was having an affair with the grotesque beast. I hadn't even thought about that. I rolled my shoulders to push off the chills the thought had brought with it.

"Are you alright, Val?" Maggie's warm hand pulled me back into the land of the living.

I shook my head. "Yeah. Sorry. I just have a lot on my mind."

"I know you do, dear. That's why we didn't call you. I

thought you could use this time to rest. How about a cup of tea?" Norma got up and walked over to the stove. She turned the burner on under the tea kettle and rummaged through the cabinet. "Here it is." She held up a pink box. "This should do the trick. I think we all need a cup of rose tea."

"Rose tea? Have you gone mad?" Sonya joined us at the table.

"That depends on who you ask." Norma giggled. "No, rose tea is something my mom used to give me to cheer me up when I was a girl. She told me if you drink a cup of rose tea, you get filled with love. It looks like we could all use a little extra love right now."

"Hmm. That's sweet, I guess. I never knew you could drink roses." Sonya placed her hand on her belly. "Hey, you guys, do you want to feel her move? She's kicking."

Maggie reached over and rubbed Sonya's belly. "Oh, she's going to be a feisty one. I think you're going to have your hands full."

"Good thing she's going to have so many awesome aunts who are going to take turns giving her mama a break." Sonya laughed as she pushed her belly closer to Lily. "Come on, Lily, I think she wants to say hi."

Lily shook her head. "Nah."

"Come on, Lily." Sonya picked Lily's hand up and placed it on her baby bump. "You're safe now, Lily. You can have one of these, too."

Lily's eyes lit up as her hand rested on Sonya's belly. "You're right. He can't hurt us anymore."

Norma set a teacup in front of me, a match to the one she gave me at the bridal shower. Our eyes met, and she gave me an approving smile and rested her hand on my shoulder, giving it a squeeze. "Here you go, dear. Drink up."

As the hot tea slid down my throat, I pushed away the thoughts so I could savor the love. She wasn't going anywhere. She told me herself her work wasn't finished. Now wasn't the time to think about what that meant. I didn't have it in me.

"What do you need us to do, Lily?" Maggie asked.

"I don't really know. I guess I need to go to the funeral home. I'm not sure his mom will be able to handle any of this on her own. She hates me, but that's only because of everything Earl told her."

"Do you want us to come with you? Maybe we should go over to his mom's house and see what she needs." Maggie looked around the table at us.

"I don't think she'd like it if we all showed up. Would you be able to come with me?" Lily's eyes dropped to the mug in her hand.

"Of course. Let's go before you change your mind." Maggie picked up her purse and got her keys.

Lily let out a sigh before she stood up to follow. "Yeah, I guess you're right. The sooner we get this over with, the better."

When Lily and Maggie left, it gave me the perfect opportunity to talk with Norma and Sonya about my decision to report Chad. I hadn't wanted to turn today into a therapy session for me while Lily was hurting, but now seemed like a good time to get a plan in place. The best part was I knew I wasn't going to have to do this alone.

"Did Norma tell you what happened?" I took a drink of tea and waited for Sonya to answer.

"Yeah, I'm sorry about your Gram."

"Thanks. I'm trying not to think about that." I looked over at Norma. "I meant the other part."

"What other part?" Sonya picked up a peanut butter cookie and took a bite.

"The part where my mom and Chad were there."

"Holy shit. Nope. She definitely didn't tell me that."

"What can I say? I'm good at keeping secrets." Norma raised her eyebrows and took a sip of tea.

"I appreciate that." I gave her a smirk before I continued. "So, as I said goodbye to my gram, my mom busted in and tried to kick me out. Luckily Norma was with me. She kicked them both out."

"That must have been awful." Sonya took another bite of the cookie.

"I was terrified at first. I was so upset about losing Gram, the thought hadn't even crossed my mind. But when I saw Norma light into them, I knew I was going to be alright."

"I can't imagine Norma being mean. You've got to be exaggerating."

"Oh, mean Norma only comes out when she has to." Norma folded her hands in front of her.

"Anyway, after talking with Norma, and Tim, I'm ready to turn Chad in."

"Turn him in? As in... for what he did to you as a kid?" Sonya raised her eyebrow. "Whoa. That's brave. Are you sure you want to deal with all that? I mean, if you get pregnant anytime soon, you don't want to deal with that stress."

"That's even more reason to do it. The longer I don't do it, the more chances he has to hurt other girls. It's already been twenty years; I don't want to think about all of the girls he's probably already done it to."

"Don't go there, Val. You weren't ready before. You can't be held responsible for his actions. What's important is that you're ready now." Norma rested her hand on top of mine.

"She's right. But have you thought about how this might affect you? I don't want to see your quest for justice tear you apart." Sonya brushed the hair out of her face before she leaned onto the table.

"Nonsense. Don't take this away from her. She's a strong girl, and she has all of us and Tim behind her now. This isn't going to break her. It's going to give her back the power he stole from her all those years ago." Norma squeezed my hand as she smiled at me. "You're a strong, capable, beautiful, determined woman. I know you have what it takes."

"Hey, if you're up for it, I'll support you. Let's make the bastard pay." Sonya stretched her arms above her head. "Wouldn't it be nice if he'd just end up dead? Like all of the others? Then you wouldn't have to deal with any of it."

"Yeah, but this is the next best thing. Maybe it's better. He's going to be exposed. Everyone is going to know what kind of person he is. He'll lose his job, and if it goes well, he'll go to jail."

"Sounds like you've given this some thought," Sonya said.

"I have been thinking about it since I read about the serial killer. I was so mad at myself for not turning him in. I imagined reading the headline of his murder, and then was angry because no one knew who he really was, except me."

"I get that. Donald Brice died without anyone knowing who he was or what he did to me." Sonya paused as she stared up at the ceiling. "But, I'm okay with that. I know he'll get his wherever he went."

"That's right. Sometimes the true punishment is out of our hands." I shot Sonya a smile as I imagined what would happen to Chad. I was ready to set the plan into action and wait for his punishment to be handed to him. He was about to have his life turned upside down. I couldn't wait.

CHAPTER FIVE

I counted the rings as I waited. The sweat had already started dripping down my forehead. Three. Four. "Hello, Stark County Victims Advocacy Program, this is Cheryl."

"Hi. I ah... was given your number by my husband, Detective Tim Phillips."

"Ah, yes, Valerie, I was expecting your call."

"You were? He told you?"

"He sent me an email to let me know. When would you like to get together? I can come by your place, or you can come here."

"I'd like to meet you there. Do you have time now?"

"Of course. I'll be here until 5:00. Do you need directions?"

"No, Tim showed me where your office was. It should take me about twenty minutes to get there."

When I hung up the phone, I picked Gabriel up and gave him a hug. "I'm so scared, buddy." I kissed the top of his head.

"Don't tell anyone. I don't want them to think I can't handle it. I *need* to do this. I can't let that prick take any more of my life." I set Gabriel on the couch and headed for my car.

I tried to push out the thoughts of Tim cheating on me with Cheryl. They were stupid, anyway. I know it's just stress making me think these crazy thoughts. But, why did he have to email her that I was coming? Did he have to warn her I was crazy or something? Did he have to repay her for helping me? One thought led to another and soon, it was all I could concentrate on. *Stop it!* Tim loves me. I know he was just trying to be supportive. I'm just glad now that I told him I wanted to do this alone.

I flipped on the stereo and let Tom Petty take me out of my head. My old standby, *Wildflowers* was on. The second Tom's voice hit my ears, I was able to breathe and push out all of the negative self-talk. I could always count on the melody to soothe my soul. When the song ended, I hit the button to play it again. Today was going to need a few songs on repeat.

Crawling Back to You began to play as I found a parking space. I let the song finish before I turned off the ignition. I had no idea what to expect. I had never reported anything like this before. I hadn't really thought too deeply into what I would have to say. I knew if my mind took me down that path, I wouldn't have come.

When I got out of my car, I straightened my shirt and ran my fingers through my hair and shook off the stress that had settled on my shoulders. At the door I saw a sign with Cheryl Sinclair's name and knew I had picked the correct door. Inside there was a young receptionist with a headset wrapped around her face. I stood in front of her waiting for her to acknowledge me.

"No, Tony, I told you we can't do *that*."

I cleared my throat and jingled my keys to try to get her attention.

"I'll talk to you later." She took the headset off and smiled. "Hi, are you," she looked down at a piece of paper. "Valerie?"

I nodded and tightened the grip on my keys, letting the edges dig into my skin.

"Have a seat, and I'll let Cheryl know you're here." She pointed to the group of three chairs in the small makeshift waiting room before she picked up the phone. "Valerie is here to see you."

The door behind her opened before she hung up the receiver. An older woman with fluffy white curls and glasses smiled at me. "Hi there, Valerie. I'm Cheryl. Why don't you come on back with me?"

A small chuckle escaped as I smiled. This was the woman I thought Tim was going to leave me for. I should know him better than that. I held out my hand. "Hi, nice to meet you. Thanks for meeting with me so quickly."

I followed her into her office as she closed the door behind her. "No problem. I'm glad you decided to come."

I pulled up the chair in front of her desk and sank into it. In the moment I felt so small. The little girl who had been violated by the people she should have been able to trust made her appearance. The tears started to fall before Cheryl took her seat.

"Oh, honey. I know this isn't easy, no matter how long it's been." She handed me a box of industrial strength tissues.

The scratchy tissue ripped as I pulled it out of the box. Pieces fell onto my lap. When I had a big enough piece, I blew my nose. "How much do you know?"

"Tim didn't share anything with me. All he said was the crime happened many years ago. I think it's best to hear it directly from the source. That way you can tell me only what you want me to know."

I squeezed my eyes together. "I don't even know where to start."

"You just take your time." She sat back in her chair and folded her hands as they rested in her lap.

"It's... I mean it was my stepfather." I swallowed to get moisture back in my mouth. "Well, it actually started when he was my therapist. I was thirteen." I focused my attention on the calendar behind her, not taking my eyes off of it so I wouldn't have to look at her. "It started with him showing me his... penis." I filled my lungs with fresh air before I exhaled through my pursed lips. "It progressed into much worse. He eventually started raping me. He told me he was trying to teach me what men want. I begged my mom to stop making me go, but she didn't listen. She ended up marrying him. When we moved into his house, I got pregnant. I finally told my mom it was his and she sent me away and made me give my baby away." I clenched my teeth and gave her a fake smile, finally able to make eye contact.

"Oh, Valerie. I am so sorry that happened to you."

"It's fine. It was a long time ago." I shrugged my shoulders as the fake smile evaporated.

"No, honey, it's not fine. I'm sure this still haunts you. If you are ready to move forward, we will have enough to press charges."

"Okay."

"Do you feel like you're ready?"

My body stiffened as I nodded.

"I do have to warn you, though. When we move forward you will have to tell your story a few times. And, you will have to give as many details as you remember."

Waves of nausea washed over me. "Okay."

"I'll be right by your side the whole time, if you want me to be."

"I'd like that."

Cheryl reached out her hand to me. She gave it the same type of squeeze Norma does when I need it the most. "I can get the detective on the phone as soon as you're ready."

"I'm as ready as I'll ever be."

"Okay." She picked up the phone. "Let's go get the dirt bag." She pushed up her glasses with her index finger before punching the numbers on the keypad. "Hey, Detective Campbell, do you have some time to stop by my office to take a statement?" She nodded her head and gave me a smile. "Great, see you in a few." The phone clicked down on the receiver. "He's on his way. Do you want a drink or anything while we wait?"

I shook my head. The migraine I had been expecting hunkered in as the magnitude of what was about to happen hit me. "Actually, can I have some water?"

"Of course." She got up from her desk and left the room. I took the opportunity to send Tim a text. I wished I hadn't wanted to do this alone. "Talking to Detective Campbell in a few minutes." I stared at the message before deciding to send it. When Cheryl came back in, I sent the message and put my phone back in my purse.

"Here you are." The cold plastic cup of water was just what I needed to reground myself. "Do you know Detective Campbell?"

"I don't think so." With my free hand I rummaged through my bag to find the Excedrin. I pulled out the bottle and placed the water between my knees. I hadn't noticed before how much my body was trembling until the unstoppable rattle of pills filled the room.

Cheryl reached her hand out. "Here, let me help you." She examined the bottle after I handed it to her. "Headache, huh? You know it's okay to feel scared or angry, or however you feel. You don't have to do this alone. Do you think you'd like to have Tim here with you?"

"Nah, I don't want to bother him. Besides, this happened so long ago. I'm over it." I popped the pills into my mouth and emptied the cup.

"Valerie, it's still okay to be affected by what happened to you. Especially now that you are talking about it. This kind of thing can take a real toll on us. When we bury the pain for so long, it is only natural for it to come back with a vengeance. Be gentle on yourself. This is a big deal, and a huge step toward your healing."

I hadn't thought about bringing anything to the surface. As soon as she said it, I knew she was right. I knew all of the feelings I had been pushing away were because of this. Not because of

Gram. Not because of Earl. Because of Chad. Because of the memories I had stuffed down as deep as I possibly could for the past twenty years. Pandora's Box was about to be opened, and I knew there was no turning back now. I couldn't let my fear hold me hostage any longer. I had to ride the rollercoaster before me in order to get out of the amusement park that had become my life. "I'm ready. I don't have any other choice."

Whistling and the ring of the bell on the front door caught my attention. "That must be Detective Campbell. He's one of the jolliest guys I know." Cheryl ruffled up her grey curls and opened her door. "Hey there, Jack, it's nice to see you."

He took off his hat and bowed his head to her as he walked past her to join us in her office. He held his hand out to me. "Hi there, I'm Detective Campbell, but you can call me Camp."

His massive hand wrapped completely around mine before he sat down. "Hi, I'm Valerie Phillips."

"Oh, are you any relation to Detective Phillips?"

"He's my husband." Embarrassment added another layer of warmth as I noticed the sweat had already soaked through my shirt.

"He's a good guy. Always willing to help out when we need him." Camp paused. "He's not why we're here, right?"

"No."

Camp wiped his forehead. "Phew. I didn't think so, but you never know."

"Valerie would like to report a sexual assault that took place when she was a child. She is ready to make a statement." Cheryl looked over at me. "You still doing alright, Valerie?"

I shook my head and rubbed the palms of my hands on my jeans. "I'm fine."

Camp pulled out a notepad and a pocket-size recorder. "You okay with me recording your statement?"

"Yes."

"Okay." Camp held the device up to his squinted eyes before setting it on Cheryl's desk. "Have you ever given a statement before?"

"No."

"Okay. Well, I'll ask you some questions and I'll need you to speak up, loud enough for that thing to hear you." He pulled the cap off his Bic pen. "Oh, yeah, I'm going to need you to say yes and no, you know? Make sure you don't just nod your head."

I nodded. "Yes. Sorry about that. I guess I'm just nervous."

"Don't be sorry, it's alright. We can go as slow as you need. Take your time and tell us as much as you can. The more I have today, the sooner we can take action."

"Take action?"

"Well, it won't be up to me what happens, but if we have enough, we might be able to have him arrested as soon as this afternoon."

I rubbed my hands on my jeans again. "Could I get another cup of water before we begin?"

"Of course. I'll be right back." Cheryl gave me a sympathetic smile before she left the room.

Camp fumbled around in his briefcase. His giant presence was more than just his size. He seemed to fill the entire room as soon as he entered it. He was what they meant when they say larger than life. I tried to picture what he might have looked like as a younger man. I imagine he was handsome and distinguished. Now, his belly rested on his lap, and his pants ended long before his boots began. I was intrigued by the attraction Cheryl had towards him. There was obvious, and uncomfortable, sexual tension between them.

Cheryl returned with two cups of water and placed them on her desk in front of Camp and me. "Alright, Valerie, are you ready to get started?"

I nodded and closed my eyes. "Sorry. I mean yes."

Camp's laugh roared through the tiny room. "It's fine. It's a hard habit to break. Just remember to take your time and be as detailed and specific as possible." He looked at his watch and clicked on the recorder. "This is Detective Jack Campbell with the Stark County Sheriff's Department, today is September 4, 2016, it is 3:35 p.m. and I have Valerie Phillips here with me today at the Stark County Victim's Advocate Center." He took a drink of water and wiped his mouth with the back of his hand. "Can you state your name for me?"

"Valerie Williamson Phillips."

"Can you tell me what it is you would like to report?"

"Umm. I ah..." I looked up at Cheryl and saw her smile and nod. "I would like to report a sexual assault that took place from the time I was thirteen until I was fifteen by my stepfather, Dr. Chad Ross."

"Can you tell me how long ago that was?"

"It was over twenty years ago."

"Can you go into detail the events that took place?"

"When I was thirteen my mom made me go to counseling, that's how I met him."

"By him, who do you mean?"

"Dr. Chad Ross. My mom thought he would be good because he had a PhD, she said that made him a real doctor." I rolled my eyes. "I didn't like him, I knew right away that I didn't want to work with him, but my mom didn't care. It started off slow. He started by touching my breasts with my shirt on, and then he had me take my shirt off so he could examine me."

"You counselor was examining your breasts?" Camp held up his index finger. "Could you be more specific?"

"Sure. He made me take off my shirt so he could look at them... my breasts. He said he needed to make sure I was developing properly. Then he started touching them. First with his hands and then with his mouth." I paused to take a breath. "Then he had me touch him."

"Where did he make you touch him?"

"His penis." As the questions continued, I found a place to go inside myself where I could remember without feeling. There were so many details to share, it felt like I was that scared little girl all over again. With each detail I uncovered, more came. Some I hadn't thought about in years. As the words left my mouth, the anger grew inside of me. I was ready to do what it took to make Dr. Chad Ross pay for what he did to me. It was time he knew what fear felt like.

As the hours passed by the sun began to set. There were still more details to share. More secrets to expose. I wanted to make sure everything was out in the open. I would no longer be his prisoner, but I was willing do whatever it took to make him mine. When I spoke my last words, Camp looked down at his wrist.

"Is there anything else you'd like to add, Valerie?"

"No, that's everything that I can remember right now."

"Okay. This is Detective Jack Campbell ending the statement of Valerie Williamson Phillips on September 4, 2016. It is now 6:12 p.m." Camp clicked off the recorder. "You did a great job, Valerie. I'm really sorry you had to go through all that."

"It's okay. It gets easier with time." I cracked my knuckles and stretched my legs.

"So, I have to ask you, do you want to press charges?"

"Absolutely." A surge of strength came from the anger that had been festering for the last twenty years.

"I was hoping that was going to be your answer." Camp looked at his watch and stretched his arms over his head. "How do you feel about us going to talk with Dr. Ross tomorrow?"

Disappointment lingered with his suggestion and it must have been painted on my face.

"Hear me out." Camp looked at his watch again. "By the time we get to his house, it's going to be late. It's going to be dark. He might come in and get out before morning. No one is going to know about any of this until it goes to trial. But, if we go to his office tomorrow morning, people are going to know. They're going to talk. He's going to be embarrassed."

My cheeks rose as my smile grew. "Okay. I like the sound of that." I imagined the look on his face when the police burst into his office and hauled him away in handcuffs. "Yeah, I think waiting until morning is a good idea."

"Alright." He rubbed his hands together. "Tomorrow it is. I'll give you a call to let you know what happened." He placed the recorder, his notepad and pen into his briefcase and buckled it shut. He reached his hand out. "It was a pleasure meeting you. I'm sorry it was under these circumstances, but I am looking forward to getting you the justice you deserve."

"Thank you for all of your help."

"No problem." He placed his hat on his head. "Tell Detective Phillips I said hi. It was nice to see you again, Cheryl."

"It's always a pleasure." Her cheeks blushed as Camp shut the door behind him.

"You like him, huh?"

"What?" She placed her hand on her neck. "Him? Oh, no, of course not. It's strictly business."

"Yeah, that's what I said about Tim, too."

She laughed. "He's a good guy. That's all. They don't come around that often these days. But, enough about that. You should get home and get some rest. You did a lot of hard work here today. Should we call Tim to come pick you up?"

"No, I'll be fine. I could use the quiet time on the drive home to unwind a little before he starts asking questions."

"You did great today, Valerie. And remember, I'm going to be by your side every step of the way. Try to relax, maybe take a hot bath or watch a funny show to get your mind off of everything."

"That's not a bad idea. Thank you for everything and for believing me."

"Why wouldn't I believe you?"

"My mom didn't believe me. Not even after I had his son. I guess it just surprises me when people who don't even know me are more supportive than the ones who were supposed to love me. I guess it just messes with my head sometimes."

"I do believe you, Valerie. I wished some of the things you said weren't true, but I believe you. I want Dr. Ross to get what he deserves, and I can tell you're ready, too."

"I am. I never thought I'd ever tell anyone what happened, and now..."

"Yeah, before you know it, this is going to be making headlines."

"Headlines?"

"Well, yeah, he's a doctor who has been treating patients all these years. So many people trust him. This is going to send shockwaves through the whole community. I wouldn't be surprised if more women come forward."

I wasn't sure if that was a good thing or not. I hadn't prepared myself for the possibility of the whole world knowing. It was too late to back out now. I had to remember what was most important. Making Chad pay. And if more people came forward, the better it would be. All I could do was wait and see.

CHAPTER SIX

I wasn't able to sleep. Every thought took me deeper down the path of self-destruction. I knew I was doing the right thing, I just had to keep telling myself that. I pictured news cameras in my face as I enter the courthouse with a swarm of people watching. Would people really care? Cheryl could be wrong. Chad might not be as loved and trusted as she thinks. Unless she knows him. What if she gave him a heads up and he takes off?

The voice in my head was probably my biggest enemy. It never failed to bring me down even further than I already was. That's something I wish I could learn to control. Therapy would do me good, but there was no way I could trust anyone, not after Chad. The circle of thoughts wove an intricate pattern in my mind. Creating problems and then solutions and then finding all the reasons they would never work.

Before I knew it, the sun was up, and Tim's alarm buzzed louder with each passing minute that he didn't hit the snooze button. Blissfully unaware of the hell I was in all night. I didn't blame him, though. I told him I was fine. And maybe I was before my thoughts got the best of me. There were still some things he didn't know about me. Like when I say I'm fine, I'm usually not. Or Stephanie Mills; he didn't know about her, and I pray to God he never will.

Shit. I forgot to deactivate that account. My pulse beat against my neck as I imagined the police linking me to that account. I can't believe I forgot. I elbowed Tim. "Hey, turn that thing off."

He reached over and smacked the top of the alarm clock. "Sorry." He burrowed his head into his pillows.

"Hey." I rolled over and put my head on his chest. "I can't sleep."

"Huh?" He didn't even lift his head.

The sigh I let out was louder than I expected but matched my frustration. I pushed the covers off of me and went into the living room. I picked my iPad up off the coffee table and logged onto Stephanie Mills Facebook page. I clicked open the conversation with Earl and read through some of the last messages. If anyone else thought of doing this, it would show that Stephanie was the last person to see him alive, and with all the technology out there, I'm sure it would be easy to figure out it was me.

I closed my eyes and thought back to the night at the cabin. I tried to picture where his phone was. I should have taken it with me and destroyed it. I wasn't thinking. I guess that's what happens when your life flashes before your eyes. My hope was since Norma left her trademark at the scene; they wouldn't look any deeper into it. But if I had his phone, I could at least get rid of the evidence that would lead them back to me. You live and learn, but this was one hell of a lesson.

There would be no more Stephanie Mills. No more secrets from Tim. No more murders. No more mistakes. There was too much to risk. I clicked on the deactivate button as Tim walked into the room.

"What are you doing?" Tim reached his arms over his head and stretched as he yawned.

"Oh, nothing. I just couldn't sleep." I closed the iPad and set it back on the coffee table.

"Why didn't you wake me up?"

"And disturb Sleeping Beauty?"

"Funny." He sat next to me on the couch. "Are you okay?"

"Yeah. Well, no, not really. I'm kind of freaking out. I don't know what's going to happen, or when."

"Just try to relax, and let Campbell do his job."

"I know. I just keep playing it over in my head. I want him to get in trouble, but I don't want the whole world watching."

"I get that."

"Do you really? I don't think you understand how much this scares me. For twenty years I held this secret close, and now, everyone is going to know. Everyone is going to look at me differently. I can't do the whole poor Val thing."

"Don't get so far ahead of yourself. We don't know what's going to happen, or how much press this is going to get. Besides, it might be helpful that he doesn't live in Lawrenceville. At least that will give you some distance from the whole thing." He put his hand on my knee. The act that would have usually comforted me, made me feel uneasy.

"I don't know." I moved my leg to push his hand off of me. "I just wish he'd hurry up and call me."

"I can give him a call if you want, but it's only 7:30. I really doubt you'll hear from him before lunch."

"Ugh. That's like five hours from now." I pushed out the sigh that was building in my chest. "I should just go to work."

"No, you should go to Norma's, or see if Sonya wants to hang out. You shouldn't go to work yet. You've got too much going on."

"Like what?" Annoyed by the sound of his voice I felt the bite from my words.

"Whoa. Val, I know you have a lot on your mind, but I'm not the enemy. I love you. I want to be here for you, but you can't push me away."

"Sorry. I just feel agitated today."

"I get it. You're grieving, and now you add Chad to the mix and anyone would be agitated."

And you add almost being killed and being at the scene of a murder to it, and there is even more reason to want to climb out of my skin. "I'm sorry. I guess you're right. I should see if the girls want to help take my mind off things today."

"You know I would if I could, but there is too much going on at work right now. I'll make it up to you, I promise."

"I know. I'm not mad at you. I love you. I just don't even like how my own skin feels on me right now."

Tim gave me a kiss and took my hands. "I love you Mrs. Phillips. I want to do everything I can to make sure you have the best life possible."

"You do. I'm grateful to have such a sweet man to call my husband. It's just the memories that I had to go back to yesterday were too much. I didn't want to tell you how much it all bothered me, because I guess I didn't want to admit it to myself."

"You don't have to be so tough. Have you given any thought to going to counseling?" The look on Tim's face let me know he regretted asking me as soon as the question left his lips. "I only ask because I know how helpful it can be, and I know how long you've been holding all of this in."

"I have been thinking about it. I'm just scared. I don't have the best luck with therapists." An uncomfortable laugh fell out of me.

"I know, but they're not all like Chad. Maybe you could find a woman that you're comfortable with. I'm sure there are a few around."

"Yeah, I have a list of them at work. I'll take a look at it sometime." I was almost positive that was another lie to add to the books. Even though I've been thinking about it doesn't mean I was planning on it. "You're going to be late for work, you better get in the shower."

Tim looked over at the clock on the satellite box. "Ah, shit, you're right. I got to get Gabe up, too. We have another long day ahead of us."

"I'm sorry." I partially felt guilty for the work all of the unsolved cases had caused him, but there was no way I was going to give up any information I had. It wasn't worth the risk of losing Norma.

"You don't have anything to be sorry for. I'm the one that's sorry. I wish I could spend the day with you. If we get lucky, we'll figure something out and I'll get my life back. Six unsolved cases." He shook his head. "I just don't get it. I don't understand how someone is *that* good. Six murders and no clues. It's a shame they don't use that skill for good."

"You don't know, maybe they do." I shrugged my shoulders as I looked out the window.

He shook his head. "The frustrating part is we probably walk past them on the street and have no idea. I wish I could get inside their head. You know, think like them."

"Nah, I don't think you'd like that. Think about the hell this person probably lived through to be able to be so good at something so awful."

"Hmm. I forgot you're on their side."

"Yeah, maybe I am. It's not like they killed anyone that didn't deserve it. The way I look at it, Lawrenceville has six less monsters. So what if there's one killer? If you're not a scumbag, you're safe. That doesn't seem like such a bad thing."

He bent down and gave me a kiss. "Hey, if you're lucky, they'll strike again after your case hits the paper. And, it will be out of my jurisdiction at that point. Kill two birds with one stone."

"Now you're talking." I gave him a smile and thought about the possibility. Maybe Norma was wrong. Maybe they wouldn't link the cases back to me.

When the guys left, I finished getting ready and went to Norma's. I didn't want to spend the day waiting for the phone call from Camp alone. The ringing of my phone made my heart drop. I had been waiting for this call but wasn't really expecting it so soon. I pulled over just a couple houses from Norma's. "Hello."

"Is this Valerie Williamson?"

"Umm. No. Well, yes. Who is this?"

"I'm calling from the Law office of Peter Berkley. He would like to schedule a time for you to come in and meet with him regarding the will of the late Marianne Cooper."

"Okay. When are you thinking?"

"The sooner the better, ma'am. He has some openings this afternoon, and a couple spots tomorrow, as well."

"Today is not really a good day, but I can probably make it tomorrow. Where are you located?"

"We are at 327 Main Street in Cedarwood. I'll put you down for 10 am."

"Is there anything I need to bring?"

"Not at this time. We'll see you tomorrow. Have a great day."

I pulled back onto the road and made my way to Norma's. Her driveway was empty, except for her car. I was excited to have the time alone with her. It was hard to come by these days since Lily had been staying with her and Maggie. I didn't want to be selfish, but I needed her to myself today. I didn't even care if we talked more about her past today. I just needed her. She was the only one who could make me feel better, and the thought of losing her made my bones ache.

I knocked on her door before I let myself in. "Norma, it's me, Val." I didn't see her in the kitchen or living room and the thought that she wasn't there took my breath away. "Norma." When my voice echoed off the walls, I noticed the pictures that usually hung there were gone. I took a few more steps in and stood at the beginning of the hall. "Norma, are you there?"

I heard the thud of what sounded like a box of books hit the floor. "Just a minute." Norma emerged from her bedroom, sweat beading off her forehead. "Oh, hi, Val, I wasn't expecting you this morning."

"Is everything alright?"

"Yes, of course it is, what's the matter?"

"Why are the pictures gone? What were you doing in there?"

"Calm down, honey. We're getting ready to paint. I let Maggie and the girls pick out a color they like. I want this to feel more like their home."

"I'm sorry. I'm just on edge today." I looked down at my phone. "I got a call a few minutes ago that didn't help anything."

"Come sit down, let's have some tea and talk." Norma turned on the lamp in the living room and went to make our tea. As I sat in the once familiar space, I couldn't help but feel out of place. Something was up. Something she wasn't telling me. I didn't have it in me to ask questions I didn't want answers to.

"Are you hungry?" Norma returned with a tray with our tea and brownies. "The girls made these last night. They're pretty good, too." She set the tray down and took her mug before sitting in the chair next to me.

I reached over and took my cup and a brownie. "I haven't been hungry lately, but who can pass up chocolate?" The tea spilled on my lap as my hand trembled. "Oh, geez. I'm such a mess. I don't know how much more I can take."

"Oh, honey. I know there is so much going on for you right now. We haven't even had a chance to talk about what happened the other night. Let me look at your neck."

"Oh, it's fine. Surprisingly the marks faded by morning. Tim didn't even notice them." I brushed the hair away from my neck and turned my head.

"Well, that's good. That would have been hard to explain." She took a sip of her tea. "But, how are you doing? It can be pretty scary being that close to... I mean in the situation you were in."

"Death. You meant to say death. I know I would have died if you hadn't showed up. It was stupid to think I could have killed him. I saw what he had done to Lily. I guess I just thought I could outsmart him."

"Can you promise me you'll stop putting yourself in risky situations? I don't want anything to happen to you."

"Yeah, I guess so. I mean, I never want that to happen again, but what happens the next time someone I love is being hurt by some jackass?"

"Val, you've got to promise me you'll never let yourself get to that place again. It's dangerous, and if you're not careful you can get caught." Norma took another sip of tea. "You've got a beautiful life ahead of you, don't let anything get in the way of it."

A heavy sigh filled the room. "Okay. But what about you? Can you promise to never kill again? I don't want to lose you. You're a big part of my life. I want to share my babies with you and come to you when things get too hard."

"Valerie, I can't make that promise. I'm in too deep to stop now. There are a few loose ends I have to tie up."

"Please at least promise me you'll keep in touch."

Norma nodded as she took a bite of brownie. "So, you were saying something about a phone call?"

"Yeah, a lawyer wants me to meet with him tomorrow in Cedarwood. I have no idea what it's about. I didn't ask. It just took me by surprise, you know, since I was waiting for Detective Campbell's call."

"Peter Berkley?"

"Yeah, how did you know? Do you have my phone tapped?"

She laughed. "No, that's your gram's lawyer. I bet they're going to talk about her will."

"Oh, you're probably right." I laughed. "That's going to piss my mom off even more now."

"What's the saying? Revenge is a dish best served cold. It's her time to suffer the consequences of ruining your life and being a shitty daughter."

I looked at my phone as it sat on the coffee table. "I don't know how much longer I can wait for that phone call. It's seriously driving me crazy." I took a drink of tea before setting it next to my phone. "So, do you think now's the time to tell me your story?"

"I do owe you that at least, don't I?" She took another drink of tea. "Just let me top this off first, okay? Do you need any more?"

I shook my head with my mouth full of the last of the brownie. The ringing of my cell phone made me leap out of my chair. My hands trembled so much picking it up to answer, it took longer than it should have. "Hello?"

"Valerie?"

"Yes."

"This is Camp. I just wanted to let you know everything went according to plan."

"You got him?"

"Yup, he's being booked as we speak. But I want you to know if he reaches bail, he'll be able to leave."

"Okay. I guess I didn't think that far ahead."

"I also want you to know that you should turn on the six o'clock news tonight. Somehow the arrest was leaked to the media and there were news crews at Chad's office this morning."

"It's going to be on the news?" The idea left me with mixed feelings. I wanted Chad outed, but I wasn't sure I was ready for the publicity yet. "Will they mention my name?"

"Oh, no, since you were a child at the time of the crime, your name will be kept out of the news. At least for a while, anyway."

The silence on my end of the phone increased the level of awkwardness of the conversation.

"Valerie? You still there?"

"Mhmm."

"Don't worry about the details right now. Let us do our job and get you justice. I just thought you'd be happy to know people are going to know really quickly who the real Dr. Chad Ross is."

"Thank you." I clicked off the phone and sat back in the chair.

"Is everything okay, dear?"

"I don't know." I looked up at her and tears started rolling out of my eyes. "They arrested him, and it's going to be on the news."

"Oh, that's great." Norma's smile made the rate of the tears increase. "The bastard is finally going to be held accountable for what he did to you all these years. This is something to celebrate. Let me see the pretty smile of yours."

"You're right. It's just a lot. I didn't expect it to be so public already."

"I think that's the best part. He can't hide behind his fancy college degrees any longer. Val, this is a good thing, trust me."

I knew I had to. She hasn't steered me wrong yet. She was probably the only person who knew all of my secrets and she still loved me. The sound of a car door slamming and laughter filled the driveway. "Looks like you're off the hook, again."

"Don't you worry, we'll get some time together soon." Norma winked at me as Maggie, Lily and the girls came through the door.

I trusted her, but I wasn't sure how much more time we'd have together. I knew she was up to something, and I also knew she wouldn't let me in on it.

CHAPTER SEVEN

Tim and Gabe were home in time for the six o'clock news to air. I hadn't considered Gabe watching with us, or even knowing about Chad. That was the one part I was most afraid of. I didn't want Gabe to feel shame or guilt for the way he came into this world. I didn't want to alter his story any more than it already had been.

The three of us sat quietly as we waited for the story to air. My heart slammed against my chest as the minutes passed by. Before they went to commercial break a picture of Chad hit the screen with the caption "Up Next." He looked miserable and surprised. I couldn't have asked for a better reaction; well besides a heart attack, but I already knew that hadn't happened.

Tim clapped his hands. "This is what we've been waiting for." The excitement in his voice annoyed me. I know I should have been as excited as he was, but I was still worried about Gabe's reaction. I knew I had some time before I had to tell him the whole story, but the thought of lying to him made me sick.

I shot Tim a smile as my hands started to sweat. After the longest commercial break in history, the story took the screen. "Local psychologist, Dr. Chad Ross was arrested today at his place of employment for allegedly raping and impregnating a patient two decades ago. The girl later became his stepdaughter. We will report more as more information becomes available."

And just like that I had been outed to the world, but more importantly, to Gabe. The room started to spin as Tim clicked off the TV. "We waited all night for that?"

I felt Gabe's eyes on me and didn't have it in me to have the conversation I knew we needed to have. "Wait." His tone was enough to make Tim see what was happening.

The tears came faster than the words I needed to find. "Gabe."

"That's my father, isn't it? That piece of shit is my dad?"

"Gabe, I'm sorry."

"Why are you sorry? You don't have a reason to be sorry. That piece of shit raped you and then they stole me from you." His anger increased with each word. "I can't believe that happened to you."

"I'm sorry."

"Would you stop saying that? Jesus Christ. You don't need to say you're sorry. You were a fuckin child. He's the one that should be saying it to you."

"Gabe settle down. I know you're angry, but give her time, okay?"

"I didn't know they were going to share all that on here. I

wanted to tell you myself. I just didn't know how." I wiped the tears away with my sleeve.

"I'm not even mad about that. I'm just fuckin pissed that he did that to you, and then ripped me away from you. I'm just fuckin furious, okay?"

"Yeah, I get that, I'm fuckin furious, too. I'd like to take care of him myself, but we can't get involved." Tim moved closer to me and pulled me into his arms.

"I'd kill the fucker if I saw him. He's lucky he's not from Lawrenceville, because it would be worth being kicked off the force."

"I love you Gabe. Just because that's how you were conceived doesn't mean I don't love you."

"I know that. I know how much you love me, I've always known. I just can't believe you'd want the reminder."

"You don't remind me of the ugly parts. You're too beautiful a person for me to ever connect you with that."

Gabe cracked his knuckles as he paced the living room. "All I can hope for is the guys in there find out what he did and beat the shit out of him."

"I'm with you on that." Tim chuckled. "I bet we could arrange for them to find out, maybe even put a little extra money in their commissaries."

Gabe rubbed his hands together. "Sounds like a great idea."

After Gabe calmed down, he went into the shower and Tim continued to hold me. I thought about them wanting to get revenge on Chad and I started to feel a little better about the secrets I held. Maybe we weren't so different after all.

I lifted my head off Tim's chest. "Do you think you could teach me how to shoot?"

"I thought you hated guns." Tim twirled my hair around his fingers.

"I do. Well, I did, but I need to learn how to protect myself."

"If you really want me to, we could go this weekend. But, are you sure?" Tim cocked his head to make eye contact.

"I don't want to be afraid anymore. Maybe if I learn how to use one it won't be so scary. I shouldn't have to depend on you to keep me safe."

"Okay. I'll get one of my handguns cleaned up for you. If you like it, I can even get you your own."

"His and hers, we can be just like Sonya and Andrew." I giggled as I thought about her pink gun.

"I'm glad to see you want to stay safe. This world just gets crazier by the day, but you already know that. With the unsolved murders, I bet a lot of people in this town aren't feeling safe."

"I don't think that's a bad thing. It's about time *those* people feel unsafe. I see it as karma." I shrugged my shoulders.

"I know. I know. And, I'm finally on board with you. I get it now, and by the looks of things, so does Gabe."

"Yeah, I think so. I didn't expect him to be so upset. I figured he'd be mad at me for lying to him."

"Val, he loves you. I think it hurts him knowing how bad you were treated. I think he understands why you didn't tell him."

"I got lucky with that boy. He's one of a kind."

"I bet his siblings will be just as amazing, especially since we'll be the parents."

"With everything going on, I don't even know if I'm late or not. Everything kind of exploded." I picked up my iPad and checked my fertility app. "Looks like we still have a couple days to wait and see."

"We can stop trying for a while, if you want. I know how much stress you must be under, and that can't be good for the baby."

"I know. I don't want to stop, though. I don't want that piece of shit to steal another day from me. I'll look for a counselor to work on stuff. I want to make sure I'm at my best when our baby gets here."

"That sounds like a great plan, but I won't be upset if you change your mind."

"I know it'll happen when it's supposed to. I'll be ready whenever that is."

Tim leaned over and kissed me. "You're one of a kind, too, you know. I got lucky when I found you."

"I guess we're just a house full of lucky ducks."

As we laughed, I thought about holding our baby, only to have the image be pushed out of my mind by the sight of me gunning down Chad. It might be the only way to have a stress-free pregnancy. I'd just have to take action sooner than later. I promised Norma I wouldn't put myself in danger anymore. If I had a gun, I wouldn't be lying.

CHAPTER EIGHT

I forgot to ask Norma to come with me to Cedarwood and hoped just showing up would be enough notice for her to come with me. Tim and Gabe were busy again, and I didn't want to be alone that long with my thoughts. When I pulled into Norma's driveway, I saw her closing the trunk of her car. I'd wished I'd been there two minutes earlier so I could have seen what she put in there. I knew she was up to something, and I didn't like any part of it.

The clicking of my directional signal echoed in the silence of the car as I rolled down the window. "Are you busy this morning?"

"I was expecting you. I'll go get my purse."

"How'd you know?"

"I knew you wouldn't want to go alone, and I know Tim's preoccupied with work. And, I promised to tell you my story."

"Great plan. There'll be no way for you to get out of it this time."

With a smile she shook her head as she walked into the house.

I had hoped we'd get to talk on the drive down there. It was over an hour away. It seemed like the perfect place to talk without interruptions. I was as eager to hear her story as I was to learn why she decided to kill. I had so many questions.

Norma came back out with her purse and two travel mugs. She handed me one through the window. "I thought we could use some caffeine this morning."

The aroma of freshly brewed coffee danced its way to my nose. She really was expecting me, so maybe there was nothing to see earlier, either that or she knew I'd be running late. I took a sip of the hot coffee and let the warm liquid ease away the tension that lingered.

Norma set her mug in the cup holder and buckled her seatbelt. "Do you know where you're going?"

"Not exactly, but I typed it into the GPS."

"I know where we're going."

I turned my head to look at her. "You do?"

"Yes, I'm the one who brought Marianne to change her will."

"You never told me that."

She smiled. "Oh, honey, there's a lot I don't tell you, or anyone for that matter."

"Touché."

"During one of our visits, after Marianne found out about Chad, she told me she wanted to make sure you were taken care of, and that your mother never saw another penny of hers. After a little discussion we decided to make an appointment to update her will. She didn't want anyone to find out, until she told you on one of your last visits."

"It was the last, actually. I meant to go back, but things kept getting in the way."

"It's okay, Val. She knew you loved her, and your wedding meant the world to her. She was grateful to have you back in her life." Norma reached over and patted my leg. "She loved you so much."

"I loved her, too. I didn't need her money, but I'm glad my mom won't be getting it."

"Oh, I think you'll be surprised."

"Yeah? What do you know?"

"Patience, grasshopper." She winked and took a drink of her coffee.

"Speaking of patience, I think I've got a story to hear."

Norma's smile faded. "Yes, that's right. I did promise you that, didn't I?"

"Yes, and I've been patiently waiting for the right time."

"I know you have." She pushed out a breath through her lips. "Where should I start?"

"How about the beginning?"

"The thing is, I don't even know where the beginning starts. But I'll try. You know, I've never trusted anyone with this before." She rested her head against the seat and closed her eyes. "My early years are kind of a blur, but I guess you could say it was a lot like yours. My dad died when I was about four, and my mom jumped in bed with the next man she found, or so I always assumed. He was nice at first, but soon he started hitting my mom. There were some days I wasn't sure she'd survive the beatings. In order to cope with it all she started to drink, and not just a glass here or there, all the time. Morning to night she had some sort of alcohol in her hand.

"My once loving mom began treating me the way he was treating her. There were days my body was more black and blue than it was white. When her husband saw how she was treating me, he started giving me special attention. You know the kind I mean. He was raping me by the time I was seven, and my mom didn't even care. If he was bothering me, he wasn't bothering her. I didn't have any friends or any other family. And since I was always covered in bruises, they kept me out of school. It's a miracle I even learned how to read.

"By the time I was sixteen, I'd had enough of it all. I enrolled in the Army and got as far away from home as possible. I thought it was the answer to all of my problems, but I was wrong. It only created new ones."

"That's why you're so good with a gun?"

She laughed. "I guess so. I've had a lot of practice."

"In the Army, or...?"

"Oh, there's still more to my story. Do you want me to continue? Or is it too much?"

"Keep going. I mean, if you're up to it."

"I promised I'd share, and I don't break my promises." She took a drink of coffee before returning her mug to the cup holder. "So, where was I?"

"The Army."

"Oh, yes. So, picture a sixteen-year-old girl being dropped off in a big pit of horny older guys. Let your imagination paint that picture, and then multiple it by a hundred. If I thought my home life was unsafe, I was proven wrong my first night there. Lucky for me I had plenty of practice being raped, so it didn't affect me quiet as much as some of the other girls. I got a reputation for being tough, and after a while it paid off. I knew I couldn't let them see me as weak. I had to be tougher than them in order to earn their respect.

"This one man, Vern St. Thomas was quite a bit older than me, but he took me under his wing. He taught me how to shoot, I was one of the best in our unit. Long story short, I fell in love with him, and he made sure no one else touched me while we were stationed. All bets were off after we got married and made a home together.

"Vern wanted children, but I was still a child myself. I wanted to wait and enjoy married life, just the two of us, but not him. Every day I didn't give him a baby he became a little meaner. He also took up drinking. It was like living at home all over again. I didn't have any friends and I hadn't seen my mom since I left. I knew Vern would end up killing me if I didn't get away.

"I hated that he drank. He knew about my past, but it didn't stop him. I lied about being pregnant, hoping that he'd stop beating me. It did work for a while, but when I wasn't showing when he thought I should, he threatened to kill me. I knew I had to get to him before he got to me. After he calmed down enough from that argument, he was sitting in the living room, listening to the radio, and I walked up behind him with his own gun and shot him right in the head. It was the best and worst feeling I'd ever had."

"Oh my God, Norma, that must have been so scary."

"It was, but it was also exhilarating. I knew I could do anything at that moment. I also knew I couldn't get caught.

We had neighbors close by, and I figured it would only be a matter of time before the police arrived. I rushed around the house and took the things I thought I would need. Before I left, I cut my arm and smeared my blood around the bedroom. I wanted it to look like there had been a struggle and I left. I never looked back."

"How long ago was that?"

"That was 1959."

"You've been on the run for over fifty years?"

"Hmm. I guess so. I never did the math."

"So, Vern was the first one you killed. How many others have there been?"

Norma shook her head. "Oh, honey, I lost count."

"What made you kill other people? I mean, I get Vern, I would've killed him, too, but when did you start killing other people?"

"It's complicated."

"I don't think it is. Remember who you're talking to. You know I understand."

"I know. I just don't like to think about it."

"Come on, it might feel good to talk about it."

A tear rolled down Norma's cheek. "Yes, you're right. I've held this in for much too long." She exhaled and pushed the tear off her face. "You see, I wasn't always as quick as I learned to be. After I moved to a new town in a new state, I started a new life. I vowed to never get married again, and spent my time looking for friends. I wanted to be with people like me, but I could never get too close to them. That was until Sylvia. We worked together and ended up spending most of our time together. She was married, and her husband was jealous of the time we spent together. She told me one day he threatened to kill me if I ever showed my face at their house.

"I didn't know it then, but I was in love with Sylvia. I think I loved her more than I had ever loved anyone. On one of our walks, she kissed me. I knew then that she loved me, too. She was going to leave her husband, and we were going to run away together. It was the sixties, that kind of thing was new, but it wasn't as taboo as it had been when I was a child.

"I begged her not to tell him. I told her to just pack a bag while he was at work, and we could figure it all out later. It was her free spirt that I loved that got her killed." Norma paused and looked out the window. "I haven't talked about Sylvia in years."

I held my hand out for Norma to hold. "Oh, Norma, I'm so sorry."

"When she told him she was leaving him for me, he shot her and then himself. Not only did he kill the woman I loved, but he also took any satisfaction I could have had by getting revenge. It was then I vowed to never wait. If I saw someone who needed to die, I took action. If someone I cared about was being hurt, I put an end to the abuse. If I read about a perpetrator in the paper, I found them and took care of the problem. When too many people were taken care of in one place, I knew it was my time to move on."

"How many times have you moved?"

"I don't remember."

"Oh, come on, you must have an idea."

"No, I honestly don't. I know it's been more than twenty, but I lost count."

"Do you assume a new identity each time?"

"Yes and no. I've recycled some of the names."

"Wow, Norma... is that even what you want me to call you?"

"Yes, Norma is fine. I wouldn't want to make it confusing for you. You know, no one can know any of this."

"I know. I promise. Your secrets are safe with me. Just like I know mine are safe with you."

"Thank you, dear."

"You're the only person who knows all of my secrets."

"Oh, I'm sure there's a few I don't know, and I don't need to. We all have pieces of ourselves that no one will ever know."

"Yeah, I guess you're right. I can't believe you were able to hold that all in for over fifty years."

"It gets easier with time."

"And you never wanted to find love again?"

She shook her head. "No, I know my true love is waiting for me. There will never be anyone as perfect for me as Sylvia. She just understood me. It's hard to put into words. I imagine it's how you feel about Tim."

I laughed. "I don't know. He's been on my nerves lately."

"Well, you've been through so much in such a short amount of time. It makes perfect sense that he'd get under your skin. The true test is if he sticks around through it all. Then you know you have the one."

"You're right. You always are."

"Careful, honey, all these compliments are going to go straight to this old woman's head."

"It's well deserved. You're my angel. You know when I tell you I love you I mean it, right?"

"I know. You're a sweet girl. And, I love you, too. I love all of you girls, but you're my favorite." She winked at me. "I'll never admit that again."

I laughed. "I'll never tell."

"Moving to Lawrenceville was the best decision I've made in a long time."

"How did you find our little group?"

"Well, that's another one of my secrets." She smirked. "When I move to a new place, I look for groups like ours. That's where I find most of my targets."

"Oh… like Martha."

"Yes. When trauma support groups started becoming a thing, it made my work that much easier. All these ladies all together, sharing their stories. It made the hunt easy. I'd solve their problems and be on my way."

"Did you always leave a trademark?"

She giggled. "Not always. I don't like to make things too much alike. I know the FBI has a database, and I didn't want them to ever be able to connect any of the murders. I wanted to keep them guessing. And, who would ever suspect a sweet, little old lady?"

"You're so smart. You've thought of everything."

"I don't know if it's smart or lucky. I'd like to think my ability to remain under the radar is just confirmation that I'm doing the right thing."

"Have you ever killed anyone you wished you wouldn't have?"

"Nope, never. Each and every one of them deserved what

they got. And the way I look at it, the world is just that much safer. Think of how many women and children were not victimized, or worse, killed. An eye for an eye. That's my motto."

"Thank you for sharing so much with me. I aspire to be like you."

"Oh, honey. Please don't. This isn't a life I'd wish on anyone. I'm lonely and angry." She laughed. "Don't let this world harden you. And don't put yourself in any more dangerous situations. I've got decades of experience. Leave it to the experts, okay?"

"I guess so. It was exhilarating when I killed Donald Brice, but it seemed to get scarier as my circle grew. The more I had to lose, the harder it got."

"Lucky for you, I was a few steps ahead of you."

"Yeah. You don't know how freaked out that made me."

"Your fear didn't stop you, though. You kept it up, even when you were afraid." She shook her head. "Do me a favor and start listening to your gut. If you're afraid, don't go. If you have a voice telling you not to trust someone, listen. We have that little voice for a reason."

"You listen to yours?"

"As a matter a fact, I do. The one time I didn't has haunted me for most of my life."

"I promise I'll pay more attention."

"That's a good girl." She gave me a smile and pointed out the window. "You'll want to turn there, his office will be on your left."

"Wow, that was a quick trip." I looked at the clock on the dash. "I guess it really wasn't as quick as I thought."

"That's what happens when you're having fun."

As I pulled into the parking space and put the car in park, I looked over at Norma. "It means a lot that you trust me enough to share all that with me. You know what I think?"

"What's that?"

"I think you should find someone to spend the rest of your life with. You are such a loving person; you should share that with someone."

Norma shook her head. "Oh, honey, that's the last thing I want to do."

"You deserve to be happy."

"Who says I'm not?"

"Oh, you know what I mean."

"Protecting the people I love is all that matters to me."

"But what if you get caught? Or worse... what if someone hurts you?"

"I've been at it long enough I don't think either will happen. And if they do," she shrugged her shoulders, "I'd be okay with it."

"Oh, Norma, that's not what I wanted to hear."

"If you love something, you have to set it free." With her hands together she made her hands fly away like a bird. "Come on, let's go see what gift awaits."

CHAPTER NINE

"Hi there, Norma. It's nice to see you again." Peter Berkley greeted us at the door. "You must be Valerie." The tall, slender man held out his hand. I tried to take my attention away from the dark brown combover resting above his glasses.

"Hi, sorry we're so early."

"It's quite alright. I expected you to arrive outside of the agreed upon time." He must have seen my eyebrow raise in disgust. "Because I knew how far you were traveling from." With his index finger he pushed up his glasses. "My secretary has the day off, so please excuse me if I get any calls. I'll need to take them. I hope you won't mind."

"No, that's fine." I followed his lead into his office at the end of the long dimly lit hall.

He flicked on the light. "Go ahead, have a seat."

Norma and I settled into the chairs in front of the massive mahogany desk. The thing was as long as the room it was in. As I looked around the room I couldn't come up with any reasonable explanation as to how it even fit through the door. The sound of Peter's ring against the wood startled me.

"Before we get started, yes, this thing was custom made, and yes it was built in here, and no, I have no idea how I'll ever get it out of here."

I gave him my fakest smile and turned to look at Norma. "Don't worry, Val, he's not a mind reader, that's how he starts every meeting." She sat back in her chair and set her purse on her lap.

"Yeah, everyone asks, so I save us both time and just get it out in the open. It's from my early days, when I'd barter my services. This thing right here is why that stopped." Peter rubbed the top of the desk and opened the manila folder in front of him. "So, I bet you're dying to know why I called you here."

"Oh, Peter, I don't think that's the right opener." Norma shook her head and closed her eyes.

He cleared his throat. "My apologies, that was uncalled for. I try to lighten the mood with laughter. Sometimes I'm not the best judge of what's funny."

"It's okay. I'm awkward sometimes, too."

His pale cheeks turned red. "Where were we?" His eyes went to the papers in front of him. "Your grandmother made some changes to her will, and she made you the sole beneficiary." He handed me a stack of papers.

A teardrop hit the paper when I saw her signature. The sting of her loss became a reality after days of trying to push the pain away.

"If you turn the page, you'll see that she had several investment accounts, and if you turn the next page, you'll see she had a few bank accounts. And, lastly, if you turn to the last page, you'll see the approximate value of her estate."

I hadn't been able to follow his instructions, grief had me in its grip. The money did not matter to me. I just wanted my gram back.

"I know it's a large number. If you'd like I can read it for you."

I wasn't sure if he was arrogant or just lacked social skills. Norma reached over and put her hand on my knee. When I was able to turn the pages, I noticed the accounts he had spoken of, and a seven-digit number on the last page. My heart dropped to the pit of my stomach. "How is this possible?"

"Your grandmother was a smart woman."

"I thought for sure my mom would have gotten her hands on this."

"Well, I assume the reason she had so many bank accounts was to throw her off. My suggestion to you is to get yourself a good financial advisor, and you'll be able to make this last your lifetime."

"Did she leave anything for my mom?"

He shook his head. "No, she made it very clear she did not want her to get a penny more of her money. I have a statement from her on file in case your mom tries to contest this."

"She thought of everything." I looked over to see the smile on Norma's face.

"She was a very smart woman. Take that copy with you for your records. I'll be in touch for the next steps."

"Thank you." Norma stood up and took my hand to help me out of the chair.

"You're welcome. I'm sorry about being so... awkward." Peter pushed his hair back into his combover.

Norma took the keys. "I think I should drive us home."

"Did you know how much she was leaving me?"

"I did, but I promised her I wouldn't tell."

"And you're the one who told her to make that statement, aren't you?"

"No, that was all her. She was fed up with your mother taking her money, and disgusted when she found out what Chad had done to you."

"I don't even know what to think. Part of me feels guilty that she's gone and now..."

"Oh, honey, don't feel guilty. She wanted you to be happy. She wanted you to live your dreams, and not be tied to a job you hate."

"Who says I hate my job?"

"What, are you trying out Mr. Berkley's jokes now?"

"Ha-ha, very funny."

"It's not hard to see how miserable you are at work. I think you should call your boss and tell her you won't be back. Travel with Tim, go see the world before you're tied down with a little one."

I thought about what Norma said. "I guess you're right, it is time to tell Jeanine to find another deceased patient coordinator." I fastened my seatbelt. "But I can't leave our group."

"You don't need that job for the group. We're still going to be your friends. Remember all those meetings at my place? All this means is you'll have more time to spend with all of us."

"I can't wait to tell Tim. Maybe he can take some time off now, too."

"I don't think either one of you will ever have to worry about going to work again."

"I still don't understand how something so awful can lead to something so wonderful."

"That's the story of life. You just have to find the joy wherever you can."

Laughter came roaring out of me. "Oh my God. You know what I just thought of?" My hand slapped my thigh. "Chad just got arrested last night... on the news... and now Mom's going to find out the inheritance she's been waiting her whole life for is mine." My head fell back as laughter swallowed me.

"Now, that's what I'm talking about. That's the jackpot of joy."

My mother's misery would still not match the pain she caused me, but it was a damn good start. Even in the depths of despair, life was starting to look up.

CHAPTER TEN

I spent the morning cleaning out my office at the hospital. Even though I didn't have the money yet, I couldn't stomach the thought of one more day there. When I had the last box loaded in my car, I walked up the stairs for the final time to Jeanine's office. The smell of lavender hit my nose before I could knock on her door.

I had my letter of resignation in my hand as I stood in the entrance to her office. "Hey, Jeanine, do you have a minute?" As much as I wanted this, part of me still felt bad for disappointing her.

"Not really, but come on in." She didn't look up at me as she punched away at the keys on her keyboard.

I sat in the chair in front of her as I waited for her to finish in awkward silence. When it was too much to bear, I spoke up. "I really need to talk to you."

"Just a minute."

I sighed as I worked up the courage to interrupt her. "Jeanine, this will only take a minute."

She looked up. "Jesus, Val, what do you want?"

"Well, you're making this much easier than I anticipated." I handed her my letter.

"What's this?"

"I ah... I quit."

"Quit? What are you talking about?"

"There's just a lot going on for me right now, I just need to take care of myself." I stood up and started to walk out of her office before she could change my mind.

"Are you serious?"

"Yeah. Thanks for everything you did for me. I appreciate it. My office has been cleaned out."

"You're not giving me any notice?" Jeannine questioned.

"No, sorry." The surge of powerful energy charged through my body as it propelled me out the door.

"You should really reconsider this, Val. If you don't give me any notice, I won't be able to give you a good reference."

I kept walking, not letting her threat touch me. I didn't care. I wouldn't need a reference from her or anyone. I took a look around before I walked out of the building as I reminisced about my time here. I wasn't leaving any friends behind. I doubted many people would even notice I was gone. The people that mattered to me were not within these walls.

The first stop I made as a free woman was the drug store. With everything happening so quickly the last few days, I had finally looked at the calendar. I was three days late. There was part of me that was anxious to see a plus sign on the test, while another part of me was terrified of either result. Positive meant I would be able to be a mother, but it also meant I had to change some of my ways I wasn't sure I was ready for just yet. Negative meant disappointment and heart break for me, and Tim, but it also meant I had at least one more month to do as I pleased.

Buying the test was the easy part, it was trying to figure out the how. Obviously, I knew how to pee on a stick, it was more of the who to tell. If I waited for Tim to be present, he'd know the results right away. That was the way it was supposed to happen. He was probably more excited than I was. He had been tracking my cycle, so I was surprised he didn't remind me it was time to test.

I thought about doing the test with the ladies and sharing the news with them. All the sitcoms show a bunch of friends eagerly waiting the two minutes while they sit around the pregnancy test. I didn't think Tim would agree to that scenario, and he'd be crushed if he found out. The thing was, I wasn't sure I wanted anyone to know, not yet.

When I arrived home, Gabriel greeted me at the door. He rubbed against my legs as soon as I walked in. He hadn't been this loving in a while, not since Gabe moved in. Gabe had stolen Gabriel's love from me. I guess it was only fair, since Tim had stolen me from him. "Hey, buddy." I picked him up and hugged him. His purring vibrated through me. "Looks like we're going to find out if you're going to be a big brother or not."

I set him down and went into the bathroom. I set the timer on my phone for two minutes and went back out with Gabriel. The seconds passed like molasses. One hundred twenty seconds felt like a lifetime. I paced the kitchen as I watched the timer count down. "I don't know what to do,

Gabriel. I do want a baby, but the timing isn't quite right. But when is it ever?" With thirty seconds to spare I went back to the bathroom and picked up the test.

"Oh shit." Two pink lines looked back at me. My heart began to race as I thought of a plan. I can't tell Tim, not yet. I couldn't tell anyone. Keeping this from Tim would be bad, but him being the last to know would be borderline unforgivable. "Congratulations, buddy, looks like you're going to get your tail pulled sooner than later."

I stuffed the test back into the box, and the box into the bag and buried it in the middle of the trash in the kitchen. Gabriel followed. "What? Don't judge me. This is our little secret, at least for a while. I have some business to tend to, and if Tim finds out, he'll never let me out of his sight... and he sure as hell won't give me that gun he's been telling me about."

I placed my hand on my stomach and closed my eyes. "I promise you are wanted and you are loved." Tears fell down my cheeks as I remembered the last time I took the test. I was scared, but I knew I wanted to bring the little life into the world. This time, I should be happy. I should be celebrating. I couldn't let Chad steal this moment from me again. "Just give me one month."

One more lie added to the list. This one wasn't really a lie though, not yet. If Tim didn't ask, I wouldn't have to lie. There was enough going on in our world that he might not ask. He might be giving me some time to grieve. I smiled as I thought about my gram. "Keep us safe, Gram."

The ringing of the phone pulled me out of my head. I glanced at the caller ID before I answered. Unknown caller. I didn't have it in me to risk answering it without knowing. I set the phone back down and waited to see if they left a voice mail. When the rings stopped, I waited, but no message was left. I grabbed a glass of orange juice and took it to the deck. Just as I shut the door, I heard the ringing again. Curiosity won. "Hello?"

"Valerie?"

"Speaking."

"This is Cheryl, from the Victims Center. There's been some developments in the case against Dr. Ross."

"There has?"

"Yes, are you sitting down?"

I took the phone and my juice and sat in the rocking chair on the deck. "Yeah. What's going on?"

"Well, we've had three other women come forward since Dr. Ross's arrest made the news. We've spoken with all of them, and their stories are almost identical to yours."

"For real?" The beat of my heart echoed through my ears, too loud to hear her next words.

"Valerie, are you still there?"

"What?"

"We're pretty confident there are others. It's just a matter of time before they come forward."

"It's my fault that he hurt those girls. I should have said something sooner."

"No, Valerie. This isn't on you. And, besides, two of the women are older than you. He's been doing this for years. You weren't the first and you weren't the last."

"But I could have stopped him."

"No, you were a child. What you did took incredible

strength. It's because of you that these women felt strong enough to tell their story. Good news for all of you is, you don't have to do this alone. The bad news is he's a serial rapist."

"Will we get to meet?"

"Yes, there will be time down the road for you all to get together. We want to keep you all separate and confidential right now, to make sure there is no way to make it look like you're all working together."

"Okay."

"We're going to make him pay for what he did to you, to all of you. Hang in there, kiddo."

The news settled in my head like a lead sinker. I couldn't shake feeling responsible, at least for the girls that came after me. What if there were other kids out there? Gabe might have half siblings. For the sake of the others, I hoped he was the only one.

This was the sign I was supposed to be paying attention to, wasn't it? The one I had promised Norma I would listen to. As the sun hit my face I looked up to the sky. "This is how you're going to keep us safe, isn't it Gram?" I laughed. "That takes all the fun out of it."

Or maybe it wouldn't. If Cheryl was right, and more women came forward there would be no way he would get away with it. There would be enough evidence to lock him up for the rest of his life. And, Tim and Gabe were right, the guys in there would know what he was in for and they'd do the dirty work for me. A smile spread across my face. "Looks like I get to celebrate you after all, little one."

"On your way home, can you grab a test?" I hit send and

closed my eyes as I imagined the joy the message alone would bring to his face.

"Test?!? Are you late???"

"Three days. I think I'll have good news for you tonight."

"OMG! I don't know how I'll be able to concentrate the rest of the day!!!"

The door swung open; Tim had a plastic bag in his hand. I went behind him and closed the door. "You're not excited, are you?"

"Maybe a little." He took the test out of the bag and dropped it before he handed it to me.

"Whoa, slow down. I won't be able to use it if you break it." I laughed as I bent down and picked it up. "How will you wait two minutes for the results?" I raised my eyebrows and smirked as I opened the box and pulled out the test.

"Come on, Val, it's not funny. I've been a wreck all day. I need to know."

"Oh, bonus points for using Tom's lyrics. That's got to get you something." I gave him a kiss and went into the bathroom.

"Do you need any help in there?" Tim tapped on the door.

"Not unless you want to pee on the stick."

I heard him sigh. I bumped into him when I walked into the hall. "What is it?" He was biting his fingernail.

"Were you listening to me the whole time?" I shook my head. "That's gross."

"Sorry. I'm excited."

"Yeah, I can see that." I wrapped my arms around him. "I love you."

"I love you, too. I just can't stop imagining our little family. I am so ready to be a dad."

"I love that you want this so bad."

"Do you think it's too early to check?" Tim's eyes went to the bathroom.

"Yeah, we can go look." I took his hand and led him to the test. I picked it up and showed him.

"What is it? What am I looking at?"

"Two pink lines means we're pregnant." I set the test back down and fell into his arms.

"Oh my God, I can't wait." Tim pulled me in tight.

"Yeah, I don't know how you're going to wait nine months when you couldn't even wait two minutes." I laughed.

"I'll be patient." He kissed the top of my head. "I just can't wait to meet him."

"Or her."

"I don't care either way, as long as he's healthy." Tim placed his hand on my belly.

I put my hand over his and closed my eyes. "You are so loved, little one."

The lesson of finding the joy in everything seemed to have some merit to it. Chad would not take this from me. From now on, I will be the thief, stealing his freedom and joy. Karma has a long shelf life, but it's oh so sweet.

CHAPTER ELEVEN

Over the next few weeks there were four other women that came forward after they saw Chad get arrested on the news. Eight in total, and that was just the ones that talked. Cheryl wouldn't give me many details, so I still didn't know if Gabe was the only child from the abuse, or if there were others. Chad's trial was still months away, and his attorney had said there would be no plea-bargain. Chad's claim was he was not guilty. He was not going to confess to anything, even if it meant he would get a lesser sentence.

Cheryl assured me it was best that he didn't make a deal, because he might have been given a slap on the wrist because of his connections. Now that Gabe knew about the case, I had all the evidence I needed; his DNA. There would no denying he was the father, and the math would prove I was a child when it happened. I wasn't sure Chad and Mom knew Gabe was in my life. I was hopeful it would be a shocking surprise and make him look like even more of a fool.

I was surprised Mom hadn't tried to contact me after the charges were pressed. I know she must have found out about Gram's will by now, and I had a bad feeling she would confront me about it. I hadn't heard a word from her. I wondered how her friends felt about what was happening, or if she was still standing by her man. How could any of her friends support her after finding out what she did to me? As evil as it sounds, I was just as excited to see Mom's life fall apart as I was Chad's. What would it take to make her snap? I often wondered that.

The perfect life they tried to portray had crumbled down around them. I was eager to light the match now that the gasoline had been poured. Still, the thought of taking Chad's life haunted me. Yes, I wanted him to pay for what he did to me and the other girls, but the thought that he would still get to live his life, even if behind bars made me crave revenge. Would this baby be safe in a world with Chad still in it? I didn't know the answer to that, and the uncertainty made my maternal instincts kick in. Surely that was a good enough excuse to stray, just this once.

Before I found out I was pregnant, Tim and Gabe took me to the shooting range. A hint of fear still lingered, but not enough to keep me from it. When I had the house to myself, I took the gun out and felt it between my hands. In the back-yard I pointed it at the tree and pretended it was Chad in the crosshairs. The rush of adrenaline left me feeling powerful and untouchable. If I were to listen to my gut, it would have told me to *do it*. I didn't know how much longer I could keep myself from acting on the desire.

Norma was the only one who would understand, but I

also knew she would not approve. Selfishly, I wished she would do the dirty work for me one last time. I hinted around at it but respected her enough not to push her into it. She was right, if she were to get involved it would be pretty easy to tie it all back to me. I knew it was her way of protecting me.

When my thoughts were too much to keep quiet, I went to Norma's house. Maggie, Lily and Norma were sitting around the living room table when I arrived. The only one missing was Sonya. She was more uncomfortable in her big belly, it seemed it was too much effort for her to join us as much as she used to. "What am I interrupting?" I stuffed myself in the chair between Maggie and Norma.

"I'm going to go live with my mom." Lily wiped away a tear. "We were just working out a plan."

"Oh, wow, Lily. That's great, isn't it?" I looked around the table to try to pick up on the mood.

Lily lifted her eyes. "Yeah, it is, but I'm going to miss you ladies."

"We can come visit." Maggie smiled as she brushed off her cheek. "The girls and I have always wanted to go to Florida."

"Just because you're there doesn't mean you lose us as friends. We'll still keep in touch. Besides, this is what you wanted. I remember you talking about how you wished you could be with your mom, but you were worried about what *he* might do." I smiled to try to soften the memory. "This is your chance to start over."

"I know. I really do need to get out of this town. No offense... there's just so many bad memories here."

"We understand, this is what's best for you, dear." Norma placed her hand on Lily's arm. "I'll even drive you down."

"Oh, I couldn't ask you to do that."

"Oh, honey, I'd love a little getaway. It's been a while since I've got to do any traveling."

I looked at Norma waiting for her to make eye contact, but she didn't take her focus off of Lily. I was the only one at the table that knew what traveling meant. "Oh, that sounds like fun. I can join you; we can take turns driving."

Norma gave me a half smile. "That does sound like fun, but there won't be any room. We're renting a U-Haul."

"That's a long drive all alone." I elbowed Maggie, waiting for her to agree with me. She did not say a word.

"I won't be alone. I'll turn the truck in down there and fly home. You can come get me at the airport. How's that sound?"

"That sounds fine." I crossed my arms to push down the vomit circling in my stomach. "How soon is all this happening?"

"We were talking about tomorrow." Norma's attention went back to Lily.

"What about Sonya? Does she know about any of this?" I tried to get Norma's attention back to me, but she didn't look away.

"No, she doesn't. You literally walked in on the plan. No one knew about it until a few minutes ago." Maggie took a drink of coffee and set her mug back down.

"Well, don't you think you need to wait until she comes over?"

"She's not feeling good, we can swing by in the morning

to say goodbye." Norma walked away from the table and put her mug in the sink. I followed.

"What's going on? What aren't you telling me?"

"Val, you know what the plan is. I'll call you from Florida as soon as I get my return ticket."

"I can't do this without you. You can't leave me." The emotion behind my words slipped out of my eyes.

Norma wrapped me in a hug. "I promise I'll call you. I'm just bringing Lily home to her mom."

"Promise me you won't leave me."

"Honey, I can't make a promise I can't keep."

Her words hit me like a brick across the face. My breath was stolen as the pain settled into my chest.

"Val, I'm an old lady, of course I can't promise you I won't leave. None of us know what our future holds. Just enjoy what you have in this moment, and don't let anything take that from you. Remember, it's important to find your joy."

I didn't find comfort in her words. I wanted to, but the thought of what was to come was stronger than the moment we were in.

"What's going on in here?" Maggie stood behind me and caressed my hair. "What's the matter, Val?"

"Nothing. It's just these hormones are out of whack."

"Oh, Val, I know this is a hard time for you, and now you have to say goodbye to Lily. But you're stuck with us, isn't that right Norma?"

Norma didn't answer, instead she pulled me closer. I squeezed my eyes shut to suppress the rest of the tears that were ready to fall. I didn't want to make today about me. I wanted to be able to give Lily the support she needed and trust Norma would return.

Maggie and I started helping Lily pack her things while Norma went to rent the U-Haul. We waited for Norma to arrive before we all went to Lily's house to finish the job. Lily's emotions were as close to the surface as mine. "I don't know if I can go through with this or not."

"I know it's scary to pack up your life and leave, but it gets easier. I'm sure there's a support group down there that you could join." Maggie handed Lily a stack of books to add to the box.

"I don't know if I want to dwell on all of that. I think it would be easier to just forget about it."

"Yeah, that's a good plan in theory." I blew the hair out of my eyes. "Sooner or later it will catch up to you and you won't have a choice."

"That's super positive, Val." Maggie shook her head.

"What? I'm trying to be helpful. Sure, maybe you're not ready to talk about it right now, but at some point, if you want to have a healthy relationship and have a family, you should deal with it." The hypocrisy of my words left a bitter taste in my mouth. "A group might not be the right thing, but maybe a good counselor. It will only hurt you to keep it all bottled up."

"Yeah, you should listen to her, I'm sure she's speaking from experience." Maggie squinted her eyes to look at the clock. "I wonder what's taking Norma so long?"

I couldn't tell if Maggie was being serious, or if she was rubbing my nose in the fact that I was giving advice I hadn't taken myself. "Well actually, I haven't dealt with a lot of the issues from my past. You ladies are the only ones I've talked to about a lot of the stuff. I really need to find someone to work with before I have this baby."

Lily stopped packing the box and smirked. "I've got an idea. How about we all make a deal that we will find a therapist and start working on our stuff. That way we can't back out of it because we can hold each other accountable."

"Ugh. I was afraid you were going to say something like that." I crossed my fingers. "Sure, I'll do whatever you say."

Maggie put her hands on her hips. "I have no idea what you're talking about. I'm perfectly fine." She stuck her tongue out and rolled her eyes.

Lily laughed and shook her head. "Great, so it's a deal."

"It's not a bad idea. We can still support each other, even from a distance." I put my hand into the middle of the three of us. "Let's shake on it."

Maggie put her hand on top of mine and Lily followed. "I'm going to miss you girls."

"We're going to miss you, too." I hated that life gave us people only for a short time. Just long enough to get close before they were taken away. The only good part of this goodbye was that we could still be in touch. It wasn't the kind of goodbye I was used to.

CHAPTER TWELVE

Norma and Lily waved as they pulled out of the driveway. As their taillights disappeared from our sight, I couldn't keep the tears from falling. Sonya's big belly bumped into me as she hugged me. "I know it's hard, but we'll get to see her again."

"I know. I just hate that we're not going to be the same little group anymore."

"What's that saying?" Maggie had her arms crossed to keep warm. "People come into our life for a reason, a season, and a..."

"Lesson?" Sonya added.

"No, it's lifetime. A reason, a season, or a lifetime." Maggie corrected her as she escorted us into the house. "Let's get some junk food and watch a sad movie."

"You won't get a protest from us pregnant chicks." Sonya rubbed her baby bump. "I think she could go for some chocolate ice cream. How about you Val?"

"Oh, she... or he... hasn't told me what they like yet. I could go for some ice cream though."

Maggie had her head in the freezer. "Looks like you're in luck. We have a new carton of rocky road."

I took out the bowls and Sonya found the ice cream scoop. "This is just what we needed. Great idea, Maggie."

"Yeah, it's been awhile since we did something like this." Sonya stopped and looked down at her belly. "Watch this." She pointed to a lump and pulled her shirt tight. "She's kicking.... that's her foot."

Maggie put her hand on the spot. "Oh, I can't wait to hold her."

"Yeah, me, either. It's at the point where everything is uncomfortable."

"She'll be here before you know it." Maggie handed off the bowls of ice cream and led us into the living room.

The sounds of our spoons clinking against the bowls accentuated the silence in the room. "Hey, can I ask you guys a question?" Sonya pushed a spoonful of ice cream into her mouth before she continued. "Do you remember the story about that lady that was missing from Maine? The one that got Norma so upset?"

"Oh god, yes. Please don't tell me you're going to bring that up again." Maggie sighed.

"Just hear me out. I won't say anything to Norma, I just want to ask you guys what you think about something. It's been driving me crazy since we heard about Earl."

I swallowed loud enough that I had to cough to cover it. "What's on your mind?"

"Well, remember I said all the ladies' perps were killed and then Martha disappeared? Well, look at our group. Almost every guy we talked about in there has been killed. Aside from Hank, who's in jail, and Chad who doesn't live around here, they're all dead. Donald, Jimmy, Seth and then Earl."

"What's your point, Sonya?" Maggie tapped the remote on the side of the chair as she waited for the explanation.

"Two groups where the guys all die? Two old ladies who don't ever share, who happen to look alike? What if Norma is Martha?"

"Oh, come on, Sonya, don't be ridiculous. Do you really think Norma is capable of any of that?" Maggie flipped on the TV disgusted by what Sonya was proposing.

"I know, that's why I can't stop thinking about it. She's so nice and caring, how could I even think that? It doesn't make sense, but it kind of does, too. People aren't always who they seem. We all know that firsthand."

"I get why you'd think that, but Norma?" I laughed and shoveled the last spoon of ice cream into my mouth.

"I'm not saying she's a bad person. I actually think whoever it is killing all those perps is a hero. I'm just saying it's weird. It's probably just a coincidence." She set her bowl on the coffee table.

If Sonya thought it was Norma, I wondered how long before someone else did, too. I remembered I told Tim and Gabe about Martha, before I knew. My heart raced as I tried to recall the conversation. I closed my eyes, but I couldn't remember what I said, or what they said back to me. They obviously didn't think there was a connection because we never spoke of it again, but what if they remembered? What if it would be my fault that Norma got caught?

"Are you okay Val?" Maggie's voice pulled me back into the living room.

"Yeah, I'm just tired." As the movie started playing in the background, I couldn't help but think about what Sonya said. I knew I needed to tell Norma, but I didn't want to. I wanted to keep her for myself, and I knew telling her would be all it took to make her leave. She saved my life, the least I could do was save her freedom.

Maggie and Sonya were lost in the movie and hadn't realized I got up to go outside. I took my phone with me and started the search for a counselor. If Lily hadn't pushed me into it, I never would have even taken this first step. I've handed out many referrals to the families I've worked with and didn't want to end up with someone who knew me.

One of my biggest fears was being judged for my past. Professionally, I know how absurd that sounds, but I couldn't shake it. I didn't want anyone to pity me, or tell me they were sorry. I didn't want to have to explain why it has taken me so long to seek help, or be told how to think or feel. Knowing I would lose Norma sooner than I anticipated, I had to get a support system in place, one where I could share things others might not understand.

It wasn't surprising that Lawrenceville didn't have a lot of options. I increased the search area and found more names the further I was willing to travel. I clicked on a few profiles and read their reviews. No one felt like a good match. I closed my eyes and pointed to the list of names before me and decided I would call Jennifer Gold. Her office was forty-five minutes from here, but it might be just far enough away to make it comfortable.

Before I could change my mind, I called the number listed on the website. After the fifth ring a perky younger woman's voice came on the line talking about where to find emergency help, and then finally requesting a name and number be left. As I waited for the beep, I clenched my teeth and debated if I should just hang up. My promise to Lily and Maggie overpowered me and I left my contact information.

The door opened behind me and Sonya stood on the stairs with a blanket wrapped around her shoulders. "What are you doing out here?"

"Oh, just making a phone call."

"Well get your ass back inside. Maggie is blubbering up a storm in there. I can't deal with her on my own."

I couldn't help but laugh as I pictured what I was about to walk into.

"It's not funny. She's been at it for a while now. I don't know what set her off, it's not that sad."

Just as I had imagined, Maggie was curled up in the recliner with crumpled up tissues all around her. She blew her nose and patted her eyes with the blanket. "What? Why aren't you guys crying?"

"It's not that sad." Sonya eyebrows raised as she rolled her eyes. "I'm hungry. Do you want to go get some lunch?"

"We've got to finish this first." Maggie blew her nose again. "How about we just order some pizza and watch the next one?"

"I've got to get going, but it's been fun." I shot Sonya a smile as she murdered me with her eyes.

"Are you sure? Just one more movie?" Maggie hit pause on the remote. "Just a couple more hours?"

"Yeah, Val, just a couple more?" Sonya sank into the couch.

"You know I'd love to, but I have to get home. Call me and let me know how the movie was."

"Oh, don't you worry, I'll be sure to tell you all about it." Sonya gritted her teeth at me and turned it into a smile for Maggie.

There was too much on my mind to just sit around. It felt like my life was slipping away faster than ever before. Norma's advice of finding the joy in every situation was beginning to be a pain in my ass. When my thoughts took me to the darkest places of my mind her voice tapped me on the shoulder and made me search for the pinhole of light. Sometimes, it was just nice to dwell in the darkness.

CHAPTER THIRTEEN

Five days had passed before Norma called me to pick her up from the airport. I was on the downward spiral of believing I would never see her again. She called me from Philadelphia where she said she was on a layover. "Hi Val, can you come get me in Burlington? I should be there by three."

"Today?" I looked at my watch. "That's in two and a half hours."

"I know. I'm sorry for the short notice."

"You weren't going to call, were you?"

"Don't let your imagination get the best of you, dear. Will you be able to come and get me, or should I give Maggie a call?"

"No, I'll be there. There's something we need to talk about anyway. I'll see you soon."

"Thank you, Val. I can't wait to see you."

There was no time to get ready, I had to leave as soon as I hung up the phone. The airport was a two-hour drive from

Lawrenceville, and I wanted to make sure I was on time. I didn't want to give her any excuse to change her plans. I sent Tim a text and was on my way.

I spent the two-hour drive rehearsing what I was going to tell Norma. I wanted to be honest with her, but I also didn't want to make things worse than they actually were, at least in the moment. With traffic in Burlington, I arrived at the airport with ten minutes to spare. I parked my car in the passenger pickup lane and watched the door for Norma.

Norma came out of the first revolving door with a small blue suitcase in hand. She was smiling and slightly swinging her bag with each step she took. Happiness poured off of her and made it impossible not to greet her with a smile. "You look like you had a relaxing trip."

"It was nice. I hadn't been to Florida in years. Lily is all settled in with her mom."

"I'm glad she is home. Maybe life will get easier for her now."

"I think it might." Norma chuckled. "Her mom threw her a welcome home party and there were a few guys that couldn't keep their eyes off of her."

"She is beautiful. I hope she finds the perfect guy and gets that baby she has been wanting."

"Oh, she will. I know it will happen for her. Good people deserve good things." She turned her head and put her hand on my arm, as if she read my mind. "Just like the happy little life you and Tim have created."

"Yeah, I got lucky."

"It's more than luck. You deserve every bit of happiness that comes your way. Don't you ever forget it."

"I'll try. You'll be happy to hear I have an appointment to meet a therapist tomorrow morning."

"That's wonderful." She smiled as she looked out the window. "You said you had something to tell me?"

I bit the inside of my lip, hoping the pain would distract me enough from what I had to say. I tightened my grip on the steering wheel. "Yeah, I guess I did tell you that, didn't I?"

"You did, and I've been curious ever since. You can't keep me waiting any longer."

I took a deep breath in and blew it out through my open mouth. "After you left in the U-Haul, Sonya started asking questions about Martha and the similarities between the two of you."

Norma squinted her eyes as she listened.

"I guess that part wouldn't be that bad, if..." I swallowed to try to push down my heart that had found its way into my throat. "I hadn't told Tim and Gabe about the case."

"You told them?"

"Well, not exactly. When I was trying to figure out who was behind the killings, I thought maybe it was the same person. I had no idea it was you. I promise. I never would have said a thing if I even suspected you for a second."

"Have they said anything since? Tim or Gabe?"

I shook my head. "No, they didn't think the cases were connected at all when I mentioned it. But when Sonya started talking, I got sick to my stomach thinking it might be my fault if you were ever caught."

"I don't think there's anything to worry about. Tim is looking for other cases that match the ones in Lawrenceville.

I don't think he could look past that detail to think outside the box on this one."

"What do you mean?"

"Well, he is fixated on that CD, he can't see any of the other connections. That's precisely why I change up what I leave behind. It's a little game of cat and mouse I like to play."

"I just feel so bad. I feel like such a failure. I should have never said anything."

"Stop it right now. You did nothing wrong. I'll be just fine, don't you worry."

I wanted to believe her, but part of me still worried someone was going to find out. I had to push the thoughts out of my mind and focus on the time we were able to spend together. Even if she didn't feel worried, something inside me told me I needed to be ready. For what? I wasn't sure.

CHAPTER FOURTEEN

I arrived at my new therapist's office right on time. I didn't want to be late and be labeled as a slacker and I didn't want to be early and talk myself out of staying. Jennifer Gold looked as perky as she sounded. The Wednesday Addams that lingered inside of me wasn't sure I would be able to be around such positivity so early in the morning.

"Good morning, Valerie, it's such a pleasure to meet you." She held my hand between her silky-smooth hands instead of shaking it.

"Hi, it's nice to meet you, too." Lie number one of the morning. I took a seat in the chair across from her and sat up straight, not allowing myself to get too comfortable. She had her long slender leg crossed over her knee where she was filling out papers on a clipboard. Her fingers were just as thin and were delicately wrapped around the pen as it glided across the page. She was perfect. Gorgeous, happy, and even had stunning strawberry blonde hair in wavy curls.

She set the clipboard down and folded her hands in her lap. "So, where would you like to start?"

"To be perfectly honest, I don't really want to be here."

She picked the paper up off the floor and wrote something down. "Okay, so then, why are you here?" She tilted her head with the pen against her rosebud lips.

"I have a lot of stuff that I need to work through." I cracked my knuckles. "I'm pregnant, and I want to work on as much stuff as I can before I have the chance to screw this baby up."

"That sounds like a good reason to be here. Have you ever been in counseling before?"

"Yeah, that's part of the reason I'm here."

"Can you explain more about that?"

"I'd rather not talk about it." I held up my hand to examine my fingernails. "But I know I have to."

"Well, you don't have to, if you don't want to. The hour is yours. You can talk about whatever you want, or nothing at all."

"Have you heard about Dr. Chad Ross?"

She nodded.

"Well, he was my first therapist, and I was the first one to report him."

"That was very brave of you."

"People keep saying that, but I don't feel brave. I wanted revenge. That was what motivated me to make the report."

"How do you feel since making the report?"

"Worse, actually. Guilty for not telling sooner. I feel like I could have prevented what happened to all the other girls. If

I hadn't waited so long, he might have already been in jail and he would have lost his license years ago."

"So, you feel responsible for his actions?"

"No. I feel responsible for my inaction."

"You say you wanted revenge. Why now? What was the thing that pushed you into action?"

"I saw him for the first time the day my gram died. My mom was with him and seeing them together brought back all of the anger I had when I left. I hadn't seen them in over sixteen years, and my mom didn't even care. She was a total bitch. I guess I should have expected that, though." I shook my head. "But, anyway, it just made me want to make them pay for what they did to me."

"It sounds like you were just as upset with your mom as you were with Dr. Ross."

"Yeah, I was. I am. It was her job to protect me, but she didn't. She let them take my baby away from me and didn't even care how bad it hurt me." The warm tears turned cold as they dried to my cheeks. "I guess I wanted to see her hurt as bad as she hurt me, and if I could get her husband taken away from her, she would know how it felt when she took my baby."

Jennifer handed me a box of tissues.

"I hope she hurts. I hope her heart is broken, and I hope she's all alone. I hope her friends all abandoned her when they found out what kind of person she really is. I hope she feels so low that she kills herself." I couldn't take the words back after they left my mouth.

"Do you ever think about hurting your mom?"

I bit the inside of my cheek and shook my head.

"Do you ever think about hurting yourself?"

"No, of course not."

"I forgot to mention earlier, that I am mandated by law to report anything you share that poses a danger to someone or yourself."

"I'm aware. I think it's pretty normal to wish bad things to the people who hurt me, or people I love, but thinking and doing are very different things."

"You're right, it is normal, and they are different things. I'm sorry if I offended you, I had to ask."

"Yeah, I know." I crossed my arms and looked around her office. "I wish I didn't even say it. I knew it was stupid as soon as I said it."

"As long as I know you are safe, you can say anything you want and it stays right here in this room."

"So, you don't think I'm evil for wishing harm on them?"

"No, not at all. I think what you are feeling is valid, and I bet there are many others who would feel the same way."

"I just feel like I'm running out of time. There are so many years I lost that I want to try to make up, but it never feels like there's enough time."

"When did you notice feeling like that?"

"Probably when my gram died." The real answer was when Earl almost killed me, but that wasn't something I could share with her, or anyone else. Having death wave from a distance was enough to make me rethink everything else in my life. "I guess when I lost her, I saw how quickly someone can slip away. Life can change in an instant, and there is nothing you can do about it. There is so much left that I haven't done yet, so many things..."

"That sounds like a good thing to work on."

"What?"

"I want you to write down a list of things you would like to do. Don't think too hard about it, just write what comes to mind."

"Like a bucket list?"

She smiled. "Yes, exactly like that."

"Alright, I can work on that."

"We are just about out of time. Is there anything else you'd like to address before you go?"

"It's been an hour already?"

Jennifer nodded. "Do you think you'd like to come back next week?"

"I think so. Today wasn't as awful as I thought it would be."

"I'll take that as a compliment." She laughed as she handed me her card. "Same time, same place?"

"Okay. I'm sure I'll have loads more fun stuff to talk about." I guided the door shut and smiled at the older woman in the waiting room. Maybe perky would work for me. She had enough energy for the both of us, and that was worth its weight in gold. I laughed at myself as the joke hit me. Jennifer *Gold.*

Inside my car, I picked up my phone to check the notifications. There were four missed calls and a text from Tim. "Call me ASAP."

Still laughing at myself I replied with, "Hi, ASAP."

My phone rang as soon as the message reached him. "Val, where are you?" His voice didn't sound like he had been laughing, but instead like the day he came to warn me about the sex offender moving into my building.

"I'm just leaving my counselor's office. Why? What's going on?"

"I need you to get home as soon as you can. Don't turn the radio on, okay?"

My heart sank. "Tim, what's going on? Is Gabe okay?"

"Gabe is fine. Please just promise me you'll come straight home. And please pop Tom into the stereo and keep the radio off."

"You know I never listen to the radio, but now I think I have to."

"Val, no. Please just get home. Please promise me, okay? This is very important."

"Yeah, okay. You're scaring me, though. Can't you please tell me what's going on?"

"I will, just get home as soon as you can."

The forty-five-minute drive home felt like an eternity as the thoughts rushed through my mind. I wanted to turn on the radio and see what he was keeping from me, but I knew I probably didn't want to know. Gabe was fine. I keep circling back to that thought. Tim and Gabe were fine. I was fine. Our baby was fine. What else could it be?

CHAPTER FIFTEEN

Tim was sitting on the stairs when I pulled into the driveway. The color had been drained from his face. The expression white as a ghost had never meant anything until I saw his face. Before I had a chance to put my car in park, Tim had his hand on my door handle. "What's going on, Tim? I can't for the life of me think what could be going on."

"Val, come on inside with me." He took my hand and led me toward the house.

"Just tell me what's going on."

The tears started falling before the words could leave his mouth. "There's been an accident, Val."

My body temperature increased as my pulse beat against my neck. I couldn't speak as I felt my body start to tremble.

"It's Norma."

"Is she okay?" Goosebumps grew on every inch of my skin as I waited for his response.

He closed his eyes and shook his head. "I'm so sorry, Val."

He wrapped his arms around me and we cried together. My head felt like a top that was spinning out of control.

"What happened?"

"It looks like she lost control of the car and it caught on fire when it crashed over the guardrails. She was found this morning."

"Where? When did it happen?"

"It was on Cliff Road; her car was found over the bank. It looks like it either happened early this morning or sometime last night."

"She was out there all night?"

"We don't really know. But it looks like she died on impact."

"Oh my God." I wailed as his words reached my core. "Does anyone else know? Maggie?"

"Yes, they went and told her this morning."

"I've got to get over there."

"I'll take you." Tim took my keys and gave me another tight hug. "I'm so sorry. I know how much you loved her."

"What was she doing in that part of town? What was she doing out so late?" The questions came, but there were no answers. I knew she was going to leave me eventually, but I didn't think this was how it was going to happen.

When we arrived at Norma's house, I let myself in. "Maggie? Maggie." Everything around me was black. My heart ached but felt hollow.

Sonya, Maggie and the girls were all in the living room. Their eyes were bloodshot and piles of crumpled up tissues surrounded them. "Val, I don't know what I'm going to do without her." Maggie's words were hard to make out, but she was saying what I was thinking. How were any of us going to live without her.

"I don't know." I held onto Tim to keep myself from falling to the floor. "I can't believe it. How can this be real?"

"I don't know." Maggie blew her nose.

"What was she doing?" I looked at Maggie for the answers I needed.

"I don't know. She must have left after we went to bed. She didn't say anything about having to go out or anything. She said goodnight to the girls and I, just like always. I expected to see her in the kitchen, just like every other morning, but she wasn't there. I looked in her room, and her bed was made and when I looked outside her car was gone. I just figured she got up early and went to the store. I didn't think anything more about it."

"She's not supposed to be gone." Sonya wailed as she rubbed her belly. "She was supposed to meet her little niece. She was supposed to tell me everything is going to be okay."

"I don't understand. Why did this have to happen?" Nausea crept up my throat at the thought of Norma alone in her car, waiting to be found. "This isn't fair. How much more is going to be stolen from me?" I stomped my feet as I let the emotion overpower me. It wasn't fair. There was so much more we had to do. So much more we had to talk about. Time and time again I kept learning the same lesson. Life isn't fair, and death is right around the corner, waiting to pounce on you, or someone you love.

"I'm so sorry ladies." Tim dropped his head. "I wish there was something we could have done."

"I'm just glad she was found, and we didn't have to

wonder what happened to her." Maggie's words struck a chord inside of me. What if? No. How?

"Are you one hundred percent sure it was Norma?" I turned my attention to Tim.

He dropped his head. "Yes, I'm afraid so. She was in the front seat."

"And, you're sure it was her car?"

"Yes, Val, I wish I could tell you something else, but we are certain it was Norma. A female was found badly burned in the driver's seat of Norma's car. We know it was her. I'm sorry."

My wish to make this a bad dream was not strong enough to turn the desire into a reality. I walked into Norma's room and sat on her bed. I closed my eyes and the hair on the back of my neck stood up. I heard her voice in my head. *"Trust your intuition."* I wished it were that simple.

Maggie joined me on the bed. We sat together and cried. The house felt empty without Norma there. "I don't even know where the girls and I will stay now. I feel so selfish for even thinking about that."

"That's not selfish, that's a reasonable fear. There are just so many unknowns right now. We'll figure it out." I took her hand in mine and held it as I looked around Norma's room. "It's so neat and tidy in here. Did she always keep it this clean?"

"It does seem extra clean in here." Maggie got up and opened the top drawer of the bureau. "Even her clothes are folded perfectly." She opened the next drawer and pulled out one of Norma's shirts. She held it up to her nose. "I don't want this to be real."

"I know, I don't, either." The thought I didn't want to think kept creeping back in. "Do you think she did this on purpose?"

"Like she killed herself?" Maggie hugged the shirt. "No, there's no way. She never would have left us like this. She would have had a plan for us. That's just how she was."

"Yeah, you're right."

"And she was so happy after she returned from her trip. I can't imagine her being so unhappy that she thought suicide was the only option."

"It did seem like she had a good time. Are any of her things missing?" I got off the bed and opened the closet.

"It doesn't look like it."

"I guess I'm just trying to figure out a way to make this not be real."

It just didn't make sense. I couldn't wrap my mind around any of it. And the only person who could help me make sense of it was gone.

CHAPTER SIXTEEN

There was no body at Norma's funeral, just an empty urn. The car fire had burned so hot there was nothing left of Norma's body; just enough to make the identification. Lily flew back for the service, making the guest count increase to nine. Norma didn't have any family, or if she did, she had never told any of us about them. From the story she shared with me, I didn't figure she would have wanted them present if she did.

The only thing that helped ease any of my pain was the thought of Norma being reunited with Sylvia. She deserved a happily ever after, even if it was in the afterlife. Even though Norma was dead, I couldn't tell her secrets. Tim and Gabe would never know who the Executioner was, at least not because I told them. *Oh my God.* The room went dark as my thoughts took me deeper.

This *was* my fault. How could I have been so stupid? I never thought telling her that Sonya was on to her would have made her take her own life. I expected her to pack up and be on her way. There was no longer any question. She took her life so she wouldn't get caught. The weight of her secret; of our secret was buried by the weight of the guilt.

Grief masked the terror I was being swallowed by. Where was the joy in this? I hated that piece of advice, but now I despised it. When I was able to feel my feet under me, I went outside to get some fresh air. The crispness of autumn reminded me there is always an end. An end to what was to make way for what will be. The changing seasons last just long enough to make me crave the next one to come, leaving me too occupied to enjoy the present moment. That was what life felt like. The desire for what was to come took all of the joy and made the darkness of depression pop like the reds and oranges of autumn. Pointing out all of the pain and sorrow.

This pain, the raw ache that burned a hole in my gut was why I didn't want to give my heart to anyone. It was what kept me closed up tight in my apartment, pushing everyone who tried to enter away. It was Norma who made me open my heart, and now it was Norma who broke it. I wouldn't give up the time we spent together to avoid this pain. It was worth far more than I can find words for.

"Val, why don't you come inside and be with your friends?" Tim placed his hand on my back.

I shook my head. "I can't. Not yet."

"What can I do for you?"

"Are you sure it was her in that car?"

"Val, we've gone over this already. I'm sorry I don't have the answers you're looking for."

My chest rose and fell under my black cardigan as my back went rigid. "I fucking hate this."

Tim ran his hand through my hair, catching a snarl I hadn't brushed out. "I know..."

"No, you don't. You've never lost your best friend. Both of your best friends in less than a goddamn month. How the fuck is this fair?" Anger kept the tears from spilling out. Rage was the only emotion I could release. "I want a redo on my whole fucking life." I crossed my arms to keep from pulling my hair.

The tears I couldn't cry streamed down Tim's face. "I'm sorry, Val. You're right."

"I just want to scream." I closed my eyes and lifted my head to feel the warmth of the sun.

"Scream. Go ahead. Get it out."

"I can't." Not here, not so everyone else could see me falling apart. I turned to face Tim and fell into him. He wrapped his arms around me and let me sob. A million questions poured out of my eyes. All the what-ifs I could muster. All the should ofs and could ofs released and left damp marks on Tim's black suit jacket.

"Let it out. Don't hold it in."

When I was able to catch my breath, we walked back into the funeral home where the others were gathered next to the handful of pictures we had of Norma. Seeing how small of a mark she had left hurt my heart. She had spent her life helping others, making sure women and children were safe, and no one could thank her. She could never be recognized for the hero she was. She was Superwoman.

I wondered how many people she had come in contact

with over her fifty-year murder spree. How many lives did she take? More importantly, how many lives did she save? Would the men she killed be waiting for her? Or would they already be in the depths of Hell? I knew Norma's heart was too pure to join them there. Too many thoughts to focus on one. They came in as fast as a freight train. Zooming by, not lingering long enough for me to board any of them. A whirlwind of questions and a lack of answers.

When we went back to Norma's house for tea and cookies, the light on her answering machine was flashing. Maggie hit play. "Hi, this is Peter Berkley, and I ah, heard about Norma's passing. Please call me at your earliest convenience." Maggie's red cheeks lost their color.

"What do you think that's about?" Maggie dropped the pen after writing down his number.

"I don't know. That's the lawyer that is handling my gram's estate."

Maggie dialed the number and waited for Peter to answer. She tapped her foot as she waited. "Hi, this is Maggie, you asked me to call you about Norma." She nodded her head in between "okays." Her eyes widened. "Oh my word."

I tried to hear what was being said on the other end, but I wasn't able to focus enough.

Maggie hung up the phone, her eyes still wide open. "Norma had a will. She left this house to the girls and me. She also had a $250,000 life insurance policy and I'm the beneficiary."

Doubt crept into my mind. The one thing we knew she

would have done before she left had been taken care of. "Wow, that's great."

"It's like she knew what was coming." Maggie and I locked eyes as the conversation in Norma's bedroom came back to her, too. "You don't think it's possible, do you?"

"I don't know." My three most used words these last few days, but I didn't know much of anything anymore. "It makes more sense now. She had things in place for a reason."

Tim came out of the bathroom and walked in on the last half of the conversation. "What are you ladies talking about?"

"Norma had a will. She left the house and a life insurance policy to Maggie. It was like she had this planned."

Tim put his hands into his pockets. "I don't think so. It was a tragic accident."

I wasn't convinced. They didn't know what I knew. I slipped back into Norma's room, shutting and locking the door behind me. I sat on her bed and opened the nightstand drawer. A journal. All of the pages were blank. Not one spec of her handwriting. A closer look revealed some of the pages had been torn out. I rubbed my finger on the page, but there was no impressions on the page.

On my hands and knees, I looked under her bed. Nothing. I crawled to check under her bureau. Not even a dust bunny greeted me. I opened every drawer in the room. Nothing was out of place. Not a clue left behind. But she was an expert at leaving. She had decades of experience. Leaving no clues behind didn't mean there wasn't anything to find out. It just meant I had to dig deeper. I had to think like Norma.

CHAPTER SEVENTEEN

The same black Jeep Cherokee was on the fourth pass by our house. Tim and Gabe had already left for work, so it was just me and my imagination. "What the heck is going on?" I asked Gabriel when he jumped on the back of the couch to look out the window with me. "How many more times do you think they're going to drive by?" As it drove by again, I was able to get a good look at the driver. An older man with a baseball hat and dark sunglasses.

My breathing increased as I took a closer look. *Was it Chad? What the hell would he be doing in Lawrenceville?* I found my phone and went back to my lookout post with Gabriel. My pulse slammed against my neck when I saw the Jeep come back by. This time he parked just a few feet from the driveway. Frozen in place I couldn't even dial the phone if I needed to reach Tim.

The man pulled his hood over his head and exited the car. He scanned the neighborhood before he started walking up the driveway. "What's happening Gabriel? You know I love you, but I really wish you were a Pitbull right now." As the man approached, there was no denying it was Chad. Before he made his way to the door, I got on my hands and knees and crawled to make sure it was locked and crawled into the hall where I was sure I wouldn't be seen.

The doorbell echoed through the house, lingering a little longer in my head. The bell buzzed again; this time followed by a knock. My heart thumped against my chest, so loud I was sure he would be able to hear me. Another knock followed, harder this time. I heard the doorknob rattle. I closed my eyes to try to escape the terror.

"Elaine? Elaine, I know you're here."

Why the hell would my mom be here? Curiosity almost outweighed the fear. *Almost.* From the slur of his words, it sounded like he had been drinking. That would make two violations on his conditions for release.

"Elaine." His voice softened. "Come on, please come home. You know I didn't do any of that stuff. You know I'm a good guy." I heard his body thud against the door. "I love you, Elaine."

When things got quiet, I tiptoed to the door to see if he was gone. He wasn't. He was sitting on the steps, his back to the door. I needed him to leave, but I wasn't sure how to go about it. I knew calling Tim would get Chad arrested, and I wasn't sure if they would keep him in jail this time. I wasn't ready to give up the opportunity I might need later, if I decided to take justice into my own hands. With Norma gone, I knew I was the only one that could do the job.

I put my hand to my stomach and closed my eyes to try to

come up with a plan. I know what I should do, but I'm not sure what I *need* to do. I waited for him to leave, but as the minutes continued to pass by, he seemed to be more settled into his spot. I went to Tim's closet and took out the nine-millimeter he had been teaching me how to shoot. I held it in my hand and observed the power on being in control fill my being. I grabbed the bullets, loaded the gun and slipped it into my waistband. I pulled my sweater over my hips to conceal it.

I shook my arms at my sides and cracked my knuckles before I opened the door. "What the fuck are you doing here, Chad?"

My voice startled him and he jumped to his feet. "Tell me where your mother is."

"I have no idea where that cold-hearted bitch is."

"Bullshit." He took a step closer to me. "She said she was coming to see you last week, and I haven't heard from her since."

With my hand inching closer to my waistband, I took a step back. "Why would she come see me? That doesn't make any sense."

"She wanted her money. She told me you were going to give it to her."

"Her money? You mean Gram's money?"

"Don't be smart. You know damn well Elaine was supposed to get that money. You just disappeared and expect to have everything?" He threw his hand up in the air.

"What the fuck did you just say?" My hand was now under my sweater, my fingers wrapped around the gun. "You have the fucking balls to say that to me? You make me your personal sex toy, and you fucking say I disappeared? You're a fucking piece of shit Dr. Fucking Ross."

"Quiet down. You're going to have people staring." He pushed the air down in front of him. "You need to lower your voice."

"You don't have the right to tell me what to do. I don't give a damn who hears what I have to say. The whole world is going to know what kind of sick fuck you are soon enough." I walked past him to stand on the lawn. "Hey, everyone, this guy right here is a child rapist. He fucks little kids and then steals their babies."

Chad stumbled down the stairs and started walking toward me. "I just want to know where Elaine is. I don't want any trouble."

"You're in plenty of trouble just being here." I snapped a picture of him. "And look, now I have proof." I waved my phone in the air. "You better get your child molesting ass out of here before I call the cops."

"Val..."

"Don't you ever call me that."

"Please don't. I just need your mother back home. I can't go through this alone."

I laughed at him. "Oh, look who the cry baby is now. You're pathetic. Get the fuck off of my property and don't ever come back."

"Val... I... ah... I just need Elaine back home."

I pulled the gun out of my waistband and pointed it at him. My hands shaking. "I said get the fuck out of here."

He held his hands up. "What are you doing?" He started to walk backwards toward his car. "I'm going, I'm going."

I kept the gun aimed at him until he was in his car and drove away. The adrenaline that pumped through my veins left me wanting more. I had never felt so powerful, not even when I killed Donald Brice. The fear in Chad's eyes gave me a type of pleasure I had never experienced before. I wanted to finish the job. I needed to. Just this last time. There would never be another.

Seeing Chad suffer was icing on the cake. I didn't expect Mom to leave him, I mean, why now? It's not like she didn't know who he was before. Where could she be? And why hadn't she contacted me about the money? I'd been expecting her.

My imagination took me down memory lane. Before Mom married Chad, she didn't have a problem finding companionship. She didn't always bring them home, but I knew where she was. She dated a lot. It would be perfect if she took off with another guy. The more I thought about it, the more I knew I had to wait to take action. I couldn't kill him while there was still misery here on Earth for him to deal with. No, he deserved all of the pain and uncomfortableness he received.

Killing Chad felt like something I needed to do. Every time I tried to talk myself out of it and wait for the justice system to take care of things, I ended up telling myself it would never be enough. There would never be enough days spent behind bars to fix what he did to me, or the other girls. Even life behind bars wouldn't be enough. He had to feel fear. And desperation. And pain. He would have to suffer. There wasn't any other way.

CHAPTER EIGHTEEN

My appointment with Jennifer Gold couldn't have come at a better time. Between Norma's death, and Chad's visit, I needed to talk to someone. Someone that would listen without telling me how sorry they were. Someone who could keep the conversation professional.

Before I sat in the same chair as last week, I grabbed the box of tissues. "I appreciate that you understand the need for the good ones. I'm so sick of ripping off half the skin on my nose. They should be outlawed."

"I see you plan on getting into some tough stuff today. I'm impressed." She set the clipboard on the floor under her chair.

"Yeah, well, I don't have to go too deep to need these." I pulled one out to get ready. "Did you hear about the accident in Lawrenceville last week? The one where the old lady burned to death?"

She nodded.

"That was my best friend." I closed my eyes before I continued. "I found out about that as soon as I got home from here. Needless to say, my week has been shitty."

"Your emotions don't seem to match your words. Can you talk a little about that?"

"I'd rather not, honesty."

"Okay. When you're ready, I think it would be something we could work on together."

"I don't want to cry, because once I start, I have a hard time stopping."

"That makes sense. Do you want to tell me about your friend?"

"She was a client, well actually, she was a member of the trauma support group I was running at the hospital. She was perfect in every way. I know people turn people into heroes after they die, but she really was." The pressure from the tears I tried not to shed was quickly turning into a headache. "She was the reason I had the last few visits with my gram. She told me I shouldn't waste my time, that you never know how much time you have left."

"She sounds like a wise woman."

"She was." I shook my head. "I hate that I have to say was. I don't want to believe it. I keep waiting for her to come back and tell me it was all a mistake."

"I think we all wish that about the people we love. It's never easy."

"I know. I spent the last decade helping people say goodbye to their loved ones, but I can't seem to use any of the tools that I know work."

"It's not the same, it's too personal for logic to work."

"Yeah, you're probably right." I twisted my wedding ring. "She saved my life. I guess I feel guilty that I couldn't save hers."

"How do you think you would have been able to save her?"

I thought about the conversation we had the day before her accident. It wasn't something I could share. Not with Jennifer or anyone else. I bit the inside of my lip. "I guess I couldn't have. I just wanted to."

"Of course."

"It's even harder that we didn't have her body for the funeral. We didn't get to say a proper goodbye. How do I make it feel real? How long before it stops hurting?"

"It takes time."

I sighed. "It also doesn't help that my gram died less than a month ago. Like, how much do I have to be tested? What lessons am I supposed to learn? Two of the most important women in my life are ripped away from me within days of each other. How is that fair?"

"You know what I'm going to say."

"Yeah, life isn't fair. Don't I know that? Oh, you want to know what else happened that isn't fair?"

Jennifer nodded.

"Chad came to my house. He was looking for my mom. He said she left him."

"Chad, as in Dr. Ross?"

"Yeah, he was drunk and wouldn't leave. I was able to tell him off. I wasn't afraid. Well, at first I was, but by the time he left, I wasn't."

"Do the police know he did this?"

"Yeah." The lie slid smoothly off my lips. "But it was exhilarating to tell him off. I was so scared to have to testify against him, but I think this really showed me I am strong enough to do what I need to do." I knew I couldn't tell her the real plan. Having a therapist was nice, but it wasn't like having Norma. She would be the only one who would have understood.

"Well, that does sound like a plus."

"I was happy to see how much he was suffering. He was whining like a baby looking for my mom. I was only eighteen when I left home, and I never cried like that. I hate her, though, so there's that."

"Did he say why he came to your house to look for her?"

"He said she told him that was where she was going. To confront me about receiving my gram's inheritance. She had been waiting her whole life for that money, and my gram left it to me. Norma was the one who took her to the lawyer to make the change to her will. That was after she figured everything out. So, anyway, Chad said she was coming to get her money. She never came. I've been expecting her. I know she'll do anything to get her hands on that money. I've been waiting, but she never showed up. I half hope she left him for another man."

"You said you were waiting for her to come. Do you think you'd want to have her back in your life if she left Chad?"

"Hell no. She had the chance to do the right thing when I was fifteen. She didn't. She chose the rapist and she sent me away. Not before calling me a whore. She wouldn't even listen to what I had to say. I wanted her to come so I could rub it in her face. I wanted to show her what she's missing out on. She's going to be a grandmother... again. There's no way in Hell I'd ever let her near this baby. I don't even want her to go near Gabe and he's a grown man."

"So, you wanted to see your mom to show her that you made it on your own? I think that's pretty awesome."

"You do? You don't think it's too... I don't know... mean?"

"Not at all. I think it's an act of empowerment."

"Hmmm. I guess I like that idea. I was just a kid and I had no one. I put myself through college and worked so many awful jobs just to have enough to eat. I never want to see another package of Ramen noodles again." I stuck my tongue out.

She laughed. "Yeah, I had my fair share of poor college kid food."

"I figure I don't owe her anything. Not one cent of that money. I kind of wanted to see the look on her face when I told her no."

"Do you want to practice? I can pretend to be her, and you can tell her everything you want to."

"That sounds stupid. You know how much I hated Gestalt?"

"Ah, that's right. You're an old pro at this." She folded her hands in her lap. "You must know how it works then?"

I rolled my eyes. "Yeah. I think I'll pass. I like you too much to call you all the names I have saved for my mother."

"Well, thank you, I guess." She smiled. "How about journaling? Have you ever written her a letter telling her everything you've ever wanted to say?"

"No. That's something I could try."

"You can either send it to her, keep it, or burn it."

"I'll give it a shot." I picked at my fingernails to break up the eye contact. "Norma was like the mom I always wanted." The tears finally released. "I loved her so much. I don't know how I'm going to make it without her."

"One day at a time. That's all we ever can do. Just put one foot in front of the other and strive for a better day than the one before it."

I blew my nose. "That's such an exhausting thought. Who knows how many steps it takes to get to where we're going?"

"My guess is you'll know."

I wondered if Norma knew. Did she set out that morning to take her last steps? Where was she going? Or coming from? Was there someone she was going to 'take care of'? The more I thought about it, the more I didn't understand. And why was she so happy? There were some secrets I knew she hadn't shared. Some secrets I'd have to uncover on my own.

CHAPTER NINETEEN

While Tim and Gabe were still at work, I logged onto our computer to see what I could find out about Norma's past; the parts she hadn't told me. With the information she did give me I figured I should have enough to connect some of the missing dots.

If she meant to or not, she let it slip that her real identity was Rose St. Thomas. In the search bar I typed in *Rose St. Thomas* and waited for the results to populate. I didn't know what state she had been living in at the time, so I had no way of pinpointing the one I was looking for.

Multiple results popped up on the screen. As I scrolled through them, I was not able to find any from the time period I was looking for. Norma had said she had been on the run for over fifty-five years. I did the math; that would have been in the late 1950s or early 1960s. I added the dates to the search bar. The same results appeared on the screen. I scrolled through the pages. When I got to the tenth page frustration grew.

Without the town, or at least the state, there would be no way to find what I was looking for. I closed my eyes and tried to go back to that conversation. There must be something she told me that would get me closer to finding out who Rose St. Thomas was. A warmth came over me as I heard Norma's voice fill my thoughts. "Don't give up, dear. I know you'll figure it out."

It was just the encouragement I needed. The name of her husband came to me forcing my eyes to pop open. Vern. Norma, or Rose, married a man named Vern St. Thomas. I typed his name into the search bar with the word *murder* and hit enter. There it was, just what I had been searching for. A picture of Vern and his wife Rose were at the top of the results. Norma was a beautiful young woman with a captivating smile with a tormented look in her eyes. The photo of her appeared to have come from her wedding day. She looked much like how I felt until I met the ladies from the group. Sad, lonely, and desperate to just blend in. Norma had a sparkle in her eyes, and the most welcoming presence I had ever experienced. She had done something right over the past fifty-five years. Living a life of crime looked good on her.

The headline of the newspaper article made my skin crawl. *Grisliest Murder in the History of Peterson, New Jersey.* With years of practice it appeared Norma had gotten better at leaving a crime scene neat and tidy. I tried to imagine the fear she must have felt as a young woman killing her husband in order to save her own life. I'm not sure I would have been strong enough to do it. I wouldn't have been able to stomach the blood, his or mine.

The next article went on to explain Vern was murdered

in 1959 and it remains unsolved. This one was dated 1999. It was a rehash of some of the most notorious crime scenes in New Jersey. It stated Rose St. Thomas was considered a missing person, although she was now presumed dead. They reported at the scene of Vern's murder there was blood of two separate people. It was believed to have been the blood of Vern and his wife Rose. There was no longer evidence from the case, so there was no way of knowing for sure who the blood belonged to. They wrote the evidence was destroyed in a fire in 1982.

As the story Norma had told me floated back to me, I couldn't help but smile. She was born for this. I never would have thought about leaving my blood behind, and this was way before she had access to the internet. I also wondered if she was responsible for the fire that destroyed the evidence. Her ingenuity left me with more questions. How would she have come up with that? And how was she able to throw away an identity and create a new one that many times without being caught?

As soon as the thought left my head, I couldn't help but question the validity of Norma's death. She was an *expert* at this kind of thing. The possibility of her doing it again was growing. Was is due to my denial? Or was it because it was a legitimate possibility? I wanted it to be the case more than anything. As hope grew it was soon squashed by the reality of what had happened. There was a body in the car. It wasn't as if the car had been abandoned.

Different scenarios played in my mind. If not Norma, who? Would could it have been? The remains were identified. They couldn't have overlooked that? Tim assured me the investigation determined it was Norma. Could she have really outsmarted the cops in this day and age? DNA wasn't something you could trick any longer. Or, was she just *that* good at what she does she was able to outsmart the system?

She had escaped law enforcement for the last five decades. The Executioner did kill six men without getting caught, and that was just in Lawrenceville alone. Could this be another smoke and mirrors trick? The reality of the delusion soon faded into an illusion. They had a body this time. When Rose and Martha went missing there was no body. Hope fizzled to disappointment. Wishing for something hard enough sometimes wasn't enough to make it so.

With a heavy heart, I clicked on Vern St. Thomas's obituary. In the family listed, there was no mention of his in-laws. There were two sisters listed; Hellen Brown and Thelma Darling. I wrote their names in my notepad and looked for Rose's obituary. There were a few for Rose St. Thomas, but none matched what I was looking for. I guess it made sense. If she didn't have family that knew where she was or that she was married, and Vern was dead there would be no one to write it.

"Honey, I'm home." Tim's voice met my ears before I heard the door shut. I closed out the pages I was on and pulled up the webpage for baby names.

"I'm in the office." I yelled loud enough for him to hear me. I wasn't able to walk away from my search yet. There were too many things I needed to look up.

"What are you doing in here?" Tim kissed the top of my head and looked over my shoulder. "Oh, baby names." He gave my shoulders a squeeze. "We do have to start thinking about that... but don't you think we should wait until we know what he is?"

"He? What makes you so sure?" I turned the computer chair enough to stand up and gave him a hug.

"Did I say he?" Tim laughed. "I'll be happy with either."

"As long as it's healthy."

"Don't patronize me."

"What, I've only heard you say it a hundred times already. I know you want a son, but be careful, she can hear you."

"Oh, so now I see what you're doing. You're trying to outnumber me."

"What do you mean? You have Gabe. I'm just trying to even things out."

"What if it's twins? Then we'll have to break the tie."

"Settle down. Let me push this one out before you get the next one in line."

"Well, we have time now." He winked at me. "Gabe is having dinner with some friends tonight. We'll have the whole place to ourselves."

"Go take a shower and I'll see how I feel."

"Gee, how romantic."

"Sorry, I've just got a lot of stuff on my mind."

"I know. I'm sorry. You're just so irresistible."

When Tim left to shower, I opened Google again and typed in *Hellen Brown and New Jersey*. Her obituary was the first result on the page. I clicked on it to confirm she was Vern's sister. He was listed as predeceased. Their sister, Thelma was listed as still alive and still living in Peterson, New Jersey. I checked to date; it was only six months ago.

I clicked out of Hellen's obituary and typed *Thelma Darling in Peterson, New Jersey*. The third one on the list gave her address and phone number. I wrote the number down and closed my notebook. I hoped she would be willing to talk to me. There were so many questions I had about Rose and even Vern. Fingers crossed she would remember.

CHAPTER TWENTY

Sonya sent me a text asking me to meet her and Maggie at Norma's. She said it was important. I couldn't stomach another tragedy. She wouldn't respond to my texts. The only way to see what was going on was to just go. The unknown that hung over my head with every text and phone call made picking up my phone fill me with anxiety. What would be next?

Sonya pulled in right behind me. She had a passenger with her. A woman, just a little shorter than Sonya, got out of the car. Her black hair was in a bun on the top of her head. Large, gold hoop earrings bounced as she walked. She looked like someone you would see on Coney Island. Her caramel eyes caught my attention when I shot her a smile.

"This is Gemini Star, she's a psychic medium." Sonya looked down at her phone. "I hired her to do a reading for us, but we have to get going, we only have an hour."

"Hi." A psychic medium? If she was legit, this would spell disaster. I felt a bead of sweat fall from my forehead.

"I've always wanted to have a reading." Lie number one, I wanted to see if she picked up on it. She had no reaction as she followed Sonya into the house.

It appeared Maggie knew what was happening, because she had candles lit on the dining room table. I widened my eyes as I stood behind Gemini and waited for Maggie to notice. She did not. Gemini sat at the head of the table and took tarot cards out of her bag. She motioned for us to sit and she started shuffling the cards.

I took the seat next to her. I wanted to be able to see her, without her being able to look at me. After a few more shuffles, she spread the cards on the table in front of her. "I asked Sonya not to tell me anything. I do not know why I am here. I will ask questions, just say yes or no. Too much information will alter the reading."

Gemini held her hand over the cards, moving her hand back and forth over them. She picked a card up and turned it over. "Oh." She put her finger on the card. "I see that there has been a lot of pain." She turned her head and looked directly into my eyes. "For all of you."

Goosebumps sprouted all over my body. Why was she looking at *me*?

Gemini pulled another card and set it on top of the previous on. "Hmmm. There are a lot of questions. I see that there are answers that have never been received." She pulled another card and laid it down. "Lies and secrets are poison. Someone knows more than they are saying." She looked around the table, stopping when she reached me. "I sense people are not who they appear. Someone is in grave danger. You must act before it is too late."

The flame from the candle flickered, growing higher and then extinguishing. "Oh my God. Did you see that?" Sonya pushed her chair away from the table.

"Don't freak out, didn't you feel the breeze?" Maggie looked for my approval.

"Oh, there are never any coincidences. Someone is trying to tell you something."

"Who? Who wants to tell us something?" I asked.

"That's for you to figure out. They do not want me to reveal their identity."

"Oh, come on. Why wouldn't they want us to know?" I rolled my eyes trying to chase away the fear brewing inside of me.

"They say you know why." Gemini pulled another card. "You can only carry your secrets for so long. They will eat you alive."

"Who is telling you this stuff?" I crossed my arms.

Gemini closed her eyes. "There is an older woman that is coming through. She loves you. She knows you will do what's right."

Sonya pulled her chair back to the table. "Norma? Is it Norma?" She put her hand to her chest.

"I'm getting a name that starts with M. Mary? Marilyn? Marianne?"

I wiped a tear away from my eye. "That's my gram. Marianne."

"She wants you to be careful. There is danger coming into your life. You need to keep your eyes open. She wants you to tell the truth. No more lies."

"What is she talking about, Val?" Sonya turned her head to look at me.

I shook my head as I felt my heart jump in my throat. "I don't know."

Gemini frowned at me as she shook her head and pointed to the card. "Oh, but you do. Hold on, I'm getting something else." She closed her eyes. "A young girl. She died a tragic death. She wants to thank you. She knows what you did for her."

I tilted my head as I absorbed the information. It must have been Carmen. I hoped she would have approved. I felt a smile spread across my face knowing she knew how much I cared about her. All the obsessive thoughts and searching was appreciated. It made everything I went through worth it. She must have been looking out for me, making sure I wasn't caught.

"We want to talk to Norma." Sonya leaned onto the table.

Gemini closed her eyes. "I'm not getting anything from a Norma."

"Why wouldn't she be here? I don't understand why she wouldn't want to talk to us." Sonya brushed her tears away.

"Maybe she hasn't been gone long enough." Maggie shrugged her shoulders. "Do you think that might be why?"

"But Val's gram hasn't been gone long, either." Sonya looked at Gemini.

"Some spirits take longer than others to figure things out."

"What if a spirit went to Hell?" I twisted my wedding ring, keeping my eyes off of Gemini.

"I don't talk to evil spirits. My guides do not let them communicate with me."

"So, if someone went to Hell, they wouldn't be able to talk to us?" The thought of Norma in Hell was too much to bear. She didn't do anything wrong. I know she did more good than she did bad.

"Who are you trying to talk to Val?" Maggie asked.

"No one. It was just a question."

"There is someone here that is angry. They just crossed over. They don't have enough energy to give me many details, but I can feel the rage. It is making me feel hot." Gemini pulled out her shirt to give herself some air. "Your grandmother is back. She cannot stress enough that you need to make right with all that you have done." Gemini flipped over another card. "New beginnings. A fresh start. They can be yours. You just have to make the needed changes. She loves you."

"I love her, too."

Gemini held her hand up and closed her eyes. "Buttercup, I'm sorry."

"Buttercup? Who said that?" My mother was the only one to ever call me that. She gave me the nickname after I picked her a handful of buttercup flowers and tried to butter toast with them. The throb of my heart echoed in my ears. The good times my mom and I shared played in my mind like a movie.

Gemini shook her head. "They said you know."

"How could they know something that only someone living would know?" My thoughts came and went like they were on a racetrack. Here, then gone, and here again.

"Well, the dead know things we don't think they should know. They see more than you can imagine." Gemini held her hands up in the shape of a ball, her bracelets clanking together.

"Can you try one more time to get Norma? I really want to talk to her. I want to know what happened." Sonya hung her head.

Gemini closed her eyes again and placed her hand on the top of her head, the other on her throat. Her eyes flinched and she moved her head around. She began to hum, the sound increasing until it was a chant. "Norma... Norma... come and talk with us."

I looked over at Sonya, who had her mouth wide open watching attentively. Maggie was looking down at her fingernails. I could not get either one of their attention. I couldn't tell if they were buying this show, or if they had as much doubt as I had.

"No, there is no Norma present with us. I asked my guides if she was here, but unable to communicate, they said she is not here. I am sorry." Gemini picked up her cards and slid them back into her purple pouch and dropped it into her bag. "Our time is up. If you'd like me to come back, Sonya has my contact information.

I stayed with Maggie while Sonya brought Gemini home. "What did you think?" I asked.

"I'm not sure. I find it hard to believe Norma wouldn't be here with us."

"Maybe she has other family she's with. Or maybe she doesn't want to see how sad we all are."

"Hmm, maybe. I guess I just thought we were her family." Maggie dropped her head. "She was my family."

"Mine, too." I rubbed Maggie's back as she began to cry.

"It's still so hard to believe. I mean I said goodnight, and then I never saw her again. I think it would have been easier to wrap my head around it if I could have said goodbye, you know?"

"We did, we said goodbye at her funeral."

"No, I mean, like if we had the chance to say it to her. To her body. To hold her hand and give her a kiss."

"Yeah, I get what you're saying. It has been hard to fully comprehend what happened." I went to the refrigerator and took out the orange juice. "Did you know this was happening? That Gemini was coming?"

"Sonya called me on her way to pick her up."

I took a drink of juice. "So, at least you were more prepared than I was. I had no idea what I was walking into until I saw her. I think I might still be a skeptic."

"I don't know what to think. She sure had a lot of messages for you. None of them resonated with you?"

"I guess some of it did. Buttercup was the name my mom called me as a little girl. No one knew about that."

"Even your gram?" Maggie asked.

"Oh, yeah, of course. She must have heard her call me that before. But why would she tell me she was sorry?"

"Maybe for leaving you? Or not protecting you?"

"Yeah, that makes sense. Now I wish I wasn't so skeptical, so I could have talked to her some more."

"We can always have her come back."

"True. Maybe Norma would be ready to talk to us then." The visit with Gemini left me with more questions than answers. Just like the message she gave me. Who was talking to me that wouldn't tell me? I went through the list of people it could have been. None left me with a good feeling.

It couldn't have been Donald Brice, I'm certain he went straight to Hell. And Jane, well, if she was still able to mingle with the good, I wasn't certain of anything. Seth was a possibility. Maybe he hadn't done enough damage to be sent packing. What was the limit of bad you could do on Earth before you weren't allowed in Heaven? Who judges what is right or wrong? Could everything Norma did be considered bad? Evil? I wouldn't have thought so, but who am I to judge. Maybe that was why my gram wanted me to make things right, so I wouldn't be sent to the land of evil. I might still have time. But, what about Norma? I didn't want her to swelter with evil. There must be something I could do to help her.

CHAPTER TWENTY-ONE

After the guys left, I got my notebook and opened it to the notes I had taken in my search the other day. Thelma Darling's phone number stared back at me. She might have the answers I need to dig deeper. How weird would it be to get a call from a stranger about your brother and sister-in-law after almost sixty years? I knew I had to stop overthinking and just make the call.

With the phone in my hand, I dialed the number. My heart raced as I counted the rings. I got to six before I heard her voice. "Hello."

"Hi, ah... is this Thelma Darling?"

"Yes. Who's asking?"

I hadn't thought this through. "Um... this is Stephanie Mills, I'm a college student doing a report on... well... ah... Vern and Rose's murders." It looks like Stephanie Mills couldn't quite be put to rest.

"How did you get my number?"

"You were listed in the files."

"Oh, okay. What do you want to know?"

Surprised she bought my lie, a surge of confidence rushed through me. "Well, I have a lot of questions. Would it be okay if I call you back once I have them written down?"

"Yes, that's fine. You must know they never solved his murder."

"Yes. That's why I wanted to do my report on the case."

"Hmm, well maybe you'll be the one to solve it."

Nervous laughter fell out of my mouth before I could silence it. "Maybe."

"I have a hard time hearing on the phone, maybe you can come over sometime."

I didn't even know where Peterson, New Jersey was, but I imagined there would be tons of traffic. Something I never got comfortable with, since there was none in Lawrenceville. "Yeah, that would be great."

"Alright. How about tomorrow?"

"Well, I'm not sure..."

"It's fine. I understand if you don't want to talk with me. Goodbye."

"No, wait. Tomorrow? Yeah, I can make it work." I wrote down the directions to her house and hung up the phone.

What have I gotten myself into now? I pulled up a map on the computer and entered Thelma's address. It was a six-hour drive. If I was going to make it by noon, I'd have to leave by at least 6:00 a.m. And Tim? What was I going to tell him? I'd be gone all day between the drive there, the visit and the drive back. My anxiety grew with each passing thought. I'd never be able to make this work.

"Val, you can do anything you set your mind to." Norma's

voice pushed away the doubt that was building. I closed my eyes to listen to what else she wanted to say, but nothing came. Except the perfect plan to get away.

I dialed Sonya's number to put it into place. "Hey, Val."

"Hey, I've got to ask you a favor."

"Sure, what do you need?"

"I need you to cover for me. I've got to get away tomorrow, and I don't want Tim to know where I'm going."

"Where *are* you going?"

"I really can't say, but I need to tell him we're going away for a day trip."

"I can come with you. That way you won't be lying."

"Thanks, but I need to do this alone. And... it's not really a lie... just a little fib."

"Is everything okay, Val? Are you and Tim okay?"

"Yeah, we're great. I just need to go get some answers, but I have to do it alone."

"You can tell him I'm with you, but I'll kill you if something happens to you."

I laughed. "Genius plan. But I'll be fine."

With that piece out of the way, I had to work on the questions I wanted to ask Thelma. I didn't want to spend the whole day in the car and forget why I was there. This couldn't be a wasted trip. I wasn't really even sure what I wanted to know, except who Rose St. Thomas was. I had to incorporate questions about Vern, too, since she was his sister.

The more I thought about Rose and Norma, and all of the other identities she had taken on in her lifetime, Stephanie Mills came to mind. She was created out of fear of getting caught. I wanted to put a distance between Valerie and the people who needed to be taken care of. I saw what happened when I got sloppy with Seth and told him my real name. It was almost the end of it for me. Norma was right, we were more alike than I knew.

I wondered if there was ever a time that she let her real identity slip. When she was with Sylvia was their relationship based solely on lies, or did she trust her enough to let her in? She let me in, but it wasn't really a choice. She could have let me die and I never would have known the truth, but she loved me. I believed that. And, I loved her. *Love* her; I will never stop.

I wasn't sure why I needed answers so desperately. They weren't going to bring Norma back. I guess part of me hoped maybe they would. With enough answers I was almost certain I could retrace Norma's last sixty years. If I could figure out a pattern, maybe I could figure out where she was now. If she really was dead, maybe I could get enough information to get her from the heat to the paradise. I owed her at least that. I needed to get her back with Sylvia so she could have the love that she deserved.

"What are you thinking about?" Tim's voice made me jump out of my skin.

"You're home early."

Tim's raised his eyebrow and looked at his watch. "I'm actually a little late."

Being lost in my thoughts had stolen the day from me. I hadn't had time to worry about the conversation we needed to have. One more lie... or fib, as I liked to call it. "Sonya and I are going to spend the day together tomorrow. One last hurrah before her baby comes."

"That sounds fun, what are you two going to do?"

"We are going on a road trip, she wants to leave by 6:00 a.m."

"Whoa, that's early. How are you going to be able to function?" Tim threw his head back with a laugh.

"Ha-ha." I swatted him with the back of my hand. "I can get up. I used to have to."

"I know. I'm just teasing you. You girls deserve a fun day." When he leaned over to kiss me a wave of guilt hit me.

The internal struggle of not wanting to add another lie to the list and needing to figure out Norma's past pulled apart my insides. The baby growing in my womb did not deserve to start life in the chaos I was so good at creating. I owed it to Tim, and this baby, and even to myself to stop all of the nonsense. There were just a few more things I *had* to do before I could rest. The trip tomorrow was one of them.

The stress from the lie I fed to Tim left me with a migraine that sent me straight to bed. I couldn't stand to look at Tim knowing he deserved better than I was giving him. I hoped he wouldn't figure it out; any of it. I didn't want him to give up on me. I couldn't even stand the feel of my own skin touching me. My karma for what was on my to-do list.

My alarm clock pulled me out of a deep sleep at 5:00 a.m. I didn't want to risk being late after driving for six hours. Thankfully, my headache was gone and the only thing I would have to worry about for the next few hours was the traffic I was sure to run into. After researching the best route, I decided it was worth the extra time and settled on Interstate 84, changing over to Interstate 287. It looked like the one with the least amount of anxiety.

It would have been a much better trip if I could have had someone come with me, and better yet if someone else could do the driving. Before I left the driveway, I made sure to put Tom Petty's Wildflower album into the stereo. If anything could keep me calm during the upcoming trip, I knew it was Tom's voice.

Leaving early helped me miss most of the traffic. For the first two hours it wasn't too bad, after that, it became a blur. The only thing that got me through some of the toughest parts of the drive was Norma's voice encouraging me. I had been hearing her since she left us. It was now hard to remember a time without it.

I arrived at Thelma's just before noon. I was thankful I had given myself the extra time. I parked my car and stretched before walking down the paved path to her door. Peterson was very different than Lawrenceville. Houses were practically on top of each other. Windows looked into neighbor's houses. If this was how it was sixty years ago, I wasn't sure how Norma could have gotten away with killing Vern.

Thelma was already at the door when I reached it. I saw her peer at me through the small opening in the curtains. I knocked anyway. The door opened before I had the chance to lower my hand. "Stephanie?"

"Yes, you must be Thelma." I reached my hand out for her to shake. She declined the gesture.

"I thought you'd be younger." She pulled her bathrobe tight against her.

"Excuse me?"

"You said you were a college kid."

"Oh, yes. I'm a graduate student. I took some time off in between."

"Oh, alright." She closed the door so only her head was sticking out. "Are you sure that's why you're here?"

I felt my body temperature rise as I thought about the possibility of her sending me home without any information. "Yes, why else would I be here?"

"Hmm, I don't know." She squinted her eyes at me. "You're not selling anything, are you?"

"Nope." I held up my notebook. "I just have some questions I'd like to ask you."

The door opened wider. "Okay. Come on in."

Inside she led me to the living room and pointed to a rocking chair. As I made my way to my seat, I scanned the room, looking for photos or any other evidence I was at the right place. The walls were lined with family pictures, but none of them looked like they could have been Vern or Rose. "Thank you for giving me your time this afternoon. I'm really hoping I'll be able to find some answers for you."

"Why do *you* think you'll be able to do something the cops haven't been able to the past sixty years?" She pulled the lever on her recliner and elevated her feet. The bottom of her pink slippers were still as white as a blank sheet of paper. Looking around her house it wasn't hard to see why. It looked like I had walked into a time warp, but everything was clean. It was almost too clean.

"I don't know. I guess I'm just hopeful." I pushed up the biggest fake smile I could find as I opened my notebook to look over the questions. "Do you like to be called Mrs. Darling?"

She crossed her arms and shook her head. "God, no. That was my mother-in-law." She puckered up her face. "You can just call me Thelma."

"Okay." My eyes returned to the list of questions I came up with last night. I wanted to find the right one to keep her interested in our visit. "So, when did you first hear about the... ah... incident?"

"Honey, if you can't say what you mean, I think there's a soap on I'd be more entertained with."

Caught off guard by her response, I felt the expression on my face change. I didn't want her to know she was getting to me. "Okay... when did you first hear about the murder?"

"There you go. It wasn't so hard, was it?" She gave me a shit-eating grin. "Well, I guess I was at home getting ready for school."

"Oh, so you were still in school?"

"Yes. Vern was twelve years older than me. I was a, what's it called? An oops baby."

"So, you were just a kid when you lost your brother? That must have been very hard."

"Yeah, I imagine it was. I didn't have a chance to think about me. My parents were a mess when they heard the news. The thing I remember the most was the sound of my mother screaming. You know those blood curdling screams the movies try to make? Well, she sounded like one of the lowest budget horror films I'd ever seen."

"That must have been scary. I can't even imagine."

"Yeah, I guess I became the adult that day. I was only fifteen. I kissed the rest of my childhood goodbye that day."

"Were there ever any rumors about what could have happened to your brother?"

"Well, he had just returned from the service with his new bride. She was a lot younger than him. Come to find out, she was closer to my age. I'd always thought it might have been a boyfriend of hers trying to get even with Vern."

"A boyfriend?"

"Yes. A boyfriend. She was young and beautiful, and it wasn't a secret that Vern was an asshole."

"You think your brother was an asshole?"

"Not just me, everyone did. He wasn't a prize by any means. I never understood how she fell for him. She was so nice."

Hearing about Norma, or Rose in her youth warmed my heart. The Norma I knew seemed to be the Rose that Thelma knew. "Did you spend a lot of time with Rose?"

"Not really, but probably more than I spent with Vern. She was the one that taught me how to bake. She baked the best thumbprint cookies I've ever eaten. Even after all these years I have not tasted one as good as Rose's."

"Did Rose ever tell you anything about their relationship?"

"No. I was the kid sister. She wasn't going to bring me into anything."

"The rumor of a boyfriend, do you think that could have been true?"

"No. I don't think she would have dared to mess around. I remember seeing bruises on her arms, and when I mentioned them to her, she made up some excuse. You know, she ran into the bureau, or into the door. Even as a kid I knew she was lying to me. I don't think she wanted me to think badly of my brother."

"Rose sounds like a great lady."

"She was. I kept hoping she'd come back. I never believed she was murdered that night."

"You didn't?"

"Nope, but I was the only one who thought that. My mother wouldn't listen to me, and once the rumor of another guy was out there, she didn't care about Rose. She blamed her."

"Your mother blamed Rose?"

"Yes. She was sure if her baby didn't bring that hussy home, he'd still be alive."

"Ouch."

"Yeah, Vern was a mama's boy. My mother was a little... hard to take."

I couldn't keep the laugh in. I tried to mask it with a cough.

"What's funny?"

"Nothing. I just had a tickle in my throat." I smiled to try to get her back to talking. "So, did Rose ever share anything about her past with you?"

"She did tell me that she had run away from home because her parents were abusive. I figured that was why she put up with Vern's crap."

"Did she tell you where she grew up or what her maiden name was?"

She squinted her eyes at me. "Why are you so interested in Rose?"

The question stopped me in my tracks. I felt my throat

start to close. "I ah... well, there are still questions about what happened to her. Everyone at least knows that Vern was murdered, and your family was able to have a funeral and say goodbye. Rose's family didn't get that chance."

"That's true, although from what Rose told me, I don't think they deserved that."

"Yeah, it does sound like that, but I still think it is important to be able to get answers for Rose."

"It has always bothered me to think she was never found." Thelma pushed her legs down and got out of her chair. "Wait right there." She turned around. "Don't touch anything."

I laced my fingers together and set them in my lap as I watched her walk down the hall. I heard a drawer open and papers being shuffled around. I didn't move while I waited. Thelma scared me. There was no way I was going to test her.

She came back into the living room with a worn envelope and handed it to me. "This should have the answers you're looking for." She returned to her chair and kicked her feet back up.

I opened the envelope and pulled out the frail, yellowed paper. It was Vern and Rose's wedding certificate. All of the answers I was looking for was on that sheet of paper. Rose Newell was born in Lynn, Massachusetts on June 5, 1940. It listed her parents as John and Mabel Newell. I wrote the information down before I handed the paper back to Thelma. "Thank you so much. That will be a great help."

"I hope so. I do think about Rose often." Moisture was building up behind Thelma's glasses. The hard exterior was finally giving way. "I'd love to see her again."

I didn't have the heart to tell her the only way she could see her would be in death. I wondered if Norma knew how much Thelma loved her, or if she ever checked up on her since she vanished. "I have a feeling you'll get to see her again."

"Is there anything else I can help you with? This is the time I usually take my nap."

If I hadn't already gathered the information I came for, I would have been disappointed that a six-hour white-knuckle drive amounted to less than an hour visit. If I left now, I could be home in time to join the guys for dinner.

CHAPTER TWENTY-TWO

After a restful night of sleep, I poured myself a cup of coffee and turned the computer on. I couldn't wait to dig in with the new information I had gathered from Thelma. I couldn't shake the thought of Norma as a young lady being sweet to her young sister-in-law. It wasn't surprising, but I wondered how she was able to just disappear when there were people who loved and cared for her so much. The more the thought lingered, I was reminded with a slap against the face; I had done the same thing to my gram.

I couldn't beat myself up over that now. The past was just that; the past. Norma's voice echoed the thought. "Good girl, Val, find your joy, let go of the past." A warm sensation encased me. I wanted to believe more than anything it was a hug from Norma and wrapped my arms around myself.

Gabriel jumped into my lap, insisting on my attention. His soft, silky black fur glided under my hand, his tail sliding through my fingers. "You're a good boy, but you're going to have to let me get some research done before the guys get home." His refusal to move made it difficult to see the screen. I pushed his tail out of my face and opened up the web browser. My search started with *Rose Newell in Lynn, Massachusetts*. I dug through the pages of results and ended up with nothing. I tried again, this time including her birthdate. Pretty much the same results appeared.

"I guess I don't know how to use Google." The heavy sigh forced Gabriel to jump off my lap. "Yeah, I can't even stand myself right now, either."

I typed in her parents' names and hit enter. At the top of the page there was an article of an unsolved murder. Clicking on the link I discovered that her parents had been found murdered in their home in 1962. They were shot, each with one bullet, and no evidence was left at the scene of the crime.

Vern's death took place in 1959, and her parents in 1962. All of the murders remained unsolved. There wasn't any doubt in my mind Norma had gone back home to get revenge. I didn't blame her after the story she had told me, but I wondered why she hadn't told me about them. She knew I wanted my mom and Chad dead, it wasn't like I was going to judge her. The nag to unearth more of Norma's secrets grew with each piece of information I uncovered.

There were multiple articles about the double murder. After reading the fourth one, I discovered they all said the same thing and stopped wasting my time. With my fingers hovering over the keys I wasn't sure what to look for next. The words *Murder Suicide Sylvia 1960* appeared in the search bar. My pinky tapped enter and I waited for the results to appear. *Holy shit.* Whoever moved my fingers had struck gold.

An article about the murder-suicide in 1960 of Darryl and Sylvia Duncan in Brooklyn, New York was the first in the search. After clicking on the link, I was greeted by the sweet smile of Sylvia Duncan, who was only twenty years old at the time of her death. My heart broke in two knowing how much her murder had hurt Norma. The photo was in black and white, but I could tell she had dark, mysterious eyes and dark hair. She was stunning. A single tear rolled down my cheek as my insides became hollow.

This was what made Norma snap. Yes, she murdered Vern first, but this momentous loss was what fed Norma's need to take action. To get to the 'bad guy' before he could hurt anyone else. A broken heart kept her cold enough to kill without thought. She was calculated and precise. I am certain each and every life she took could be justified by the big guy upstairs.

What she was doing was killing out of love. She used her own heartbreak to stop others from experiencing the pain she carried. My adoration for Norma grew. I wished I had known all of this while she was still alive. Maybe I could have helped her find love again. Maybe I could have healed her broken heart.

With my eyes full of tears, I wrote down the information I had found about John and Mabel Newell and then the newest information about Sylvia and Daryl Duncan. I started a timeline with what I had. The search to find out the journey of Rose and all of her aliases had begun. I hoped I would have the guidance I needed to find her next stop.

In the search bar I typed *unsolved murders 1960, East Coast* and hit enter. There were five cases listed. I clicked on and read the first few lines in each one. The first three did not fit the previous murders. The fourth one matched. It was a man in New York that was arrested for raping a young woman. Everything about the case had Norma written all over it. The location seemed to fit where she would have been at that time, too. The last one was also a no-go.

I entered the same search, only changing the year to 1961. There were three unsolved cases, but none fit the criteria I was searching for. I searched again, this time 1962. Norma's parents were part of this search. I looked for more cases in either New York or New Jersey. Three fit what I was looking for.

All three men had been charged with some sort of violent crime against women or children. I wrote the information in the notebook and continued the search. Year by year, I made it to 1971 before I heard Tim and Gabe. By that time, I had two pages of notes. I wrote down the location and the names of the victims. I also printed out a map that I was using as a guide of where she had traveled. I wasn't able to find out the names she used, but I was pleased with the results that came up. So far I found enough evidence to lead me to believe Norma had murdered over twenty-three men, plus her mother by 1971. There was also a good possibility that some of the murders had been solved and pinned on other people. There would be no way to add them to the list.

I had enough to map out her early years. In an odd way, it felt like I was on the journey with her. I had only murdered two people and the fear of getting caught still haunted me. That and the question if *they* were haunting me. I hadn't had anything to make me think that, yet, but the idea that it could be a possibility left me newly afraid of the dark. Knowing there were probably hundreds more deaths I was going to find, I wondered if Norma had crossed one too many lines to be forgiven. That would be my next project; learning ways to help spirits ask for forgiveness.

The roller-coaster of grief had me strapped in tight. I was dancing between denial and bargaining. One moment I was telling myself she wasn't really gone, while the next I was ready to do anything to either bring her back to me or get her safely to Heaven.

Before Tim and Gabe were able to find me, I closed up the notebook and stuffed it in the back of a drawer. I snuck into the bedroom and got on the bed with a book. "I'm in the bedroom." I yelled as I heard Tim whistling.

"What are you doing in here? It's such a beautiful day." Tim came and sat next to me on the bed.

"I was just tired, so I thought I'd try to rest a little." I wasn't sure where these lies were coming from or what the purpose behind them were. I didn't like that I had awoken Stephanie Mills. *She* was the one I couldn't trust. This was just more evidence that I needed to get the last of my to-do list done as soon as possible. I needed to make sure Stephanie Mills had her own funeral well before our baby arrives.

"That makes sense. You did have a long day yesterday. Have you checked in with Sonya to see how she's doing?" Tim rubbed my back and gave me a sweet smile.

"No, I probably should, though." I matched his smile to try to wash the worry off my face. "How was your day? You seem happy."

"Why wouldn't I be? I get to come home to you."

"Ought-oh, what did you do?"

"What? Nothing. I just couldn't wait to see you today. I'm just so happy being your husband, and according to my math, you are eight weeks today." He held up his fingers. "So, only seven more months until we get to meet our baby."

"You're not nervous? Not at all?"

"Of course, I am, but I'm more excited than nervous. I mean lots of people have babies and they do just fine."

"Yeah, we'll be good. All you really need is love. I think I remember someone told me that once." I winked as the doubt crept in. Being a bad person was what made me the most nervous. With the taste of justice I had, I wasn't sure how to get it off my palate. I think I need to find a twelve-step program to get the urge out of my system. Just once more. That was all I needed.

CHAPTER TWENTY-THREE

"Val, turn on the channel six news." Tim's words blasted through the receiver as soon as I answered.

"Well, hello to you, too."

"I'm serious. They're talking about your mom."

My heart swam up my throat. "What about her?"

"She's been reported as a missing person."

I clicked on the TV and watched the report. Chad was the one that reported her missing. I knew from his visit that she had left him. I knew it was no more than that, but Tim didn't know. "I'm sure she just took off. She's an adult, she has that right."

"You don't think Chad had something to do with this?"

"No. Why would he kill the one person who believed him all these years? She's just like him. A perfect pair."

"You don't think he would have killed her to keep her from testifying against him, do you?"

"Hmm. That's a good point. I don't think so, though. I'm

sure she's fine. I honestly don't care is she isn't." I felt a chill go down my spine and tried to shake it off.

"Woah, okay. I'm sorry, I just thought you'd want to know."

"No, it's fine. I just don't give a shit about either one of them. Personally, they'd be better off dead."

"I understand. I just thought you should know. I wasn't sure if it was something Chad had done, and I was a little worried he might be desperate."

"Thank you for letting me know. I love you. I don't think you have anything to worry about. Chad's a coward. He only goes after young, helpless girls. He's a rapist, but I don't think he's a murderer."

I kept watching the news coverage after Tim was off the phone. Chad was about to speak. I wanted to see the pain in his eyes again. I wanted to see him beg for his life back. He was only getting what he deserved. He stole so much from so many of us. When the cameras went to Chad, I felt my lips turn up into a smile. His face was worn, and his eyes were sunken into his head. "Please, Elaine, if you see this, please come home." His pleas increased in desperation as the interview went on. I turned the volume off and just watched the poor, pitiful man beg for his life to go back to normal.

The longer I watched, the more the anger festered. The only reason he was given the airtime was because he knew someone at the station. He knew someone everywhere. Even though there were eight of us with similar stories, I knew he was going to get a slap on the wrist. He would never be held accountable for any of his actions. I knew I would have to take justice into my own hands. The last thing on Stephanie

Mills' to-do list. I just wanted to let him suffer a little longer before I crossed it off the list.

As I went to turn the TV off, I stopped to read the red headline at the top of the screen. *"Hank Dawson, an inmate at Stark County Correctional Facility has escaped. Do not approach. Call the Vermont State Police if you see him. He is six feet, two inches tall and 245 pounds. Not considered dangerous."*

Holy shit. That had to be Maggie's husband. Without turning off the TV, I grabbed my keys and raced to my car. I had to get to Maggie before Hank did. My phone started ringing before I was out of the driveway. "Val... he's out..."

"I know, I'm on my way over there now."

"I think it's okay. I don't think he has any idea where we are." Maggie sounded calmer than I was feeling.

"I don't think we should take any chances. Where are Lexi and Sammy? We need to check their social media accounts."

"Lexi is at her boyfriend's house, and Sammy is in her room."

"You need to get Lexi to come home. She needs to know that she might be in danger."

"Val, I don't think it's that big of a deal. I think we're going to be fine."

"Why aren't you scared?"

"I know I can protect us now."

"I'm glad you feel that way, but what if he shows up?"

"I didn't want to tell you." She paused. "Sonya taught me how to shoot. I bought a pistol."

"Oh my God, Maggie. You have a gun in the house with the girls?" The judgement oozed off my words.

"Yes. I wanted to be able to defend myself and protect the girls. I never wanted to be in danger again."

"We can talk more when I get there." I tossed the phone onto the passenger seat as I continued the drive to Maggie's. So, we all know how to use a gun now. I guess I couldn't be upset with her. I liked how powerful I felt after Tim showed me. I, like Maggie, never wanted to have my life threatened ever again. If I shot first, I'd always be the one to walk away.

Maggie was sitting on the front steps when I pulled in. She was thumbing through a magazine. It appeared she didn't have a care in the world. She was not the same woman I met at our first group. She was strong and confident. I took a few moments to enjoy seeing her in this new light. The old Maggie would have been on the floor in pieces and her insides probably would have matched mine right now. But this new Maggie was in control. No one was going to mess with her and I loved it. Seeing her calm composure helped ease a lot of my fears. I didn't have to run to Maggie's rescue. She was now able to take care of herself.

Maggie stood up and started walking to me. "Val, I know..."

"No, it's okay. You don't need me to lecture you. You have this under control."

"Hmm." She put her hands on her hips. "I wasn't expecting you to react like this. I was ready to explain things."

"No need to. I know you don't need me. You've come a long way."

Maggie smiled. "I have, haven't I?"

"Can we still talk some things over? No lectures, I promise." I placed my hand over my heart.

"Sure, let's go have a cup of tea... for Norma."

"Oh, that sounds lovely. Is there any more of the rose tea? I really liked that stuff." If Norma were still here, I knew Hank would be history. That was one of the unfinished pieces of business she told me she needed to take care of before she left. It's funny how he decides to escape so soon after his assassin is dead.

Maggie turned on the tea kettle and pulled out two teacups and I opened the tea bags. "I think she'd want us to use the fancy cups. You know, since you only live once, we should always use the fancy stuff."

"That does sound like something she'd say."

"I miss her. The house is so quiet without her." Maggie took a sip of tea.

"I miss her like crazy, too. Life isn't fair sometimes." I pushed out a sigh.

Maggie laughed. "We're experts in that lesson, aren't we?"

"Yeah. What a great thing to excel in; bad luck."

"With the bad comes the good." She turned to look at me.

"Remember to find the joy." We said in unison.

"She left us with some good lessons, didn't she?" Maggie took her cup to the living room.

I followed. "She did. You know, I keep hearing her voice."

Maggie took a sip of tea. "You do? What does she say to you?"

"Um, well, it really depends on what's going on. She's

reminded me to look for joy a time or two. She hasn't been talking to you?"

"No, I don't think so. I guess I wasn't really expecting her to."

"Maybe I'm just going insane." I laughed. "That's a possibility, too."

"No. You've been through a lot these last few weeks. I'm sure she's with you. She'll always be our guardian angel." Maggie reached out her hand.

I gave her hand a squeeze. "I like the thought of that. I feel safer knowing she's watching out for us."

"Yeah, me, too," Maggie said.

"Did you have a chance to talk with the girls and let them know Hank escaped?" I asked.

"I did. I also checked their social media accounts, and everything is locked up tight. I don't think he'd have a clue where to find us. I'm confident we're safe."

I held the warm mug between my hands. "I know you are."

The phone rang and made us both jump. "Okay, I guess I'm still a little jumpy." Maggie laughed and headed to the kitchen to answer the phone.

I overheard the tone of Maggie's voice change and went out to see what was going on.

"Are you sure?" Silence followed as the color left Maggie's face. "Okay, thank you for letting me know." She shut the phone off and placed it on the counter.

"What's wrong? Is everything alright with Lexi?"

"Yeah. Everything is fine." Her eyes widened and a smile spread across her face. "They found Hank."

"Oh, that's great news. I guess I didn't have anything to worry about."

"The great news is they found him dead. Someone shot him."

"Holy shit, Maggie. I'm sorry, or congratulations." I threw my hands in the air. "This is good, right?"

"It's amazing. We're free. My girls are safe."

I gave Maggie a hug and felt the weight lift off of her shoulders. "Maybe it was our guardian angel."

"Nah, Norma was too sweet to hurt anyone."

"Yeah, you're right. Looks like karma caught up to him."

"About time." Maggie's hand covered her mouth. "Oh my God. I almost forgot about Hank's life insurance policy. I'll be able to send the girls to college, buy them cars, hell, I can buy myself a car."

"Everything is falling into place, isn't it?" I couldn't shake the thought that Norma had something to do with this. Do angels kill people? Can dead people kill people? I guess it didn't matter. All that mattered was that Hank was dead and Maggie was safe. Wherever Norma is, I'm sure she is smiling.

CHAPTER TWENTY-FOUR

The search for my mother was called off after they were able to trace her credit cards and cell phone. They found her in southern New Hampshire, about two hours from here. When she was contacted, she told the police she didn't want to be found, and that she left on her own freewill. I wished they'd hold another news conference to share Chad's reaction to the rejection.

I was still expecting her to confront me about the inheritance, even more so now that she had been located. The only thing that could possibly keep her away was if she ran off with a man with money. Money was her motivation. I half hoped she would at least rub her new love interest in Chad's face. The possibilities of prolonging Chad's suffering were endless, and I wanted to take advantage of each and every one of them.

The count of women who came forward since my report was now at nine. It seemed his news appearance backfired on him and got two more ladies to talk. I had a feeling the longer we waited until the trial, the more people we would have to testify. Cheryl had pulled some strings to let the ones who wanted to, to get together and talk. Since we had all given our statements and they were on record, she thought it would be good for us to meet.

My meeting with Jennifer couldn't have come at a better time. It seemed as though the weeks since we started meeting the chaos in my life had exploded. It almost felt like the floodgates had been opened and permission had been granted to let the shit hit the fan. The saying that God only gives you what you can handle used to make me roll my eyes. Now, I had to believe it. I was being tested in every aspect of my life, but I knew I could handle whatever came my way. I was strong enough now; or at least that was what I was going to believe.

Jennifer's office door was open when I arrived. I knocked on the side of the wall and poked my head in. "Is it okay if I come in?"

"You're early today." She gave me a smile before I had the chance to turn what she said into rejection. "Come on in."

I sat in the same chair and sighed. "I don't even know where to start."

"Wherever you'd like." She set her travel mug on the floor by her feet and crossed her legs.

"Well, my week started with my mom being a missing person, only to turn into a found person. One of my best friend's husbands escaped from jail, but he was found dead. Two more women have come forward against Chad. And now Cheryl... from the victim center has been given permission to let us all get together and talk." I let out the breath I had been holding.

"Wow, that does sound like an action-packed week."

"Oh, yeah, since you can't tell anyone... I also drove to New Jersey to meet..." I stopped before I finished. "For research and lied to my husband about what I was doing."

"Is that a habit?"

"What?"

"Lying to your husband."

"Whoa... so much for no judgment." I cracked my knuckles. "No, not really. I hate doing it... but there are a few things I can't tell him."

"No judgement here, I was just asking a question."

"There are just some things he can't know, and this was for a friend, so it's not something I can talk about with him anyway."

Jennifer nodded as she took notes.

"I just hate how it feels. I don't want to have a marriage built on lies. I just don't know how to get around it in certain situations."

"You don't think he would understand?"

I laughed. "Nope, I know he wouldn't. I just have one more and then I'll stop."

"One more lie?"

"Yes. There's one last thing I need to do."

"So, you're premeditating the lie?"

"Premeditating? You make it sound like a crime."

"No, just a question."

"I don't like your questions."

"Why do you think that is?" She tilted her head.

"Because. I don't have answers. I mean, I know why I do what I do, but I also can't tell you for the same reasons. It's complicated." I spun my wedding ring. "I would like to talk about how I'm feeling about meeting with the other women that have come forward, though."

"Okay."

"The thing is, I don't know how I feel about it. On one hand I'm kind of pissed off at the girls that came before me. You know? I mean if they had told on him when it happened, it never would have happened to me. But on the other hand, I feel guilty for not reporting it sooner... for the same reasons."

Jennifer nodded. "Do you think the others are feeling the same way?"

I shrugged my shoulders. "I guess. Why wouldn't they?"

"What would be the worst thing that could happen if you met with them?"

"They all blame me. For not reporting it sooner and for reporting it at all. It's been over twenty years for some of them. I guess I'm worried that I stirred something up that shouldn't have been stirred up, like kicking a hornet's nest. Now I just want to run and hide but I also want to get the biggest can of Raid I can find."

"I like that." She smiled.

"Like what?"

"Your analogy with the can of Raid."

"I want to watch him fall, but I don't want to be the reason other people are hurt. I don't want them to be angry at me."

"Valerie, you do understand what happened to you and the others has nothing to do with you. Dr. Ross is the one at fault for all of it. You are not to blame, and if one of the women feel that you are, then give them my business card."

"Logically I know that. But, I can't shake it. I know I didn't make him rape any of us, but I also feel like he might not have if I had told before. It's just a mess."

"Have you been using any of the breathing techniques we've been working on?"

"Not really."

"When your thoughts start carrying you away, give it a try. Focus on something in the room and count your breaths. It helps me, and I think it might help you get grounded when the world is spinning out of control."

"How did you know that's how it feels?"

"Because, it's a normal reaction for what has happened to you, and I've experience it myself."

"You're messed up, too?"

Jennifer leaned her head back as she laughed. "I guess you can say that. But I like to say that I've lived an eventful life. I don't like the word messed up or crazy. It's a normal reaction to trauma."

"Hmm. That does sound better. Normal. Huh. I never thought I'd fit into that mold."

"Embrace it. Once you start looking at yourself differently, things in your life will start to shift. The chaos will quiet. The panic will settle. You just have to be ready to say goodbye to the old mindset."

"Huh. That sounds easy."

"It takes a lot of work, but I know you can do it."

"I'd like that. Let's work toward that, okay?"

Jennifer nodded as she took a drink from her mug.

"Do you think it's normal to hear dead people?"

"How do you mean?"

"Well, since my friend Norma died, I hear her voice in my head. It's like she's talking to me. It actually really helps me. I don't think I'm ready to make it stop."

"I do think it's normal. People process their grief differently."

"I was hoping you'd say that." I laughed. "I'd hate to lose the normal title already."

"You're the only one who can take it away." Jennifer's eyes went to the clock behind me. "Well, it looks like this hour slipped by quickly today. I'll see you next week?"

"I wouldn't miss it." With my hand on the doorknob, I turned around. "Thank you."

"For what?"

"For not being a jerk, for making me do the work, and for helping me see I'm not a lost cause."

"Oh, but I didn't do any of that. Next time you look in the mirror, tell that to the woman looking back at you."

Normal. I still couldn't believe a professional didn't think I was screwed up. To be fair, she doesn't know the *whole* story, but I'm not going to let that thought take this away from me. I'm not crazy. I'm not damaged. I'm *normal.* A sense of peace entered me and pushed out the self-doubting, self-blaming thoughts that had left me feeling uneasy. I was ready to meet the others.

CHAPTER TWENTY-FIVE

"I don't have anything to wear!" I threw the entire contents of my closet onto the bed. "I'm such a fat whale."

"Stop it, Val. You're beautiful and you're not fat, you're growing our baby."

"Ahh." I pulled at my hair. "I guess I just can't go." I fell onto the pile of clothes on the bed and started to cry.

"Let me go with you. I can't imagine how hard this is for you." Tim found a spot on the bed to sit next to me.

"You can't. You have to work." The annoyance rang louder than my words.

"No, I can take some time off. There's nothing going on right now. As long as the Executioner doesn't strike again, I should be able to start taking time off."

Emotion boiled out of me. The Executioner could never strike again. She was dead. The thought alone was enough motivation for me. She wasn't here to do my dirty work any longer. I had to. I sat up and wiped my face. "Yes. I would like you to come."

"Thank you. I'm glad you changed your mind. I didn't want you to take that drive alone after today. I know it's not going to be easy."

"Nothing is *ever* easy. These last few weeks have really sucked. I'm so sick of everything lately. It wasn't good enough to take my gram. Nope. They've also got to take my best friend. Oh, yeah, you might as well throw me in the middle of a trial with my rapist. Oh, but wait, there's more." I stopped when I realized Tim didn't know about the 'more.' That was something no one could know.

"It has been rough. You definitely deserve a break."

Thankfully he didn't notice the slip. I guess that's the upside to being a mess. *Jesus Christ* I can't even stop the self-doubting bullshit. I let out a scream. "I can't take much more."

"I'm sorry, Val. Let me help. Whatever you need."

"I'd love the Executioner to take care of Chad. I mean, is that too much to ask for?" I threw my hands up in the air.

Tim gave me a smile. "There's still time. Let's get dressed, and maybe if you're up to it we can go shopping later today."

"Shopping? Who are you?" Tim found my smile, the one I hadn't been able to find in a few days. Today was going to be a step in the right direction. The direction of ending my relationship with Stephanie Mills once and for all. And ending Dr. Chad Ross.

Cheryl had reserved the conference room at the Stark County Court House for us since there were too many of us to fit in her office. It made my stomach churn when it hit me; there were too many of Chad's victims to fit into her office. He had hurt so many people we had to get a bigger room for all of us to fit.

My heart began to race as Tim found a parking spot. "I don't know if I can do this."

He took my hand in his. "Breathe with me." He inhaled and I followed his lead. "Every one of you in there today doesn't want to be here. You shouldn't have to be, but since you are, why not find some friends who understand what you went through. These ladies had their lives affected, too. You each have a story, and unfortunately, they're similar. You need to work together and get that piece of shit in jail."

"Ugh. I guess you're right. I'm just scared. What if what they went through is worse than I did? And they're able to deal with it better than me? What if..."

"Val, it's not a competition. This isn't about who got fucked over the most. Think of this as finding a group of people who understand you."

"Yeah, but what if they don't?"

"My guess is they wouldn't be here. Let's get in there and get it over with. Once today is over, I bet you won't be able to wait to see each other."

I took his hand in the parking lot and walked behind him. The dampness from my palm made it too uncomfortable to keep holding. I wiped the sweat onto my skirt and pulled down my cardigan. "My God, I'm so fat."

"No, you're not. Stop it." Tim held the door open for me and we waited to go through the metal detector. When Tim walked through the bells started going off. He pulled out his badge and they let us both go through.

"I guess that's another bonus to being married to a cop."

Tim's cheeks turned red. "There are lots of bonuses. You'll see." He winked as he reached for my hand.

Cheryl was outside of the conference room on her cell phone. She nodded and waved before she pointed into the room. When we got inside there were already three women. So far Tim was the only man there. Tim pulled out a chair for me and sat next to me. The silence in the room allowed my thoughts to unravel out of control.

I felt everyone's eyes on me. Right now, no one knew I was the one to make the first report. I wasn't sure I wanted anyone to know. They didn't have to come forward, though. I hadn't forced that on any of them. They were here because they felt they needed to be. Two more ladies arrived. Tim was no longer the only guy here.

Five minutes after we were scheduled to be there, the last lady walked in. Cheryl closed the door and returned to her seat. "Before we begin, I want to make sure it's okay that the support people are in here. Is everyone okay with this?"

A unanimous yes circled the table. Tim and the three other men were given permission to stay. I was relieved and annoyed. I wanted him by my side, but I wasn't sure I wanted the other guys in here. I guess it was only fair.

"I'd like to start by going around the room and introducing ourselves. You can just give your first name if you'd like." Since the last remaining seat was by me when Cheryl came in, I knew I would pull the unlucky straw. "Valerie, would you like to start?"

I blew the air out of my lungs and folded my hands in my lap. "I'm Valerie, also known as Val."

The rest of the women went around the table, and by the time we were back to Cheryl, my nerves had calmed down. Everyone else did seem to be just as nervous as I was.

"When I was given permission to get you ladies together, I didn't want to wait. I believe the stories you have each shared with me will help each other. What you all went through should have never happened." Cheryl lowered her head as she shook it. "Each and every one of you is incredibly brave." She placed her hand to her heart. "Today, I'd like you to start to get to know each other. We will be spending a lot of time together when the trial starts, and I think it would be helpful if you were able to use each other for support and strength."

One of the women, I forgot her name raised her hand.

"Yes, Tonya?" Cheryl jogged my memory, although there was no way I was going to remember all nine names.

"Could we wear name tags? Just in here? I don't think I'll be able to remember anyone's name without them."

The ladies around the table smiled in agreement. Hmm, I guess we are more alike than I thought.

"That's a great idea, Tonya. I actually have some right here." Cheryl took out the stickers and a sharpie and handed them to me.

Now that we each had our name stuck to our chest, the meat of the gathering could begin.

"I'd like to know who the first one to speak up was." Tina looked around the table.

I closed my eyes as I tried to find enough strength to speak. "I did." My voice just louder than a whisper found its way out.

Tina turned her attention to me. "I just want to say thank you. If you weren't brave enough to come forward, I would never had said anything."

"Same." Tonya uncrossed her arms.

"Yeah, me, too." Melissa chimed in.

The ones who didn't say it were nodding and smiling. They didn't blame me. I hadn't ruined their lives. The weight that had settled onto my shoulders lifted and I felt my posture improve. "I thought you'd all be mad at me."

"No, I didn't think anyone was going to believe me. I mean, he is a doctor. He made my mom think I was crazy, so when I tried to tell her when it was happening, he suggested she place me in a psychiatric hospital. They had me so drugged up I decided to never say anything again." Alexa wiped a tear off her cheek and smiled through her long brown hair.

"Yeah, he did the same thing with my mom." Hattie bit at her fingernail. "I thought I was the only one."

"I did, too." Alexa frowned as she looked around the table. "I trusted him, even after he raped me. He made me believe I was special and that he loved me."

"I trusted him, too. I guess I was just stupid." Tina hung her head.

"Not unless the rest of us are," Alexa said. "We were children, we weren't stupid. He made us tell him our weaknesses and then used them against us."

"Did any of you get pregnant?" I couldn't keep the question in any longer.

"I did." Beth pulled her sleeves over her hands. "He

forced my mom to bring me to a home for girls, and then they gave the baby away."

"Sawyer's Home for Unwed Girls?" My foot began to tap under the table.

"Yeah. You, too?"

"Yeah. Can I ask you how long ago that was?"

"It was seventeen years ago." Beth's answer was like a punch to my gut. I could have stopped it.

"I was sent to Sawyer's, too." Tonya spoke up. "Twenty-three years ago. They took my daughter, too. Chad turned my own mother against me and then stole my baby."

"Twenty years for me." I lifted my eyes, heavy from the tears I was fighting, to look around the table. He did the same thing to three of us. I had a sick feeling there were more. "He was married to my mom when he got me pregnant. They're still married... well they were, I think she left him when everything hit the news."

"Good. Serves the prick right." Emma slapped the table. "I hope he suffers."

"Me, too." At least three of us spoke at the same time.

"Do any of you get nightmares?" Nicole asked.

"I do, and it's been over twenty years," Tina answered. "I wake up sometimes and it feels like he's still on top of me."

"I get them, too. I have to take stuff to help me sleep, otherwise I just lay in my bed and listen to every sound. I've never stopped being afraid." Liz joined the conversation. "I don't trust anyone... no offense." Her eyes danced around the room, not connecting with any of us.

I felt her pain, and I knew the fear she was talking about. "I'm still afraid a lot of the time, too. I look over my shoulder all the time. Loud noises... well, any noises make me jump. I couldn't trust anyone, either... not until recently."

"He destroyed my life. I ran away from home when my mom wouldn't help me. I ended up moving in with an abusive asshole and got pregnant when I was seventeen. The state took my baby when I almost overdosed." Emma put her head down. "I'm clean now, but it's always a struggle."

"I struggled with drugs, too. It was the only thing I could find to get my mind off of what happened. I can't even have sex without seeing his face." Tina pushed the hair behind her ear.

"I drink more than I should. It helps stop the memories," Beth said.

"Does anyone else have a hard time with..." Melissa looked around the table before she finished. "Sex?"

We all nodded.

"I didn't have sex for over nineteen years. The idea of it made me feel dirty." I took Tim's hand and gave it a squeeze.

"I'm still a virgin... well, when you don't count *him*," Tonya said.

"I'm a lesbian." Alexa dropped her eyes to avoid eye contact.

"Me, too." Liz added. "I can't stand the thought of a guy touching me. If I never see another penis again, I'd be happy."

The room filled with nervous laughter. "See, this is why I thought it was important for you all to meet. You are so much alike, in so many ways. From the trauma you experienced then, to the way it still affects you."

Cheryl was right, it was a good idea for us to come together. After two hours of talking and asking questions, it felt like we had known each other for years. We shared so much. From the way our innocence was stolen from us, to the way our freedom is still elusive at best. Before we parted ways, we shared our contact information, and planned another time to get together. My circle tripled in size. These were my people now, and the desire to protect them took over everything else.

We will never be free from Chad until he is dead. Jail is not enough to keep us safe. Death is the only way I will be sure he will never hurt anyone again. I was ready to check it off my list and start living; for us all to start living.

CHAPTER TWENTY-SIX

The women in the group started a private group on Facebook. This was the best way for all of us to keep in touch and build our relationship. The oldest in our group was thirty-nine, and the youngest was nineteen. For at least twenty years, Chad had been using his power to take advantage of his young clients. We were all just children, and now we were damaged adults. There was hope for us, just around the corner. It just wasn't time yet.

With Tim back at work I had the house to myself for the day. With a cup of rose tea, I went into the office and turned the computer on. While I waited for it to turn on, I dug out my notebook. I was on page five now and over one hundred unsolved murders. My last search ended in 1990. There were still over twenty-six years to search through. The map where I was recreating Norma's journey already had New Jersey, New York, Massachusetts, Connecticut, Florida and Rhode Island. I still wasn't sure if Florida was Norma, but everything added up to the rest of them, and I remember she had said something about having been there before. I was leaving it on the list for now.

It seemed the more murders she had under her belt, the better she became at them. She obviously knew what she was doing, since she got away with all of them. I understood now why she couldn't tell me how many murders there had been. It was an overwhelming list, and if the pattern continued, the murders would increase as the years went on. You could see when she became comfortable. The murders grew from one a year, to a couple, to a cluster of three or more in one location.

She also seemed to move out of the state the murders took place to a nearby state. So far it didn't appear she stayed in the same state after the job was complete, but she would return in a year or so. The path that I had traced so far, for the first half of her career was unpredictable. There was no way to know where she would go, or how many murders would take place before she left.

With the search bar up and ready I typed the same search I had been using; *Unsolved murders, East Coast 1991*. When I had the information I needed, I just changed the year and hit enter again. It took time to weed through the cases. The more I researched the easier it became to pick the cases that seemed like something Norma would have been responsible for. The newest search revealed four murders in Northern Vermont. The towns listed were only about an hour from Lawrenceville. It made me curious if this had been her first time here, or if there was a reason she ended up here.

I spent the rest of the day entering the same search, changing the date each time and recording my findings. The one case I had discovered in Florida I found by accident. I had forgotten to put East Coast and found the cases. I couldn't imagine how much time it would take me to dig through the unsolved murders in the whole country over the last sixty years. If there are too many gaps in my findings, I'm sure curiosity will drive me to it.

After six hours I had made it to 1998. My prediction that there would be more as the years went on proved to be accurate. In the seven years searched today, I added another five pages. Without counting, my guess was there were over two hundred names in my notebook. From the cases I had read, it did appear all of the victims were perpetrators of one kind or another. Would that be enough to get her a pass out of Hell? As the list continued to grow, so did my apprehension about the future of Norma's eternity.

The meeting with Gemini Star played out in my mind. I wasn't sure who was trying to talk to me. She said I would know, but I didn't. I still couldn't figure it out. The only dead people I loved were Gram and Norma. Gram came through, and I was grateful to hear from her, but I needed to talk to Norma. Maybe enough time has passed for her to come through, and if not, without the others there I would have more freedom to ask the questions I needed answers to. If Gemini was legit, she probably knew what I was hiding anyway. It's not likely the police would listen to her, and if they did, there was no evidence. And if she turned Norma in, it was already too late. My need for answers outweighed the risks.

I typed in Gemini's name into the search bar and I was directed to her Facebook page. I sent her a message. The bubbles appeared on the screen to let me know she was replying. I bit my fingernail as I watched them dance on my screen. "I have an opening tomorrow at 11 a.m. We can meet at my office or at your place."

"Your office is best."

She sent me directions to her office and a link to send her payment. I wrote down the address and sent the payment. An hour to talk with Gemini was $200. She said she was giving me a repeat customer discount. I wondered how much Sonya had paid for the last visit. The cost didn't matter to me. I would have paid anything.

I started dinner before Tim and Gabe arrived. I hadn't felt up to cooking the last few weeks, but I thought it might help pull me out of the slump I had fallen into. Since I hadn't been cooking, I also hadn't been shopping. A quick search through the cupboards and freezer planned the menu. Spaghetti, garlic bread and broccoli. It was simple, but probably better for us than another mushroom and pepperoni pizza. If I didn't start eating vegetables this baby might grow a second head.

When I opened the fridge the six pack of Sam Adams stared back at me. So far not being able to unwind with a beer was the hardest part of being pregnant. If you asked Tim, I'm sure he would say it was my mood swings. A healthy baby was worth more to me than a beer. When I closed the door and left Sam Adams in the dark, I remembered hearing the ladies from the other day talk about drinking or taking drugs to escape the memories. That's probably why I started having a beer to calm my nerves. I guess I can add that crutch to the list of things Chad did to me.

With the water boiling, I dumped the spaghetti noodles

into the pot, water splashed out on to my arm. *Jesus Christ.* Tim and Gabe were standing behind me when I rushed to run cold water over my burn.

"Whoa, Val, are you alright?" Tim stood over me to inspect my arm.

"Yeah, I'm fine. I just have a lot on my mind." I shook the water off my arm and dried the rest with a towel.

"You don't have to make dinner."

"Why? You'd rather have pizza again?" I rolled my eyes. "Fine. I'll just throw it away."

"I didn't say that. You said you had a lot on your mind. I thought it would be easier for you." He came closer and reached for my hand.

Gabe was standing behind us, his head looking at his feet.

"No, I want to make dinner for us. It's been too long." I tossed the towel on the counter and stirred the pasta. "How was your day?" I turned and smiled at Gabe.

"It was okay. Nothing exciting today." Gabe stuffed his hands in his pockets. "I love spaghetti."

"I'm glad you're so easy to please." I gave him a smile. "Why don't we sit down later and make a list of meals you like? I'll go shopping tomorrow."

"Okay, that sounds good. I'm not really picky, I'll eat most anything."

"Hear that Tim? He's not picky. Maybe you could learn how to try new things from Gabe."

"Ouch." Tim twisted off the top of his beer and pressed it to his lips.

When he set the bottle down, I gave him a kiss. "God, I miss that." I licked my lips.

"Not in front of the kids." Tim laughed.

"I was talking about the beer."

"Double ouch." Tim took another drink and held his hand out to keep me away from him. "You're not going to use me to get to Sam."

"Ha-ha. I'm sorry I'm so bitchy. It's the hormones."

"It's okay. I still love you. I knew what I was getting myself into."

"Triple ouch." Gabe raised his eyebrows and moved his hand across his neck. "Dude, you never say stuff like that."

"You're going to make someone a great husband." I gave him a kiss on the cheek and went back to making dinner.

"About that." Gabe's ears turned red. "I met someone. We're going on a date this weekend."

"Oh, that's exciting. Where did you meet her?" I set down the spoon and turned around to see the excitement on his face.

"I met her at the gas station. Random I know. But she's super sweet and cute."

"Which gas station? I might know her."

"I don't know. She just moved here. Her name is Carmen."

I whipped my head around making my neck crack. "Carmen? What does she look like?"

"She's cute. Short, sparkling blue eyes."

My heart was doing somersaults in my chest. The image of Carmen in her hospital bed flashed before me. It couldn't be her. She was dead. I saw it with my own eyes. "What's her last name?"

"I'm not sure. We literally just met."

"What color hair does she have? Where did she move here from?"

"She's a redhead. That's a random question." Gabe cocked his head. "Do you know her?"

"No, I was thinking of someone else. Where did you say she was from?"

"She just moved here from California. She's still got a tan." Gabe licked his lips before his face was plastered with a smile.

"She does sound cute. I hope you two have a good time. But not too good. Do we need to have *the* talk?" I crossed my arms, pulling my cardigan over my belly.

"Val, I'm twenty. I've done my fair share of practicing."

I covered my ears and closed my eyes. "La-la-la-la. I can't hear you."

Gabe laughed. "I'm not a little kid. I'm a man... you just said I'd make someone a great husband. And if I've got things figured out, I think I know what husbands do." Gabe looked down at the baby growing in my stomach and winked.

"I know. You're a good boy."

We ate dinner as a family and I tried to be present. I tried to push out all of the thoughts I hadn't been able to shake and enjoy the time with my son and husband. Life passes by so quickly, I wanted to make sure I devoured moments like these. Everything can change so fast.

CHAPTER TWENTY-SEVEN

Gemini's house was only a twenty-minute drive from mine. I turned onto Star lane and parked my car in front of the small wooden camp. There was an old Volkswagen bus with flat tires rotting in the yard. It was filled with boxes that looked like they had been there for decades. Bird feeders lined the walkway and surrounded the front of the house. A stack of aged firewood rested next to a small fire pit.

The smell of sage and wood smoke met me as I knocked on her door. A gold horseshoe hung under a tiny peephole. The door creaked open and Gemini held it open for me to enter. She was wearing the same clothes as she was the first time we met. A black cat that looked like Gabriel rushed out between my legs and ran into the yard.

"Should I go get him?"

She shook her head. "She's fine. She spends most of her time out there."

"She looks like my cat. What's her name?"

"Celeste. Come on and have a seat." She pointed to a small table set against the wall in her kitchen. An antique stove filled most of the space.

"It's so cozy here." I took off my jacket and placed it on the chair before I sat down.

Gemini handed me the stack of tarot cards. "Shuffle them. Think of what you want to know, who you want to talk to as you touch them."

I closed my eyes and rubbed my hands together. With the cards in my hands I asked Norma to come talk to me. I asked what I had to do to help Norma get to Heaven. I thought about Norma and Sylvia spending eternity together. I tried to repeat the thoughts over and over as the cards passed through my hands.

"When you are ready, hand them to me." Gemini held her hand out.

I closed my eyes again and thought about Norma coming through today one last time before handing them back to her.

Gemini held the cards with both hands before she started shuffling them. This was not what she had done the last time, so I was hopeful for a different outcome. Gemini blew on the cards before she set them down in a stack. "Do you have any questions?"

I nodded as I sat on my hands. "I have a lot of them." I felt a tear drop hit my cheek.

"Today is not like before. You can ask me what you want to know. Your spirits have been talking to me. I knew you'd be back."

"They have? Who?"

Gemini shook her head. "They still do not want me to tell you. You must figure that out on your own."

"I don't understand why you can't tell me." I tried to bury my annoyance.

"Some things have to be discovered when you are ready. Now is not the time."

"How did you know I was coming back?"

"I told you. I've been talking to your spirits. They told me."

"How did they know?"

With an expressionless face her eyes pierced my soul. "They have been watching you. They're always watching you."

My body stiffened as I thought about what *they* had seen, and who *they* were. "They see what I do? Like, all the time?"

"What do you have to hide?" Gemini raised her eyebrow.

I knew she *knew*, I just wanted to hear it from her. I cleared my throat. "What do I have to do?"

"You have to stop lying. You'll never get the life you want if you don't stop."

"I will. There's just one more thing I have to do first."

Gemini pounded her fist on the table. "No. You must not."

"Was that *you*?"

"No, that was them. She says you must not follow through with your plan."

"How am I supposed to listen when I don't know who is talking to me?"

"You'll know in time. She said she's not ready for you to

know yet. Things have to be figured out first. You're not ready yet. Information has to come forward first."

"Okay. Let's say I get the message. Can I ask a question now?"

Gemini placed her hand on the tarot cards. "Go ahead."

"Is Norma here?"

She closed her eyes as she swayed back and forth in her chair. "Not yet." She turned over a card. "The Fool. This represents new beginnings. There is something up ahead and you must jump whether you feel ready or not. Take a leap of faith and trust the universe."

I knew I had to take care of Chad in order to get to the new beginning. It seemed to contradict what was said before, but no other jump that I needed to take came to mind. "Is there a way to help someone get to Heaven?"

Gemini tilted her head and picked up a card. "Justice, this represents fairness and truth. If someone has acted in alignment with their Higher Self, there is nothing to worry about. If they acted against this, I'm afraid it is up to them to make it right."

"What if they were doing something wrong to make something right?"

"I am not the judge of what is wrong or right. Only they will know. Only they will be able to right their wrongs."

A heavy sigh filled the room. "So, there is nothing I can do?"

"If you were not the one who acted, you are not the one who has to fix it. People who pass over have the chance to learn the lessons they did not learn here. Only few people are truly evil. The God you are taught to believe loves truer than you could imagine. There are very few spirits banished to Hell. It is not as black and white as it is here. Your friend you are worried about." She turned over another card. "She is not in Hell. You don't have to worry. The Sun, this represents positive, radiant energy. Wherever she goes, this will follow her. She has a gift that she shares with the world."

"So, you can see Norma is okay?" Relief replaced the worry.

"She is where she needs to be. Her gift is still needed."

I wiped away my tears. "Is she with Sylvia?"

Gemini closed her eyes. "No, not yet. Her work is not finished yet."

"Can you please tell her I love her? And thank her for everything she did for me?"

"You can tell her yourself."

"How?"

"Just tell her. Talk to her. She will hear you."

"Thank you." I placed my hand to my chest. "This has been so helpful; I can't even put it into words."

"Your lesson here has not been learned. Something is coming to a head for you. She wants me to tell you to stop the lies. Take responsibility for your actions. Danger is coming for you. Watch your back."

"Okay. I will."

The question of who was sending me a message left my mind as soon as my tires hit the pavement. What I wanted to hear was all that I needed to take from the visit. I don't know who was talking to me. It was not something my gram would have said, and if I didn't know who it was, it wasn't worth worrying about. The pain in my heart eased when I heard what I already thought. The work Norma had done was a gift. It was her calling, her purpose. Murder isn't always bad; not when it saves more lives than it takes.

Knowing that Norma was safe lessened the need to know every detail of her past. I could let that part rest for now. There was plenty of other things to focus my attention on. The nine other women that have come into my life could now become my focus. I wanted to know what they went through and how much they suffered. It would help me when the time came to make Chad pay for what he did to me, to us.

There were at least three babies he stole from the children he raped. Three children who carried his baby. He didn't want any of us to have an abortion. I couldn't understand that. Why wouldn't he want us to get rid of the evidence? Unless he was being paid by the adoption agency. I've seen a *Dateline* episode that talked about something like this.

My mother would have been onboard with getting the money, but Gabe's adoptive parents didn't seem like the type that would have paid for a baby. Gabe had a great life. This wasn't a road I wanted to go down. The idea that not only did he steal my baby, but he sold my child infuriated me. He did not deserve to breathe the same air that any of us did. There was no way I could let any of the women he hurt look at him again. He didn't deserve to know how he hurt them.

After hearing some of the stories from the other ladies, it was clear he was raping some of them while he was still raping me. It wasn't good enough that he had one little girl, he had multiple. I couldn't understand how that many mothers could look the other way. Was he fucking them, too?

How did my mom get him to marry her? Did she know what he was doing before I told her? Did she use me to get what she wanted? The thoughts spiraled out of control. The moment of peace I had as I left Gemini's house flew out the window with the last black fly of the season.

The hate I held for Chad and my mother increased tenfold. Each thought took me deeper, and darker into what might have happened. I was nothing more than the carrot dangled in front of a pervert's nose. My own mother prostituted me out for a place to live and then sold her grandchild. I pounded my hand against the steering wheel.

The need to end Chad's life was moved to the top of my list. My mother's name was added, too. I didn't think I needed her gone, but I *knew* now that she had to pay, too. She was just as guilty as Chad. The sooner I got it over with, the sooner I could start my new, honest life. No more lies. No more hiding stuff. My happily ever after was just beyond a couple of bullets. The time was now.

CHAPTER TWENTY-EIGHT

"Do you have any way of finding out where my mother is?" I asked Tim as he flipped through the *Village News*.

"What do you mean?" He looked over the paper at me.

"Well, on the news they said she was located in southern New Hampshire. If they know that, would they know where she is?"

"I guess they might. They probably just checked with her bank and saw she had made charges down there. Same with the cell phone records. I think since she's an adult and left on her own there is nothing they can do. So, long answer to your question is no. Why?"

"Oh, I don't know." I took a drink of coffee before holding it between my hands. "I guess I just wanted to talk to her."

"You do?" Tim set the paper down. "Why?"

"I want to ask her if the reason they stole Gabe from me was to sell him."

"Sell him? What are you talking about?"

"You heard the other day. There were at least three of us who were sent to Sawyer's Home. All of our babies were taken from us. I was just thinking with so many of us, maybe there was something in it for him."

"Hmm." Tim scratched his head. "I don't know, I mean I guess it could be a possibility, but do you really think he would have been that stupid? Selling the babies from the underage girls he raped?"

"It's been done before, I've seen it on *Dateline*."

"I know it happens. I just don't think the adoption agency, or Gabe's parents would have been involved with anything like that. They all seem like nice people."

"People aren't always who they seem." I moved the mug between my hands. "Seemingly nice people do shitty things all the time."

"I know." Tim reached for my hand. "What are you expecting to get out of this conversation with your mother?"

"I don't really know." My shoulders fell in defeat. "I guess I just wanted to hold her accountable." *And shoot her.*

"I don't think it would phase her, honestly. I mean, not from everything you've told me about her. She just seems like an evil person."

"You're right. It was a stupid idea."

"No, it wasn't stupid. Meeting with the other ladies was a lot. Chad is an evil person, too. What he did to you and all the other women is despicable. He is the lowest of the low. We can only hope he spends the rest of his life in jail."

"I'd love for him to suffer as much as he made us all suffer. And you know what makes me the sickest? I *know* there has to be more."

"You're probably right." Tim shook his head. "I can't begin to explain to you how angry I felt listening to everyone's stories. I'm so sorry, Val, for everything he did to you."

"It's okay. It's not your fault."

"I know, but I'm sorry that humanity sucks so bad. That bastard was trusted and he blatantly took full advantage of so many people, just because he could."

"Mostly children. Don't leave out that part."

"Yeah. It's disgusting. I'd kill anyone who hurt my child. I can't even imagine looking the other way."

"Hmmm, I think I remember you having a different opinion a while ago."

"Yeah, about that." He ran his hand through his hair. "I'm sorry. I get it now. I totally understand why the Executioner does what he does."

"You're forgiven." I stood up and stretched before placing my hands on the tiny baby bump under my sweater. "If anyone hurts this little one, I feel better knowing you'll take care of them. Because if you don't you can bet your ass that I will."

"Looks like he or she is going to be in great hands." He walked over and put his hand over mine before wrapping me in his arms. "I'm sorry that no one took care of you."

"But, you are now, and that makes it all better." Tim really did make most things better. I couldn't wait to start living an honest life with him, and that could happen as soon as my to-do list was complete.

While Tim was in the shower, I called the nursing home where Gram had been staying. "This is Valerie Phillips. I am Marianne Cooper's granddaughter and I was hoping you could give me her daughter's phone number. I lost my old phone and I don't have any way to get ahold of her." My plan to call on the weekend and get staff that aren't up to snuff with the rules paid off. I wrote the number down and dialed it before Tim was finished.

The call went straight to voice mail. I knew it would. She didn't know it was me, and even if she did, she wouldn't have answered it. When the voicemail instructed me to leave her a message, my anger intensified. Parts of me missed the mother I should have had, while other parts loathed her. Just the sound of her voice made my blood boil. The phone clicked off before I was able to leave a message. I called back and when her voice came on the line, I cleared my throat. "Hi, ah, Mom, this is Valerie. I would like to talk to you. I'm willing to give you some of the money." There was no way in Hell I was going to give her any money; it was merely the carrot to dangle in front of her nose.

I wasn't sure she would ever call me back. I wasn't sure I'd be able to find her, but I wanted to at least try. The more I thought about her getting away from all of the commotion and Chad, the more determined I was to find her. She had no right to find happiness. She was just as guilty as Chad. She needed to be removed from the equation before her new grandchild was born. I didn't want Gabe to meet her, either; not even Gabriel.

CHAPTER TWENTY-NINE

After Tim and Gabe left for work, I took the keys out of the nightstand and removed the pistol from the gun cabinet. I picked the one Tim had taught me how to shoot with, it was the only one I was confident enough to use on my own. In the top of Tim's closet I found the bullets I needed and took the whole box and tucked them into my tote bag.

The vibration of my pounding heart sent shockwaves through my entire body. With my eyes closed I imagined standing in front of Chad and aiming the gun at him. I brought my hands up, holding the gun out in front of me, like I did when he came by a few weeks ago. "It's show time Dr. Ross. This won't hurt for long." A smile grew on my face as I pictured him begging for his life. "*Bang.*" The word echoed off the walls. I held the gun up to my mouth and blew on it before I put it in my bag.

I shut the door behind me. It was now or never, and never wasn't an option I was willing to settle for. I put Chad's address into my GPS and set off down the road. It was my childhood home, but I had spent the last sixteen years trying to erase all of my memories from that time. The hour and a half drive was enough time to work out the plan. There were never any thoughts of not following through or backing out. This was probably the murder I most wanted to complete. To see his life evaporate before my eyes would bring me the greatest joy.

I popped Tom Petty and the Heartbreakers into the stereo and sang along to the Greatest Hits. I turned the volume up and sang along with *Runnin' Down A Dream* and turned it up again to sing along to *I Won't Back Down*. Tom knew exactly how I was feeling. I would never back down again. I knew what I wanted, and I wasn't going to stop until I reached the desired results.

The winding roads through the mountains brought me back to my childhood and to the pain. My throat closed when I thought about the last time I drove this route. It was when I left home. I had not been back since. I had never expected to follow the curves of this road again. So much had changed since I left over sixteen years ago. I wasn't the same girl who ran away all those years ago, today I wasn't running away, but I was rushing into a battle zone. Party of one, your order is up.

The sound of the gravel under my tires as I pulled into the driveway sent chills down my spine. *This was it.* I parked my car under the huge oak tree, the same one I used to sit under and read when I needed to escape. I rolled my shoulders to shake off any of the sentimental feelings that tried to attach to me. I took a deep breath and pushed it out through my lips as I cracked my knuckles.

When I got out of my car I put on the black, leather driving gloves Norma had given me for Christmas. I pulled out the pistol and dug out the bullets and proceeded to load the gun before slipping it into my waistband. I let all of the air out of my lungs and started for the entrance. I lifted the rock by the front door and found the key. You'd think after all this time they would have come up with a better hiding spot.

I glided the key into the lock and gave it a turn before pushing it open. "Honey, I'm home." The sarcasm in my words gave me a little jolt of power. It was me who was in control now. I walked through the kitchen and into the living room. "Oh Chad, you have company." The melody in my words kept me on my toes. The adrenaline pumping through my veins made me feel light on my feet.

The wooden stairs creaked under me, bringing me back to the nights I laid in bed with the covers tightly pulled over my head, knowing Chad would be in to do his 'business.' The memory alone was enough to make me pull out the gun and hold it in front of me as I turned the corner at the top of the steps. "Chad, I have something very special for you." I pushed the bedroom door open and saw Chad lying in bed. "Rise and shine sleepy head, we have work to do." The same words he spoke to me came out of my mouth, like someone else was speaking them.

He didn't move. I made my way closer to the bed and kicked him. Still nothing. "Chad, what the fuck. Get up." I held the gun with one hand and pushed him over with the other. "Fuck. Fuck. Fuck. Oh my fucking God." The blood had dried to his hair and soaked the pillowcase. His eyes were wide open. "Holy fucking shit." I took a step back and fell to the floor. When I reached down to push myself back up I saw *it*.

What is going on? I picked up the copy of the Dixie Chicks album, *Fly*, the same one Norma tossed on the floor next to Earl's body. I turned the CD over to see if there were any clues, any message, or anything. The only thing was a red X in the top right corner on the front of the case. I held the CD close to my heart and began to cry. *Norma*. She wasn't dead. *I knew it*.

I stood up with the album still in my hand and pushed Chad back over into the position he had been in. I took the bullets out of the gun, returned them to the box and put everything back in the bag. I replaced *Fly* where I found it and started back down the stairs. With my hand on the front door, I ran back up to the bedroom and took the album. I didn't want the Executioner linked to this murder. It was too close for comfort, and if Norma is still watching me, she knew I was coming. She most likely left it for me.

My heart was still racing when I tried to put my key in the ignition. My hand was shaking so much it took three tries before I actually heard the hum of my engine. *Holy shit*. I can't believe Norma did this for me. It was the one thing I had asked her for, but she told me she couldn't. What changed her mind? And now that she was presumed dead it was even more risky. Or, maybe it wasn't. The more I tried to wrap my head around it all, the more tangled it all became.

With my foot on the brake, I slide the shifter back into park and picked up *Fly*. There had to be a message inside. I knew Norma would want to talk to me. I pulled the inside cover out and opened the booklet. I turned each page, examining everything. There was nothing there. I popped the CD out and placed it on my lap before I tore the case apart. Maybe she left a note inside. Nothing.

Disappointment filled my body as my shoulders fell. *I don't understand.* I put the case back together and returned the booklet to the front. I ejected Tom Petty and replaced it with the Dixie Chicks. It was my last hope. The hair stood up on the back of my neck when the song started to play. *Ready to Run.* Was this my message? Was Norma ready to run? She wasn't coming back. All the things she was talking about finishing before she could leave were now complete.

I pounded my hand on the steering wheel. *Hank.* She *was* the one that got to him. She had to have been. And now Chad. She was ready to run. Mission accomplished. I left the CD in the stereo and turned out of the driveway to return home. If I had only gotten there a few hours earlier I might have been able to see her. How was she able to read me so well, even when we were separated, that she knew I was on my way here?

With my childhood home in the rearview mirror, the words to the next song reached my ears. *If I Fall You're Going Down With Me.* Was that the message I was supposed to get? Was I thinking too much into this? Did she really know I was coming? Was it left for me? The questions came at me quicker than the trees passed by the windows. No longer able to hear the words to the music, the voices in my head were louder, stronger, and more powerful than I was. I couldn't push them out.

I needed to get off this road and away from the memories. I needed to get home and return to the safety of my own bed. The migraine settled in and I was unable to form another rational thought. The road led me back to Lawrenceville. Thankfully I was on autopilot.

The thrill I had been after left me as soon as my mind took over. I wanted to kill him. I wanted to be the one to watch his life vanish before my eyes. I wanted to hear him scream and beg for his life. I wanted him to suffer. It didn't look like he even saw what was coming. He didn't have to feel afraid. He didn't have to be overpowered. He didn't have to be in the shoes he forced me into. He got away with it again.

I hit the eject button and returned *Fly* to the case before slipping it into my bag and heading into the house. I retraced the steps I took a couple hours ago and returned the gun and bullets. I put the CD in my dresser, under my pajama pants. I was the only one who took care of laundry, so it was the safest place in the house.

Defeat carried me to bed, where I kicked off my shoes and pulled the blankets over me. I couldn't stand the feel of my skin touching my body. Fumes of anger heated me from the inside out. I buried my head into my pillow and screamed. I bit into the softness and yelled again, louder. I sensed a presence at the door, watching me. When I uncovered my head I saw Gabriel. He looked at me as if he didn't know me.

"Come on, buddy." I kissed for him to come. He wouldn't budge from the doorway. "Gabriel, come on." His rejection intensified my fury. I burrowed my head deeper into the pillows and cried until I fell asleep.

"Go to Hell you piece of shit." I held the gun in my hands as I stood over him.

"No, please, no. I'll do whatever you want." Chad covered his face as I stood over him.

"I don't remember no ever working." A sinister laugh filled the room. "Pull your pants off."

"No, stop it. You can't make me." Chad's body curled into the fetal position.

"I said take your fucking pants off. Come on, I want to see if you're a man. What are you? Scared?"

"No, Valerie, no. I'll do anything. Please let me go." The fear in his voice made him smaller. So small, I was now double his size.

"You're not going anywhere until I'm satisfied. That's what good boys do." I picked my foot up and pressed it into his stomach. "If you don't do what I say, you're going to have to be punished."

He withered up under my foot, getting smaller and smaller. The roles reversed, I was the one in control. I was the one with the power. I aimed the gun and pulled the trigger. Blood spattered as the bullet hit his groin. Screams mixed with laughter; my laughter swirled in my head.

The room began to fill with blood. The level kept rising. Chad was gasping for air, no longer able to hold his head above it. The moments of feeling powerful were swallowed up by fear as the blood reached my neck. I swam to stay above, but the room was disappearing. Chad's blood was going to kill me. He took his power back, even in death.

I felt a hand reach for me. I grabbed onto it and was pulled outside, where everything that had happened *vanished. The sun shone down, heating my skin and I saw my mother swinging on the old swing in the backyard. She was smiling and kicking her feet. Was she the one who saved me?*

I looked down and saw my hands were smaller. I was a girl. The desire for my mom to hold me came over me and I ran to the swing. The more I ran, the farther away she got. "Mommy." The joyfulness of the moment was gone when I realized she wasn't coming back for me. I was alone.

I spun around in my dress before I fell to the ground. With my head hiding between my knees, I felt something push the hair out of my face. "Valerie." The familiar voice reached the core of my soul. "Valerie, come on out and play."

When I lifted my head, I saw a young woman in a beautiful flowered dress. Big, beautiful roses in pinks and red surrounded us. The sweet smell of summer encased me. I reached for her hand and felt the warmth of her love. "There, there, you're safe now. There's nothing more to worry about." She kissed my forehead before she was gone.

When I opened my eyes, Tim was sitting on the side of the bed. "Hey there. Are you okay?"

I rubbed my eyes. "What? What time is it?"

"It's 5:15. Gabe and I got out a little early. We thought you'd want to join us for some pizza."

"I'm not really hungry. I'm not feeling well today."

"What's wrong?" His hand went to my forehead. "You don't feel like you have a fever."

I pushed his hand off. "Can you guys get it to go? I don't really want to be alone."

"Sure." Tim looked around the room. "It's just that Gabe

wanted us to meet Carmen. I don't know how he'd feel about bringing her back here."

I sat up with the blankets still wrapped around me. "I guess I can go. Do I have time to take a shower?" I could still smell Chad's house in my hair.

"Yeah, sure. We can always do this some other time. Let them have another alone date before the parents crash it."

"Nah, I think it'll be good. It can take my mind off of stuff."

"Is there anything you want to talk about? Anything I can help with?"

"No, I'll be fine. A shower should help wash it all away." I hadn't even taken time to make sure I didn't get any blood on my shoes or anywhere else. I could be a walking piece of evidence.

I couldn't figure out what the dream was all about. Maybe it was to show me it wasn't so great to be the one to kill Chad, because it ended up almost killing me. Norma did me a favor, but I would have liked to at least had the chance to talk to her. And who was the beautiful young woman that saved me? And why couldn't I get to my mom?

As I rubbed the shampoo into my scalp, the image of the woman from my dream came back to me. It was Norma. It was the same picture I had seen of her in all of the news stories when Rose St. Thomas went missing. The roses. Of course, it made sense. And she did save me, just like she saved all of us. She solved all of our problems. Was she on to another group now? She was done with us?

I knew she loved me, she loved all of us. How could she just leave us all behind? If we really mattered that much to her, how could she just leave? I felt like a jilted lover. I needed her to need me. I didn't want to think about anyone else having *my* Norma.

The hot water continued to hit my back when I heard a knock on the door. "Val, are you doing alright in there?"

I twisted the lever and turned the water off. Standing naked and alone in the middle of the shower. "Yeah, I'm fine. I'm almost done." When I stepped out of the shower, I noticed my reflection in the mirror. Through the steam, I barely recognized the eyes staring back at me. I rubbed off a small circle and saw the tears streaming down my cheeks. "It's gone. It's all gone."

My problems were over. They were done. There would be no trial. There would be no testifying. There would be no more chances of Chad arriving at our house. There would be no more monster to haunt me. Or would there? Was it that simple? Did his death really solve anything? The memories still haunted me. I had a feeling they always would.

I gritted my teeth and stared back at my reflection. "It's over." I pounded the sides of my head. "Get out of my head. Get the fuck out."

"Val?" Tim was outside the door. Was he listening to me? I guess I was louder than I had thought.

"Just a minute. Almost done."

"Can I come in?"

"No, I don't want you to see me like this. Hang on, just give me a second." I pulled the rough side of the towel across my skin, somehow thinking the pain would make it stop. My skin becoming raw with each pull. When I was dry enough, I put my clothes on and threw my drenched hair into a messy bun. The water dripping down my shoulder.

When I opened the door, Tim was sitting in the hall, his back against the wall.

"What are you doing out here? What's the matter with *you*?" I was angry at him for not knowing how much pain I was in and then I was angry at myself for all of the lies. I just wanted to let him in and tell him all of my secrets. But I couldn't.

"I'm just worried about you. What's going on?"

"I just... don't feel well. I told you that." I brushed the drops of water off my shirt.

"You seem like something else is bugging you. Do you want to talk?"

"I'm sick and tired of everything. I fucking miss Norma. I'm so pissed off at her for leaving me. What the fuck did I do to make her abandon me? Why am I not enough for anyone?" The words that came were not ones I expected. I fell onto the floor next to Tim and sobbed as he stroked my soaking wet hair.

"Oh, Val, I know you miss her. She didn't leave you; she died. It wasn't her choice."

"We don't know that for certain. We don't know anything really."

"Val, I saw her body. I *know* she is dead. She loved you very much. She would have never just left you."

"I don't know about that. She probably hated me. She probably..." I stopped before I said something I shouldn't.

"I love you, Val. Gabe loves you. We're not going to abandon you. You're stuck with us." He wiped the tears off my face. "And soon we're going to have a little person that's going to love you more than anything."

The baby. I had to pull myself together for the baby. The amount of rage and stress pumping through my veins was enough to poison my unborn child. It depended on me to give a safe place to grow, and I couldn't even do that right. I put my hands to my abdomen and felt my heartbeat. "I think I need help."

CHAPTER THIRTY

"I think I'm falling apart." The words left my mouth before Jennifer had a chance to sit down.

"I'm glad you were able to make it in today."

"I didn't think I could wait until our next appointment. I think I'm going crazy."

"Why? Can you tell me what's going on?"

"I don't know." I was trapped between what I needed to say and what I could say. "There's a lot happening right now, I guess it's just too much." I twisted my wedding ring and looked at the braided rug. "It's just that... I really miss Norma."

"Losing someone important can be difficult."

"Yeah, I know. It's just that I'm angry at her for leaving. It feels selfish, like she didn't have to go. Then I get mad at myself for being upset with her. It's just one big fucking circle of chaos."

"It's okay to be angry. You have a right to feel anything and everything. There is no right or wrong way to grieve."

I twirled a piece of my hair around my finger. "The real issue is I don't believe she's dead. Like, I know they think she's dead, but how do we really know?"

"What makes you think she's not gone?"

"That's the thing. I'm not sure." Except I was sure. I knew for a fact she wasn't gone. "Another thing that is getting harder is keeping all these secrets. They just keep growing. I don't know how many more I can hold onto."

"Secrets can be heavy. Is there something you want to let go of today? Remember, what you tell me stays here, unless it is poses a threat to you or someone else."

I bit my bottom lip and adjusted myself in my chair. "I don't think so. I really want to talk about it, but I don't want to get anyone in trouble."

"Is there anything you can talk about that would help?"

"I'm angry at my mother. I feel like her and Chad made me give up my baby because they sold him. When I met the other girls there were two others who went to Sawyer's Home for Unwed Girls, and they both had their baby taken from them, too."

"That's a lot to take in, and now you're pregnant again. I can see how this could be upsetting."

"It's way more than upsetting. I'm angry... like seeing red angry. I have moments where I want my mom to suffer as much as I did. The thought that she got to run away from everything makes me furious. She got to have the good time and happy life. Now that it's over she can just pack up and move on to the next one. It's like everything she did to me doesn't matter anymore. She got to ruin my life, but she isn't even fazed by it. It just shows me how little I actually mattered to her."

"That doesn't seem fair, does it?"

"No. It's not fair at all. I just want her to know what it was like. She was supposed to be the one person that loved me, but I meant nothing to her." I focused my attention on the bookcase behind Jennifer's chair. "I'd never do that to my child. I don't care what they did. I'd never leave their side. I'd give up my life for them. How could you not?"

"Unfortunately, some people were not meant to have children. They are selfish and abusive. That's why there are people like me. We are here to help remind people like you that you are worthy. The good news is you know what kind of mother you never want to be." Jennifer pushed the cap of her pen into her chin.

"True. I guess losing Norma made me remember the pain of losing my mom." I rubbed the palms of my hands on my thigh. "And add my grandmother into the mix, and I guess it's a perfect storm"

"Valerie, you have a lot going on; all at once. You forgot to mention the trial with Chad, and the new life growing inside of you. I honestly don't know how you are doing as well as you are."

"You don't think I'm crazy?" My eyes started to water.

"Not at all. For everything you've been through, and are currently going through, you're a superhero."

I laughed as I pushed the tears out of my eyes. "That would be one hell of a movie. We could call it Two Deaths, A Baby, and A Rape Trial."

"Definitely has blockbuster written all over it." Jennifer

smiled. "What can we do today to bring this joy back to you? I love to see you smile and able to enjoy life."

Find the joy. "That was what Norma used to tell me. I do have to find the joy. I just don't know where to start."

"I think you do. Here, let's make a list." Jennifer picked up her notepad and flipped to a clean page. "Let's name off some of the important people in your life that you can reach out to if you're feeling down."

My shoulders fell with a sigh. "Tim and Gabe are always willing to listen. Then there's Sonya and Maggie. I can call or text Lily, so I can add her to the list." I bit my fingernail. "I guess that's it."

"Well, let's add my name to the list. I'm part of your team now, too. Can you think of anyone else you'd like to add?"

I shook my head. "I can't think of anyone else."

"That's okay. This is an impressive list. I bet if you were to write this a couple years ago it would have been a lot smaller."

"You're right. It would have been empty. I wouldn't have had one name on that list."

"See how far you've come? Give yourself credit, even if you don't think it's a big deal. Own the accomplishment and celebrate."

"I can try that. I guess it is a big deal to go from having no one to having a decent support team; even though I already lost two of them."

"It always comes with a risk. Love isn't always easy, but if it was real, it is always worth the risk."

"Do you write Hallmark cards in your spare time?"

She laughed. "No, do you think I should?"

"Absolutely, but only if you promise to keep doing this, too. You really helped me today. I wasn't sure anyone was going to be able to."

"I didn't do anything. You did all of the hard work."

After talking with Jennifer, I did feel better about some things. I had a better understanding as to why I was so angry at Norma for leaving me. It felt too much like what my mom did to me. She did go out of her way to take care of Chad for me. I guess I could forgive her for not waiting for me or letting me know she is okay. I didn't love her any less; maybe a little more.

And, Jennifer was right, I would be nothing like my mother. The joy I could find in my shitty childhood was that my children would have a good mother; a mother who loved them. It felt better knowing I wasn't going crazy or losing my mind. It is all a normal part of grieving. I guess you can still grieve someone who is still living. I used to do it all the time and who knows, maybe she will reach out to me once she feels it's safe. It didn't hurt to dream.

CHAPTER THIRTY-ONE

The familiar piercing ring of the telephone pulled me out of sleep. Tim took the day off to take me to our ultrasound appointment. We were going to get to find out if I was carrying a beautiful little girl or a handsome little boy. I elbowed Tim to make the noise stop. He tossed his arm around me and pulled me close for a hug. "Let the answering machine get it," he mumbled as he drifted back to sleep.

When the ringing stopped, Tim's voice started to play on the machine in the kitchen before the 'beep' sounded. "Hi, Valerie, this is Cheryl from the victims' center. I tried to reach Detective Phillips at his office, but they told me he had the day off. When you get this, please call me. It's urgent."

I knew what she was calling to tell us. Tim would be pulled away from me on one of the most important days of my pregnancy. I might not have pulled the trigger, but I initiated it. The knot began tying in my stomach as I looked over at Tim. "It was Cheryl, did you hear the message?"

Tim pulled the pillow over his head. "Mhm, just give me a few more minutes."

"She said it was urgent. Aren't you at all curious what it's about?"

"Not enough to get out of bed."

I stared at the ceiling while Tim continued to sleep. I wasn't curious. I knew what the call was about. I guess there was no hurry to ruin our day. I rolled over and lifted Tim's arm and snuggled into him. Between us, I felt the baby moving. It wasn't the first time, but the sensation was getting stronger. This was where I wanted to be. *Needed to be.* I didn't want Chad to interfere with this. Even in death he was going to prove to be an inconvenience.

Tim pulled me closer and kissed me on the lips. I still melted every time I felt the warmth of his skin next to mine. "I guess I'll give her a call." He sighed as he stretched. "I really don't want to."

"I know. I don't want you to, either."

"No? You're not curious what is so urgent?"

"Nah, I mean, at least not today."

Tim reached over for the phone. "Yeah, I know. I'm sorry. I feel like I need to call her before she freaks out." He sat up, his legs off the side of the bed and dialed the number. I pushed closer to him to try to hear the other side of the conversation. "Hi Cheryl, this is Detective Philips returning your call."

I couldn't make out what she was saying, but Tim went quiet. His complexion went white as his mouth dropped open. I placed my hand on his back, but he didn't respond to my touch.

"Thank you for letting me know." Tim set the phone back down and rubbed his eyes before he turned to look at me. "She was calling to tell me Chad's dead."

"He's dead?"

"Yeah, he was found murdered. It was a lot like the cases here in Lawrenceville. It looks like you got your wish."

"Holy shit. That's the best news I've heard in a long time."

"I guess it is."

"Do you have to help with the investigation?"

"No, the town of Benton is handling it."

"But, if it's like all of the unsolved cases here, shouldn't you guys help?"

"Maybe, at some point, but right now it's in their hands."

"So, you still get to come with me today?"

"I do. I wouldn't miss it for anything. I can't want to meet the little guy."

"Or girl. I don't know why you're so sure this is a little Tim." I rested my hands on my baby bump.

"Timothy Jr. does have a good ring to it." He laughed and fell onto the bed, pushing me over with him. "Valerie Jr. just doesn't have the same ring to it."

"Eww. I'd never do that to a child. I just can't wait to be able to refer to the baby as something other than it."

"Just a few more hours and we'll be able to see what you've got cooking in there."

"Did Cheryl say anything else?"

"Not really, just that she wanted to get you and the others together soon to talk about what happens now."

"That makes sense. This is great news for us. I really

didn't want to have to testify and be picked apart by his lawyer or see them do it to the other girls."

Tim scratched his head. "Yeah, except that can't happen until you've all been excluded as suspects."

"Wait... what?"

"Since all of you have plenty of reason to want Chad dead, they'll most likely want to talk to each of you. They'll want to get your whereabouts for the time of murder."

"My whereabouts? Like my alibi?" I felt the migraine start to take residency above my left eye.

"Yeah, but you've got nothing to worry about."

"Why do they need to do all that? I mean, if the murder is like all the others, won't they just link them all together?"

"Maybe. I guess it depends on what they find at the crime scene. I mean if the famous trademark is there, then it's probably a closed case since that hasn't been released to the public. Don't worry, I don't think any of you have anything to worry about."

"Should I tell any of the others?"

"No, I wouldn't do that. Let Cheryl give them the news. I'm sure the police will be by to talk to all of you within a day or so, if they decide they have to. You have nothing to worry about."

"It sounds like I have a lot to worry about. I don't want to talk to the police. I'm alone all the time, who is going to vouch for me? It's not a secret that I wanted him dead."

"Val, calm down. You don't have to worry. You didn't do it; you've got nothing to worry about."

"How do you know? I mean, how do you really know?"

"Because I just do. Try to relax and let's have a good day together. I want to go shopping after we find out today."

"It's easy for you to say. I mean, you didn't tell your therapist you wished some guy was dead... and then he's murdered." My body quivered as I recalled the conversation.

Tim took my hands. "Val, it's perfectly normal for you to have wished him dead, but it doesn't mean you're the one who killed him."

"I don't know. I'm really freaking out right now."

"Trust me, you've got nothing to worry about. You're safe now." He reached over and kissed the top of my head. "Now, go get dressed so we're not late."

It was easy for Tim to tell me to calm down. He wasn't the one in the house who kicked a dead body. He wasn't the one who stole the one piece of evidence linking the murder to all the others. *Shit*. Nothing is ever easy. If chaos is water, I'm drowning in it.

When we arrived at the radiology department for the ultrasound, my body hadn't stopped shaking. Mix that with the gallon of water they had me drink for the appointment and I was ready to crawl out of my skin. Ten minutes after the time I was scheduled to see the technician, my full bladder turned everything into a catastrophe. My foot tapped under my chair as my eyes went to the clock on the wall. "What's taking them so long?"

"I don't know, maybe there was an emergency."

"There's going to be one soon if they don't get me back there."

"Want me to go check with the receptionist?"

"Yes. I have to pee so bad. I don't know how much longer I can hold it."

"Oh, that's right. I forgot you had to drink all that stuff. Hang on." Tim knocked on the glass in front of the woman with the headset on. He turned around and pointed to me and then to his watch before he returned to his seat. "She said they're running a few minutes behind, but you're the next one in line."

"How much longer."

"She said it should be less than five more minutes."

"It better be, or I'm going to pee right here."

Tim laughed and took my hand. "I'm sorry. It won't be much longer."

"Why don't you go drink a bunch of water and you can be uncomfortable with me?" I squirmed in my seat to try to find a position that didn't cause me pain.

"I should have. I'm sorry. You shouldn't be the only one in pain."

"Ha. Give it a few months. Are you going to feel that pain, too?"

"Valerie Phillips?" The technician came out just in time to take the heat off of Tim.

"About time," I sputtered under my breath.

Tim took my hand as we followed the woman into the first exam room. She handed me a hospital gown and told me to undress from the waist down. I found some relief when the pressure from my pants was gone. She rubbed some jelly on my stomach and pushed the wand into my skin. The pain I had been feeling evaporated when I saw our baby up on the screen.

"You can use the bathroom now." The technician wiped the jelly off of my belly.

"Wait, can we find out what the gender is?" I wiped the tears out of my eyes.

"That's the next part. I just thought you'd be more comfortable after you used the restroom."

I swung my feet off the exam table and held the gown closed behind me as I made my way into the bathroom. When I stood up to wash my hands, tears filled my eyes as I saw my reflection looking back at me. "Get it together Val, this baby needs you." The whisper was drowned out by the running water. "No more stupid shit." I turned the water off and dried my hands before returning to the table.

After the gel was spread on my abdomen, she pressed the wand back into my skin and started pausing in areas to take measurements and pictures. The longer I was able to watch the life growing inside of me on the screen, the more I fell in love.

"Did you say you wanted to know the gender?"

"Yes." Tim and I answered together. It was the first time I had noticed the tears in his eyes. It looked like he was just as in love as I was.

"Okay, are you two ready?" She looked over at us. "It's a... girl."

"I told you." I reached my hand out to take Tim's.

"I guess it's time I finally admit you're always right." He kissed the top of my hand.

We were having a little girl. Even more reason she needed her mother in her life. There were so many things and people to protect her from. She was going to have the best safety net around her. I couldn't wait to hold my baby girl in my arms and show her how important she is to me; to us. She was going to be one lucky girl. I have history to rewrite. The line of family trauma stops here.

"She's beautiful." Tim's eyes sparkled in the glow of the computer screen. "Valerie Jr., it is."

"No. I think Marianne Rose is a better choice."

CHAPTER THIRTY-TWO

Since the police department in Benton were as understaffed as the Lawrenceville department, they called on Tim and his crew to help with the investigation. I wasn't sure if this was a good idea or not. They did know the cases pretty well after investigating the six murders here. I knew if they saw the crime scene, they'd be able to tell it was the same person; but since I took the trademark, I wasn't sure. Was that the only piece of evidence that linked it all together?

The hours passed like molasses as I waited for Tim to arrive home. The Chief in Benton was going to wait before he interviewed anyone until he had the chance to talk with the Lawrenceville team. Depending on what they found today would determine if the girls from the trial would be interviewed or not. I didn't know which scenario would be better. I did linger in Chad's driveway longer than I needed to. I could have been seen by anyone driving by. For some reason my desire to kill him took over all of my common sense that day.

I sent Sonya a text. I needed something to distract myself while I waited. We hadn't seen each other very much the last few weeks. Her daughter was due any day, so she was trying to get as much rest as she could while she still could. "We're on the way to the hospital!!!"

"Oh my God! Is today the day???"

"It better be! I can't take another day of this crap!"

"Do the others know? Can I tell them."

"We just got in the car, so you're the first to know. You can tell the others. I'll let you know when you can come by."

"Good luck! Let us know if you need anything." I made a group text for Maggie and Lily and shared the news. We had all sort of drifted apart since Norma died. She was the matriarch keeping it all together. It seemed all of our lives went in different directions since that fateful day. With Lily in Florida it was hard to keep her in the loop. And with Hank gone, Maggie had a new sense of independence that kept her on her toes. I knew they'd be there if I needed them, but I felt more like a burden these days, since I was the one with all of the drama.

Both texts went unread. Looks like I'd need to find something else to do to pass the time. I logged onto the iPad and curled on the couch. I had a lot of baby shopping to do now that we knew we were having a girl. On Amazon I started filling my cart with all of the cute pink outfits and the softest looking blankets. A twinge of regret tugged at my heart as memories of our last shopping trip floated back to me. Nothing was the same.

Everything had changed since that day. Marriages, funerals and murders really change a person... well a group of friends. I wanted the feeling from that day back more than anything.

When I heard Tim's car pull into the yard I jumped off of the couch and greeted him at the door. "So? What did you guys think?"

The bags under his eyes were darker than the storm clouds brewing. "I can't say much, but I don't think he's going to want to interview any of you."

"So, was it the same killer?"

He ran his hand through his hair. "There were similarities. That's all I can say."

"How are you doing? You look exhausted."

"I am. It's exhausting. I'm not sure I even know how to do my job anymore. I mean, if this is the serial killer, we're up to seven unsolved murders."

"Well, serial killers are a different breed. They seem to know how to get away with it. I wouldn't say it means you don't know how to do your job." I put my arms around him. "I'm glad you're home. I missed you."

"I'm just glad that piece of shit is dead." He squeezed his eyes shut. "I know I shouldn't say that, but I just can't help it. I hated the idea of you having to relive all that shit all over again. You didn't need that and neither did she." He placed his hand on my baby bump.

"Did you feel that?" The baby kicked when she felt the pressure of his hand. "That's our daughter."

"Oh, wow, that's so cool. You're lucky you get to hang out with her all day."

I rolled my eyes. "Yeah, real lucky. You're not the one who's getting as big as a house."

"You're beautiful. I can't wait to have her here on the outside."

"Me either. Speaking of kids, where's Gabe? Shouldn't he be home by now?"

"Oh, shit, I forgot to tell you. He's going over to Carmen's place to have dinner tonight."

"Dinner, huh? He's spending a lot of time with her lately."

"Relax, Val, he's a grown man. He's allowed to have dinner with a woman if he wants to."

"Ugh. I don't like the thought of it. And what if dinner leads to dessert? Then Marianne will be an aunt before her first birthday."

Tim laughed. "Well, it's not an impossibility. He's old enough to be a dad."

I covered my ears. "La-la-la... I don't even want to think about that." I shook my head to push the thought out. "So, you're sure the Chief isn't going to want to talk to me? And the others?"

"Nah, they pretty much determined it was the work of the Executioner. There's just a few more things to tie up."

"Things to tie up?"

"Oh, you know, he's got to get the approval from the rest of the department. Then Chad's case gets added to the stack in Lawrenceville."

"Why did they let you investigate the case when they wouldn't let Gabe?"

"They didn't put it together that I'm your husband. I'm

not really sure where they dropped the ball, but I wanted to make sure I was in on it. I wanted to make sure the cases were connected and make sure you didn't have to worry about anything anymore."

"Could they throw out the case if they figure it out?"

With the refrigerator door open Tim turned to look at me. "Nah, I don't see why they would. I mean, it's pretty open and shut, we're dealing with the same guy. Now we just wait for him to strike again in Benton, or the surrounding towns. When that happens there will be no doubt."

"What about the trademark?"

"What about it?" Tim twisted the cap off the beer.

"What happens when it isn't there?"

"How did you know it wasn't there?" Tim's eyebrows shot up.

"You told me, silly." My mouth went dry as I tried to undo the mess I just created.

"No, I didn't. I told you I couldn't tell you much. I know I didn't say anything."

"You're just tired. It must have slipped." I felt my cheeks start to burn.

"I wouldn't have. I know that's the piece I never talk about. It's the most important piece. It wouldn't have slipped." He rubbed his mouth before he set his drink on the counter. "Did I? It's been a crazy day."

My pulse beat against my neck as relief washed over me. "Sounds like you need to get to bed early tonight." I took his hand and led him to the living room where we sat on the couch together. "I missed you today. It seemed like you were gone forever."

"I know. I hate being away from you. I'm not sure how I'll be able to leave you and the baby all day."

"Maybe you don't have to. Once the inheritance is all settled, we will have plenty of money for us both to stay home with her."

"I don't know. I love what I do."

"I know, but maybe you'd love not doing it, too."

"That's very true. I guess we'll just have to wait and see what happens."

My phone vibrated on the coffee table. It was Sonya. "Get your butt to the hospital... bring Maggie." I almost dropped the phone as I read the text.

I bolted off the couch. "Oh my God! I've got to get to the hospital! Sonya said it was time."

Tim cocked his head. "Time? For what?"

"The baby is coming." I sent Maggie a text and grabbed the gift bag I had prepared for her daughter's arrival and rushed out the door. "I love you. Don't wait up for me."

At Maggie's I beeped my horn to alert her of my arrival. She was pulling on her sweatshirt as she closed the door behind her. She tossed a pink gift bag in the back seat and pulled on her seatbelt. "I've been waiting for this day since she told us. I can't want to get some baby snuggles." She caught her breath. "It feels like it's been forever since I saw you."

"I know. It does seem like it. How have you been?"

"I've been great. Since Hank died it feels like my life; our life has improved a hundred and ten percent. I finally got the call about his life insurance policy. We'll have the money soon. I've been thinking about moving back home to Texas."

"Wow, Maggie. That's exciting. Have you been talking to your family?"

"Yeah, my sister and I reconnected. We've been talking a lot, and I think it would be good for all of us to just start over. Plus, I think it would be nice to let the girls meet their family."

"I'll be sad to see you go, but I can't wait to see all of the new adventures you're going to have."

"I'm nervous, but really excited. I've been talking to one of the guys I dated before I met Hank."

"Wait... what? Oh my God... that's awesome! I knew you had a glow about you."

She glanced over at me. "I do?"

"Yeah, and now you've got those cute red cheeks."

"Ha-ha. Funny, Val." She looked out the window. "The thing that's bothering me is I'll have to sell Norma's house. It doesn't feel right to just take her money and run."

"She'd want you to be happy. She wouldn't want you to give up your chance at happiness just to be nice. Stop being nice and start living your life." I knew Norma was doing the same thing. I hated I couldn't share any of it with her.

"You think so? It just feels... weird. Like I used her or something."

"Stop it. She loved you and the girls. She wanted to make sure you were taken care of. The house doesn't mean anything to her."

"How can you be sure?"

"Just trust me."

"Do you want to come over and take what you want of Norma's things?"

"I'd love that."

When we arrived at the hospital, I sent Andrew a text to let him know. He met us in the waiting room. "You're just in time to meet her."

"She's here already?"

"She is, looks like she is going to be just as impatient as her mama."

Andrew led us into Sonya's room. The lights were dimmed, and she was lying in bed with her precious newborn on her chest. "Oh, Sonya, she's beautiful." I reached down and rubbed her tiny, wrinkled foot.

"No one told me it was going to hurt so badly." Sonya smirked as she stroked her daughter's hair.

"I do think someone told you... but you didn't want to hear it." Maggie laughed. "Look at all that hair."

"I know. I guess they were right about the heartburn. Do you want to hold her?"

Maggie stepped in front of me. "You know I do." She held her hands out to cradle the little bundle. "Oh, Sonya, she's perfect."

"Well, you do know who her mom is, right?" She giggled.

"What's her name?"

"Unity Valley. Unity to represent all of us, and the best group of friends a girl could ask for, and Valley after you, since you're the one who brought us all together."

Goosebumps sprouted on my arms. "That's beautiful. I don't know what to say."

"I didn't want to tell you before. I knew you'd try to talk me out of it."

All of our lives were changing. Life was pulling us apart

but bringing us closer together. The bond we formed in our first few trauma support group meetings was showing me just how important it is to find your tribe. I'm grateful to have the small, but mighty group of women in my circle, even if we can't physically be in each other's lives.

CHAPTER THIRTY-THREE

Tim drove me to the Stark County Courthouse where the other ladies and I were going to be able to see each other for the first time since Chad's murder. This time I wasn't nervous. A charge of energy pulsated through me. I couldn't wait to be with others who would celebrate his death with me.

"I feel like we should have brought champagne." My leg bounced as Tim parked the car.

"Easy now, Mrs. Phillips. The little miss can't drink."

"I know... I was kidding... kind of. It just feels like we should be throwing a party. I know I'm not the only one."

"This is true. I'm sure there will be plenty of celebrating as soon as we get inside, but let's try to act civilized until we get in there."

I put my hand to my chest. "Why, I never. I'm civilized. What are you talking about?"

"You know, bringing balloons, cake and bubbly to talk

about some guy's murder might look a little strange to some people."

"Screw 'em. It's not *some* guy, it's a sexual predator." I laughed. "How perfect is it that the serial child rapist was murdered by a serial killer?" I threw my head back and laughed.

"Hmm. Ironic, isn't it?" He joined me in our own private laughter fest. "Okay, let's pull ourselves together and get in there."

We walked into the courthouse and I felt unstoppable. Power surged through my body. No one was ever going to take this feeling from me. You mess with me or my family and your days are numbered. I had the angel of death looking out for me.

When we entered the room, all of the other ladies were already in there. The room was not buzzing with the same joy I was swimming in. "Hey ladies, how is everyone?"

"Hi Valerie, we were hoping you'd join us." Cheryl stood up as we sat down and closed the door behind us.

I tried to read the energy in the room. I couldn't tell if they were happy or if I missed something. This was only the second time we have all been together. All of our other contact had been online, and that had been shut down when we found out about Chad's murder.

"I just wanted us all to get together and talk about the new developments in the case." Cheryl returned to her seat.

My heart sank. What was she talking about? New developments?

"It turns out the Benton police think Dr. Chad Ross was murdered by a serial killer. They will not need to speak to any of you, like they previously had thought." Cheryl folded her hands in front of her.

I had forgotten I had inside information. The other ladies didn't know any of the details of the case. I was the only one who knew today was cause for celebration. A weight lifted off of me. When I looked around the room, it appeared it had lifted off the others, too. They were here, unsure what they were going to hear, while I had the luxury of *knowing* we were all off of the hook.

"So, does this mean the trial is over, too?" Emma asked.

"It does. This means that none of you will have to testify." Cheryl ended her answer with a smile.

"The bastard gets off easy if you ask me." Tina crossed her arms. "I was looking forward to the prison beatings... and rape." She laughed as she looked around the table.

"I know. I was hoping he was going to get to feel the same fear he made us feel. This is a close second, though." Beth's lips turned up in a Grinch-like smile.

"I'm not sure what to think." Hattie hung her head. "I want to feel happy about it, but it doesn't feel real."

"It's real. The monster is gone. We're all free from him now." I tried to cheer her up.

"It's been so long since I felt safe." Hattie picked at her fingernail.

"Me, too." Nicole pushed her messy blonde hair out of her face. "I know what you mean, Hattie. I think it's just going to take some time to really sink in."

"How did a serial killer find him?" Hattie asked.

"Well, the case was all over the news. I'm sure you could have found him in a quick Google search." It was probably a good idea I didn't waltz in there with an arm full of party supplies. I hadn't even considered the possibility of this being hard on anyone.

"Do you think they'll be able to find out where we live?" Hattie flicked the fingernail she peeled off onto the floor.

"No, of course not. The serial killer only kills pieces of shit. A vigilante. You've got nothing to worry about. The opposite, really. The murder happened to make sure no one else was hurt by him." The conviction in my voice was enough to ease her worries. I saw her face soften.

"Yes, Valerie is right. None of you are in danger. The case files have been sealed, and no one will ever know who any of you are. We would like to extend the offer of counseling to each of you. Just because Dr. Ross is dead does not mean what you went through isn't important. I really hope you all will consider the offer." Cheryl handed out a rack card explaining the program.

"Does this mean we can start talking with each other again?" Melissa asked.

"Yes, there are no restrictions for any of you. Well, except it is still important to keep the information you learned about each other confidential. I'll still be around if any of you need anything, or if you have an issue with contacting a counselor. I'm extremely proud of each and every one of you for your courage and your willingness to come together. I wish you the best in your future endeavors." Cheryl looked down at her watch. "I'm sorry, ladies, but I have a meeting to get to. Please stay in touch."

Just like that, the trial looming over our heads was gone. We didn't have to face the relentless defense attorney. We didn't have to be victim blamed and shamed. It was over. As we exited the building and went our separate ways, I hoped the friendship we had created was going to be strong enough to last. Too many things in life were not long enough, while others seemed to last the duration.

"Well, that didn't go as planned. I thought there would be a lot more positive reactions." Tim held the door open for me as I got into the car.

"Trauma's a funny thing. You never know what it's going to do, or how you'll react to it. I am a little disappointed that Chad will never have to suffer. I was looking forward to him getting a taste of his own medicine... literally."

"Eww... gross." Tim shook his whole body and stuck out his tongue.

"Yeah, it really is. I'm bummed he won't ever have to fall asleep with his hand over his butthole or have to look over his shoulder when he's in the shower."

"You'd rather him be alive?"

"No. I just like to fantasize about him being tortured. I can only hope it's happening wherever he is now. Maybe the devil has his pitchfork shoved up his ass." I laughed at the image. "A girl can dream, right."

Tim chuckled. "Yes, you have every right to feel that way."

Norma got to him before I did, just like before. I wonder if she plans on striking again, or if she's already moved on. The unfinished jobs were complete. We were all living in a world where our abusers no longer existed. Norma created the perfect world for each of us. I only wish I could repay the favor.

CHAPTER THIRTY-FOUR

With my car full of boxes, I took the familiar drive to Norma's house to help Maggie get ready for a yard sale before their move. With her love interest intensifying, the date of the move had been pushed up. She wanted to be in Texas before the snow started to fall. I hated Vermont in the winter, so I didn't blame her for wanting to skip out early.

Sonya and Unity were sitting in the rocking chair in the living room when I arrived. "Sorry I'm late, I had a hard time squeezing in all of the boxes into my car. I should have borrowed Tim's."

"Hey, we wouldn't know what to do if you showed up on time." Sonya smirked as she patted the baby's back.

"Ouch."

"Oh, you know we love you. I'm just teasing. You're not late, I just couldn't stand being cooped up in the house any longer."

I reached my hands out. "Give her to me. I need some

baby love." I cradled Unity in my arms and looked down at her sweet face. She was fast asleep. I couldn't wait to be holding my little girl. Just a few more months. "She's such a beautiful baby. She looks like a doll." I rocked her in my arms as I stood.

"She is pretty, isn't she? I think she's going to be a redhead, too."

"Uh oh... looks like you might have your hands full very soon." I laughed as I imagined Unity toddling around telling her mom 'no.'

"Especially if she's anything like me." Sonya laughed.

"Yeah, that was what I was talking about," I said.

"You look good holding a baby, Val." Sonya took a drink of ice water and smiled.

"You think so? I'm getting nervous."

"You'll be fine. You're going to be a great mom, and Tim... you two are like a sitcom family."

"I don't know about that." I moved the blanket out of Unity's face to get a better look.

Maggie came in and swooped up the baby. "I haven't had my turn with this sweet little doll yet." She kissed the top of her head and danced her around the room.

"You look pretty good with a baby, too, Maggie. Are you thinking about having anymore?" Sonya asked.

"Oh, God, no. I love babies, but the best part is giving them back. I did my time with Lexi and Sammy. I still am, I'm just on parole now."

"Yeah, she doesn't want to share her time with that new hunk." Sonya moved to the couch to spread out.

"His name is Jeffrey." Maggie's cheeks turned pink.

"Oh, leave her alone, Sonya. I'm happy for her. I'm going to start in Norma's room, if that's okay." I took a box and closed the door behind me. This was my last time to find anything Norma might have left behind.

Her bed was made, just like it was the first day we got the news. Maggie hadn't changed anything in here. It was easier for me this time knowing Norma wasn't really dead. I pulled out the drawers to her dresser and dumped them on the bed. Before I returned the drawers, I felt around inside each opening. I *knew* she had to have left some type of clue behind. She knew what she was doing, otherwise she wouldn't have had the will or life insurance policy in Maggie's name. There was no way this was a spur of the moment decision.

The search yielded zero results. After I had all of her clothes folded and placed in the boxes, I pulled out all of the clothes hanging in her closet. Before I folded each item, I checked every pocket I could find. When the closet was empty, I ran my hand along the wall. There was nothing there. I tipped over an empty tote and pushed it in front of the shelf. I reached my arm as far back as I could and used the flashlight on my phone to light up the dark corners.

I took the books off of the bookshelf, making sure to flip through each book. Nothing fell out. I went back through the books a second time to make sure I hadn't overlooked anything. The findings came back the same; nothing. With every space uncovered I sat on the floor, my back against the bed. I closed my eyes and tried to think like Norma. She had no problem reading my mind. Like the search results of her room, nothing came. She was CIA level at keeping secrets.

Something, or someone, told me to look under the bed. It

seemed like the most predictable hiding spot. There was no way she would have hid something so easy to be found. I pushed the mattress off the bed. I was right. There was nothing there. As I started to put the mattress back onto the box frame, the nudge to keep looking pulled me to the frame of the bed, under the box spring. I ran my hand along the wooden slats. My fingers met a sharp, cold object. My heart leapt into my chest. *This was it.*

I pushed the mattress the rest of the way to the floor, the box spring followed. A copper key with *MASTER* engraved on the round head. It looked like the kind of key that comes with a padlock. Disappointment crashed down washing out the wave of excitement from the find. For a moment I had high hopes. What the hell am I going to do with *this?* I tucked the key into my pocket and went back to packing.

Norma's room was pretty bare. It held just the essentials. The morning I came to go to Peter Berkley's office came back to me. I pulled in as Norma was closing the trunk of her car. Maybe what I was looking for wasn't here after all. For the life of me I couldn't figure out where she might have taken it, or even what *it* might be.

Why wouldn't she have at least left her number for *me?* She knew I could never tell her secret; she held too many of mine. There was no way I'd ever talk. She must have known that. Why would she just leave me? And, who was in the car, if it wasn't Norma? Was this a test? If I figured out what she wanted me to, would I be able to have her back in my life? A game of cat and mouse. I just wasn't sure which one I was. Am I the one running to or from? I didn't even know anymore.

After Norma's bedroom was packed up, I joined the others. Maggie was sorting through the kitchen. Two large boxes sat on the floor in front of her. "Do you want any of this stuff? We won't have a lot of room in the U-Haul."

I picked up one of the teacups and held it in my hand. "You really don't want any of these?"

"I do... but I don't know if it will make the trip."

"Come on, take at least one. So, when you're drinking your cup of tea you will remember us, and the memories we shared." I held the cup out for her to take.

"That's a great idea. Let's make sure Sonya gets one, too. And I'll pack one up for Lily." Maggie pulled two more cups out of the box and set them on the counter.

"Even better. Maybe we can all plan a time each week where we just sit and have a cup of tea. That way we can still get together, kind of."

"I love that idea, Val." Maggie pushed the tears out of her eyes. "I hate the thought of leaving you guys."

"I know, but just think about the future that awaits you. You and the girls deserve great things. There are so many more opportunities for all of you in Texas."

"You're right. It's just hard to say goodbye." Maggie held out her arms for a hug. "I'm so glad I met you."

"Ditto. I don't know where I'd be if I wasn't forced to start that group. It was the best decision of my life so far." I helped Maggie wrap dishes in newspaper and load the boxes on the floor before getting new ones to fill. Maggie wasn't keeping many of Norma's belongings. Knowing how little the items meant to Norma made me not want them, either. I wanted information, not things.

"Our little group was like a wishing well. We walked into that room as strangers and walked out as family. We threw everything we had in there and let fate do the rest." Maggie crossed her arms and smiled.

"I love how that happened." I set down the stack of plates I wrapped. "Have you found anything of Norma's that might have given any clues about where she was going that night? Or anything else?"

"No, not really. I haven't found any photos or paperwork, other than the usual bills. I wonder where she kept that stuff?" Maggie picked up another glass to wrap.

"That is a little strange, isn't it? Everyone has at least something kicking around." I blew the loose strand of hair out of my face. "No birth certificate or bank book?"

Maggie shook her head. "Not that I've found. But she didn't talk about her past at all. Maybe there were things she didn't want to think about, so she just didn't keep it here. Maybe she had a safe deposit box or a storage locker."

Oh my God, she was on to something. I put my hand in my pocket and felt the key. "Have you found any bills for a storage unit?"

"No, I did look, too. I didn't want to see her personal information be sold at an auction or something. I haven't been able to find anything."

A storage unit made perfect sense. That was probably where she took whatever she put in her trunk that day, and where her message to me was. How many storage units could there be in Lawrenceville? If it's even in this town. Norma sure knew how to keep me on my toes.

CHAPTER THIRTY-FIVE

"I know I said I wished Chad was dead, and to be honest, I am glad, it's just that it didn't fix everything."

"What did you think his death would fix?" Jennifer pressed the end of her pen into her chin.

"I don't know. I guess I thought if he was dead my life could go back to normal." I twisted my wedding ring and looked down at my hands. "I thought if he died, I'd feel safe. Or at least the memories of what he did to me would vanish with him. Instead, I keep having nightmares. He's always after me. Sometimes he has a gun and he's running after me, other times he is beating me with a big stick. I can't get away from him. I try not to let him cloud my thoughts when I'm awake, but I don't have any control when I'm sleeping. It's like he's haunting me."

"Why do you think he would be haunting you?"

I couldn't tell her the real reason. I couldn't tell anyone. "It's just what he does. The mother fucker stole so much from me, and now I can't even sleep." I sat on my hands to keep from fidgeting. "Why can't I dream about my gram? I mean, that would be cool to see her again, but no, I have to dream about that dirt bag."

"Have you tried asking to dream about your gram before you go to sleep? If you fall asleep thinking about your gram, maybe she would come to you."

"Maybe, but it's not like I'm thinking about Chad and then he appears. He just highjacks my dreams. I'm so sick of being afraid."

"What are you afraid of?"

I bit my bottom lip and stared at the ceiling to fight off the tears. "I don't know."

"Oh, I think you do. Go to the place you are hiding from and you'll find your answer. Close your eyes and let's go together." Her voice softened as I closed my eyes. "Remember you are in control. You can go to your safe space we talked about earlier. Do you remember where that is?"

"Yeah." I adjusted myself in my chair, forcing my eyes shut.

"Go back to your first memory where Chad made you feel afraid."

The tears streamed down my face as the image of Chad and my thirteen-year-old self came into focus. "I don't want to do this." My words barely distinguishable through the pain. I choked on the breath I tried to take, unable to reach my lungs. "My mom just left me in his office. I knew in my gut I didn't feel safe. He made me feel dirty and like I was bad. He wouldn't listen when I told him no." The tears took over the words.

"Take a deep breath and put your hands on your legs. Can you feel your feet on the floor?"

"Yeah." I wiggled my toes in my shoes.

"Go to your safe spot if you need to. Repeat after me, 'I am safe. I am in control.'"

"I am safe. I am in control." With my eyes still closed, I pushed out the pent-up air through my lips. "It hurt so bad. I told him no, but he kept forcing himself on me."

"Go ahead and tell him no. Tell him you are in control of your body."

"No. Get off of me. I'm in control. Get the fuck off of me."

"Picture yourself cutting the string that attaches yourself to him. Cut it, and watch him float out of the room, out of your life."

In my mind, I pulled the image up of a giant pair of red scissors and watched myself cut the thick black cord that connected us. As the scissors sliced through the cord, I watched as he floated away like a deflating balloon. I felt a smile spread across my face.

"Tell him whatever it is you want him to hear."

"I fucking hate you. You destroyed my life. You stole my mother from me. You hurt me and made me scared to trust anyone. I fucking hate you. I hope you rot in Hell. You can't hurt me anymore. I'm in control." A weight lifted off of my heart as he drifted out of view. A surge of power filled my body, starting at my toes and it didn't stop until it reached the top of my head.

"Now, I want you to picture yourself surrounded by a circle of white light. Let that cover every inch of your body and repeat after me, 'I am safe. I am protected. I am strong.'"

"I am safe. I am protected. I am strong." I believed these words more than ever before. "He can't hurt me." I pushed the last of the tears out of the corner of my eyes and opened them.

"You're right, Valerie. He can no longer hurt you." Jennifer folded her hands in her lap and smiled. "How are you feeling?"

"That was incredible. I would have told you that was bullshit, but I think it worked."

"If you start to feel him creeping back in, go back to that space and tell him to leave you the fuck alone. The more you do it, the better it works."

"This would have been nice to know about, say... twenty years ago." I stretched my arms over my head and let myself relax into my body. For the first time in many years I felt connected to myself. Fuck Chad and everything about him. That ghost is history.

When I arrived home, I went to my bedroom and laid down. I tried to recreate what Jennifer and I did earlier. This time I wanted to release the ties I had to my mother. I wanted to get rid of her once and for all, and murder wasn't an option since I couldn't find her. As I closed my eyes to stir up the most painful memory from my mother, the urge to call her one last time shot through me. Maybe the reason it worked so well with Chad was because I knew he was dead. I needed to take out all of the trash before this baby arrives.

I reached over to my nightstand and got my phone. I scrolled through my recent calls until I found her number and hit the button. One. Two. Three. I counted the rings as I waited. My heart did a somersault in my chest. The flutter felt like butterfly wings rubbing against my breastbone. Before I reached four, the ringing stopped. My tongue swelled up in the back of my throat as I tried to listen closely, waiting to hear her speak.

"Hello?" I forced the word out. Breathing on the other end was the only reply. "Mom, is that you?"

No answer, just more breathing. I stayed on the line and listened until the other end of the line went dead. Did she know I was responsible for Chad's death? Well, not exactly me, but my wish was Norma's command. Why did she answer? I know she knew it was me. I left a message last time. There was no way she didn't. I called the number again and waited for her to answer. This time it went straight to voice mail.

I put the phone back on the nightstand and tried to go back to the task I set out to master. I *needed* to get my mother out of my head. I needed to erase all of the hurt and years of neglect. I needed to squash all of the desires that lingered in the corners of my heart for the mother she should have been. I took a long breath in through my nose and pushed every bit of it out of my mouth. I imagined the pieces of her floating out with my breath and vanishing.

When I pulled up the most painful memory, the one that came was one I had not remembered before. I saw myself as a seven-year-old girl. I was in my bedroom and I saw her standing in the doorway. Her arms were crossed as she watched *him* crawl on top of me. I felt the tears hit my neck as I cried, his hand over my mouth. And still, she's just standing there. The chills that ran through my body became replaced by a boiling rage. Chad wasn't the first one. Nausea rushed up my body and made me jump to my feet.

I grabbed the phone and hit the call button. My hand shook as my heart pounded. Five rings later I was sent to voice mail. "I fucking hate you. I know what you did to me. I know Chad wasn't the only one. I know. I know everything. You're the reason my life is so fucked up. I fucking hope you die you stupid, good for nothing piece of shit. I hope you die a painful death and rot in Hell."

I tossed the phone on the bed and paced the room. How could I have forgotten that? How could she have just watched? I felt the blood pump through my veins. I could feel everything. I needed to find her and make her pay. I needed to end her. Wishing her out of my life was not going to be good enough. She needed to suffer.

CHAPTER THIRTY-SIX

Maggie had a buyer for the house after it being on the market for less than a week. Her plan to move was pushed up by a couple of months. When I arrived to help her finish packing, my heart dropped when I saw the U-Haul sitting in the driveway. The realization of what was *really* happening hit me for the first time. There wasn't any more time to pretend it wasn't. Our little circle was shrinking by the day. Sonya and I were going to be the only ones left in Lawrenceville.

I let myself in for the last time and found Sonya sitting in a folding lawn chair feeding Unity. "This sure doesn't feel like the same place, does it?"

"I know. I'm trying not to think about all the good times... and bad times we had here. My heart hurts a little." Sonya wiped the tears off her cheek.

"Mine does, too. I hate how life keeps moving full speed ahead when I'm not ready for it to." I stomped my foot down and crossed my arms. "It's not fair." I laughed as I walked over to get a closer look at Unity.

"Hey, Val. I'm so glad you're here. The movers will be here any minute." Maggie handed me an envelope and sat on the floor, her back against the wall. "I found this in an old phone book."

When I opened it, I saw an old black and white photo. When I pulled the picture out, a young woman's smiling face stared back at me. I knew right away this was from the internet searches I had been doing. "Is it okay if I keep this?"

"Yeah, sure. I wasn't sure what to do with it. Do you know who it is?"

"No, but you know me, I love old stuff."

She raised her eyebrow as she pushed herself up off the floor. "Really? I didn't know that."

"I guess it's a new thing." I forced laughter as I put the picture away. Sylvia was just as beautiful as the photo from the article I saw online. I was looking forward to returning it to Norma. I'm sure she is missing it. "Is there anything you need help with?"

"No, I just want you two... I mean three here with me. I want to soak up as much time as I can with you all before we have to go. Lexi and Sammy are off saying their goodbyes."

"How are they doing with it all?" I asked.

"They seem excited. They'll still be able to stay in touch with their friends with all that social media they're always on, and I told them I'd let them come back and visit a couple times a year if they wanted to."

"I hope that means you'll be coming with them." Sonya handed Unity to Maggie.

"I'll bring Jeffrey with me, too. I think you ladies will love him."

"As long as he's good to you, he'll be just fine." I winked at her. "I'm going to miss you... and us. We've come a long way."

"We sure have. I never thought I'd ever want another man in my life after Hank. Seeing you and Tim together, I knew I wanted that."

"It is pretty amazing. I got lucky. I didn't have to weed through a bunch of dirt bags." I walked over and rubbed Unity's back. "Can we make a pact? To always stay in touch? I don't want to drift away."

"I'd never dream of it. I need you both. You're my sisters. You won't get rid of me that easily." Maggie kissed the top of the sleeping baby's head. "Aunty Maggie has a couple of nieces to watch grow up."

When the last of Maggie's belongings were packed into the U-Haul, we said our "see you laters." Sonya and I stood in the driveway and waved as Maggie drove off with Lexi and Sammy. I swallowed the tears knowing they were off to bigger, better things. They were leaving, but they were not abandoning me. It was a different kind of goodbye than I had been used to. I trusted we would see each other again.

When I returned home, I pulled the picture of Sylvia out of my pocket and studied her face. I tried to imagine Norma and her together. It was likely this was taken by Norma. The sparkle in Sylvia's eyes spoke volumes about the love that they shared. I needed to find Norma and get this back to her. She must have been in such a hurry that she had left it behind.

I pulled out the notebook from the previous searches and

tried to find a pattern. Like the last time I looked, I couldn't find any predictability in where she went. It seemed as random as throwing a dart at a map. "Oh, Norma, I could really use a talk with you right about now." I hadn't been hearing Norma's voice since I found Chad. I'm not sure why it started, or why it went away, but I would even settle for that right about now. I needed her to help me figure out how to find my mother, and how to deal with the new memories I awakened.

As I thumbed through the pages of my previous research, I was immediately overwhelmed. It seemed hopeless. I wished I was able to think on my toes like she was. As the frustration grew, so did my anger. It was a tricky balance I walked upon. On one hand I understood why Norma had to go, but on the other I didn't understand how she could just leave without even saying goodbye. As I danced between acceptance and rejection, a migraine started to brew. Before I let it take ahold of me, I tucked Sylvia's picture into my notebook and buried it under a pile of books in my desk drawer.

I curled up on the bed and tried to take a nap. Gabriel jumped up next to me and purred as I ran my hand over his silky fur. "Oh, look who's back for some loving. I thought you were mad at me." The emotions for the past few days fell onto his back, matting up his fur. He pressed his body closer to mine and hummed me to sleep.

"Valerie, nothing is what you think." My gram sat in her recliner as she tried to warn me. "Don't let your mind play tricks on you. You're a smart girl, I know you'll be able to figure it out."

I walked toward her and watched her disappear before I

was able to reach her. I sat in the middle of her living room with my head in my hands and sobbed. "Gram, come back to me." When I opened my eyes, Sylvia was sitting in her place.

Her laughter echoed around me. "Rose." Her voice danced as it reached my ears. "Come out, come out, wherever you are."

I stood up to walk to Sylvia, but she vanished as I got closer to her. The laughter returned. I covered my ears to block it out, but the sound penetrated my hands.

"Rose... I'm waiting for you." Sylvia twirled around the living room, her dress flowing with her movement.

"Where is she? Where is Norma?"

"I don't know Norma. I'm looking for Rose." She held out her hand and as I reached for it, I saw Norma walk through the door.

"Norma." My voice pulled me out of the dream and back into reality. What did it all mean? Why was Norma joining Sylvia? I knew she was safe and sound, somewhere. Maybe Sylvia wanted to help me find her? I rubbed the disappointment from my eyes and stared at the wall as I tried to make sense of it all.

CHAPTER THIRTY-SEVEN

The hot water from the bathtub wrapped me in comfort. It had been a while since I soaked in a bubble bath. I popped the bubbles with my toes as I examined my changing body. Marianne was taking up more and more space with each passing day. I watched her foot kick my belly and traced the outline of her body with my finger. The smell of the lavender soap eased the tension I had been wearing.

"Tim, come in here." I watched the door for him to enter. "Tim!" I wasn't sure my voice would be loud enough for him to hear over the TV.

I saw the door crack open. "Is everything alright?"

"Come watch Marianne swim around. She's so active tonight."

"Chinese must agree with her." He kneeled next to the tub and put his hand on my belly. "Wow, she's strong."

"Tell me about it. Some days it feels like she's going to rip her way out." I relaxed under his touch as I imagined having her on the outside with us.

"It won't be long before we get to meet her."

"I know. It's crazy how fast the time went. Just a couple more weeks and we're going to be parents." I smiled as I pictured our family photo. Tim, Gabe, Marianne and me. If we didn't hurry, we'd have to include Carmen. "I mean, parents to a baby, not a full-grown man."

"I know what you meant. Gabe's getting a life of his own. I think it's great he wants to settle down in Lawrenceville. That means we get to continue to be part of his life, and he'll be able to enjoy his little sister."

"You're right, it's just hard to have him so preoccupied so suddenly. I am glad he's happy. Everyone deserves to be loved."

"He still loves you. Just because Carmen is in his life doesn't mean he doesn't still love you. He's just following his... ah... you know." Tim winked as his eyes went to his crotch.

"Gross." I closed my eyes to try to push the thought out of my mind. "Hey. Can you go grab me some pajamas? I forgot to bring them in."

"You sure you just don't want to go get them yourself?" He wiggled his eyebrows at me.

"No. You don't need to see any more of this than you already have."

Tim was gone longer than I expected. I got out of the tub while I waited for him. After he didn't return I wrapped the towel around me, covering as much of my skin as I could. "Hey, what took you so long?" I asked as I entered the room.

Tim turned around to face me. It seemed like he was moving in slow motion. "Where did you get this?" His voice shook as he held the copy of the Dixie Chicks album I had hidden in my drawer.

My tongue swelled up as it rolled to the back of my throat. Unable to produce any words I stood next to him, water dripping around me.

"Val, where did you get this?"

"Um... I ah... I don't remember. I've had it for a while."

"Val, don't lie to me. Tell me where you got this." He shook the CD in the air.

"What? I'm not lying." My cheeks burned as I slipped on an oversized t-shirt. "Is it a crime to listen to the Dixie Chicks?"

"Come on. Just tell me why you have this." I noticed the tremor in his hand as he held up the item in question.

"I did tell you. I don't remember. Why are you so upset?"

"I'm not playing games. This is serious. I *need* you to tell me where you got this."

"Oh my God. What the hell is wrong with me having a CD in my drawer? Why are your panties in a bunch?" My attempt at humor was lost on him. I was trying to lighten the mood. I knew he was aware of the connection of this album, I just didn't want him to know I was, too.

"Val, I *know* where you got this from. I need you to tell me." His voice cracked.

"I don't know what you mean." I shrugged my shoulders as I pulled on my pajama pants.

"Fuck. Val, come on. This is fuckin serious. I don't have

time to play games." The change in his mood scared me. It was the first time I had seen him angry.

"I can't tell you." My eyes dropped to the floor.

"See this red X right here?" He pointed to the corner of the CD. "This is how I know you aren't telling me the truth."

My heart shot up into my throat as what he just said fully sunk in. "It was you?"

"Fuck." He threw his head back. "Why do you have this?" He pushed the tears off his face. "Please, just tell me."

I pushed out the breath I was holding and looked into his eyes. "It was you?" I collapsed onto the bed. It was Tim and never Norma. I couldn't process what was coming at me. "You're the one who kill Chad?"

He came and sat down next to me. "I had to. I couldn't let him hurt you anymore. He was a monster."

"Why didn't you tell me?"

"Tell you that I murdered a man?" He put his face in his hands and rubbed his eyes. "There was no way in Hell I was going to get you involved in all of that. How did you get this? And why?" He held up the CD again.

"It's a long story."

"I think you owe me at least that."

"Uh." The word lingered with a sigh. "I was planning on doing the job myself."

Tim dropped his head. "Okay. I guess that makes sense. But why would you take this?" His eyes shot open. "Fuck, Val, don't tell me..."

"It's not what you think."

"I don't even know what to think right now."

"I'm not the Executioner, if that's what you think." I put my hand on his knee.

"Then how would you know this was such an important thing to take?"

"It's not my secret to share."

"Wait... so you know who the Executioner is?" He squinted his eyes. "All this time you've known and you couldn't tell me?"

"It's complicated." I felt like I was betraying Tim by holding onto the secret, but if I released it, I would be betraying Norma. "Seems like we've both been keeping secrets from each other."

"You know who it is and you didn't tell me?" Tim's eyes filled with tears again. "Are you cheating on me?"

"No, it's not like that. Not at all."

"Why else would you keep something like that from me? You know how much this case has been driving me crazy. You've watched it eat away at my sanity and you couldn't even tell me?" He pushed my hand off of him and stood up. "I don't understand." He paced the floor in front of me.

The sting of his disappointment wrapped around my heart. I didn't want to lose him. "If I tell you all that I know, will you promise to keep it between us?"

He wrung his hands as he continued to pace. "Fuck." His hands went to his head and he returned to the bed. "There's no way in Hell I'm protecting your lover."

"Tim, you know me better than that."

He pushed out a fake laugh. "Do I?"

"Promise me? This stays between us."

"Okay." He turned to look at me.

I reached my hand out for him to take. He refused the offer. "Do you remember the man you found dead? The one with his pants off? You said it looked like he died of natural causes?"

"What does this have to do with anything?"

"I have to start at the beginning to get to the end. Donald Brice, do you remember him?"

"Yeah, I guess."

"He raped Sonya when she was a little girl. He was an awful man. He was the first one."

"First one?"

"That I murdered."

Tim's eyes widened.

"After Sonya shared her story, I couldn't stop thinking about what he did to her. I searched for him online and when I couldn't find him, I found him through the medical records at the hospital. I didn't go with the intention to kill him, at least not right away, but I was so angry. He hit on me, and I saw all the pictures of the little girls on the wall, something inside me snapped. I killed him."

"How? The medical examiner said he had a heart attack."

"All those *Snapped* episodes came in handy." I picked at the bedspread. "I gave him an overdose of insulin."

"Holy shit. That was a while ago."

"It was. Please don't stop loving me." I closed my eyes tight to keep the emotions from spilling out.

"This is why you were so hung up on sticking up for the vigilante killings." He ran his hand through his hair.

"Partly. Also because I know what it's like to be on the other side of things. I know what it's like to be their victim." I cleared my throat. "Remember how I told you Jane came by the hospital and told me she murdered Carmen? And you said there was nothing you could do?"

"Oh my God, Val."

"I killed her, too. I bought some of her pills from Seth and crushed them up and put them in her orange juice and I left her to die, alone."

"You bought drugs from Seth? Jesus." He hung his head.

"Yes, but I didn't kill him. I tried, but someone, the Executioner beat me to it. I walked into his apartment and found him. He came by the hospital and pulled a gun on me. He told me he was going to turn me in."

"Jesus, Val. You should have told me."

"How? Oh, hey, Tim, the drug dealer I bought the pills I used to murder Jane with threatened to kill me if I didn't pay him $10,000. Yeah, that would have went over well." I looked up at the ceiling. "That wasn't the reason I was going to kill him, though. Maggie told us in group that Lexi had hooked up with him. He was almost twice her age. I couldn't sit back and watch the same thing that happened to Carmen happen to her."

"You could have been killed." Tim finally reached over for my hand.

The warmth of his skin next to mine gave me the strength to continue. "So, let's see. The next guy I went to kill was Jimmy. He was threatening to hurt Sonya. It was right after she told us she was pregnant. I couldn't stand the thought of anything happening to her or her baby. I had to take action. Jimmy and I had planned on meeting at the park by the river, but he never showed up. The Executioner beat me to it again."

"Why did you keep planning to kill people, when you knew the Executioner was going to do the job?" Tim asked.

"The thing was, I didn't know. I didn't know who it was or how they were finding out about all of these guys. Not until..." My hand went to my neck as I remembered the night at Earl's.

"Not until when?"

"Not until I went to Earl's. Lily shared her story with us while he was in jail. When he got out, he got to her again. He had really messed her up. She didn't want to go to the police, and I encouraged her not to. I knew if you guys heard about what happened, he would have went back to jail."

Tim arched his eyebrow. "Ah, if he was in jail you couldn't have killed him."

"Bingo. At this point I thought I had figured out who the Executioner was. I was almost positive it was Andrew."

"Sonya's boyfriend?"

"Yeah. It made the most sense to me. After Seth and Jimmy were both murdered, I figured it had to have been someone who knew our stories. Someone who was close to our group. I couldn't figure out why he would have killed the other guys. I just assumed it was because he was trying to get rid of all the child molesters after hearing about Sonya's past. I didn't think he was going to take care of Earl, and I didn't think I had time to wait and see. I knew Earl was going to kill Lily if I didn't kill him first." I closed my eyes and took a deep breath before continuing. "When I got to Earl's place, he was still alive. I got cocky and didn't take into consideration how dangerous he was. My plan to inject him with insulin backfired. He came after me. He would have killed me if it wasn't for the Executioner."

"Holy shit, Val." He squeezed my hand.

"He had his hands around my neck and he pushed so hard I couldn't breathe. Everything went black and I saw the light. As I walked toward it, I heard someone tell me it wasn't my time yet. And, that's when I looked down and saw someone had shot him. He was on the floor by my feet when I came back. And that's when I figured out who the Executioner was. And what the trademark was."

"The Executioner saved your life?"

I felt a smile spread across my face. "And that's why I don't want to tell you who it is. I don't want to be the reason they go to jail."

"Val, I promise I won't share anything you've told me. This is between us. I could lose my job... hell, I'll go to jail if anyone knew what I did to Chad."

"I know. I can't lose you, too."

"Who is it, Val? Who can I thank for saving your life?"

"Norma."

"Norma? Wait. Val, how can she go to jail?"

My shoulders fell as I was reminded of the reality. The real reality. "I guess, she can't. When I found the CD at Chad's, I was so excited to think she was still around, somehow. You know? I took it from the crime scene because I didn't want the Executioner connected to anymore of the people in our group. I figured someone would trace it back."

"Oh, Val. I'm sorry."

"I was really hoping it was her. I was hoping she had somehow figured out a way to beat the system again. I wanted to think she was still out there hanging under the radar riding the planet of scumbags."

"I still can't believe the Executioner was a little old lady. Where did she learn how to shoot like that?"

"She was in the Army." I left Norma's story at that. Nothing else mattered to this narrative. I wanted to keep as many of her secrets as private as I could. "So, that's all I have been hiding from you."

"That's a lot, Val. Holy shit." He rubbed his eyes. "My only secret was that I murdered Chad and tried to pin it on a little old lady." He threw his head back and laughed. "Holy shit."

"You're forgiven."

"So are you. I know why you kept that to yourself. I don't like that you didn't think you could trust me, but I get it. I think it's time for a career change."

"That sounds like a good idea. Marianne and I need you home with us." With all of my secrets out in the open, the weight of the guilt I had been carrying lifted off of me. We could start fresh and have a marriage free from deceit. "Thank you."

"For what?"

"For risking everything to protect me."

"You are worth more than anything to me. I would do it again in a heartbeat."

"Can we agree right now that we're both done with murdering?"

Tim laughed. "Deal." His index finger and thumb framed his chin. "That's why you haven't wanted to watch *Snapped* lately, isn't it?"

"Yeah, I guess it takes the fun out of it when you're the one who's snapped."

CHAPTER THIRTY-EIGHT

"I told Tim all of my secrets." The door had just closed behind me when I shared the news with Jennifer.

"You did? How did it go?" She sat in her usual seat at the same time I sat in mine.

"It went well. Amazingly, surprisingly well."

"And you're still married?" Jennifer smiled.

"Yeah. Crazy, huh?"

"How does it feel?"

"Like a million tons of pressure has been lifted off of my shoulders. And, he didn't leave me. He was a little upset, at first, but they were some doozies."

She raised her eyebrow. "Doozies?"

"Ha-ha, yeah. My gram used to say that. Some impressive ones. But doesn't doozy sound better?"

"I suppose it does." She pressed her pen cap into her chin as she smiled. "You seem to be doing well."

"I think I am. Maggie is safe in Texas with her new boyfriend. Sonya is doing great at being a mom to Unity. Lily is happy to be home with her mom in Florida. Gabe is in love, so I'll probably be a grandma soon. Marianne is due to arrive any day." I rested my hand on my baby bump. "And Tim and I are stronger than ever together. He told me his secrets, too. It feels so much better to have everything out in the open."

"That's so great to hear, Valerie. I'm proud of the work you've been doing."

"Thanks. I'm glad I found you when I did. I don't know if I could have made it without you."

"Oh, I'm sure you would have been fine. You did all of the work. I'm glad you felt it was helpful."

"There is one last thing I'd like to work on. Well, two actually." I twisted my wedding ring. "I'm finally ready to admit that Norma is dead." My eyes dropped. "I was trying really hard to make her death disappear. I was making all these scenarios up in my head where she was still alive. Creating these stories of how she could have faked her death. But none of them really made sense."

"It's hard to lose someone you love."

"It is. And Norma saved my life. She came into my life at just the right time and she gave me the courage to live. She was the one that pushed me into going to see my gram. She was like the mother I never had. I think I'm ready to let her go." I pushed the tears out of my eyes. "I'm grateful for every-thing she did for me, and everything she was to me. I'll never forget her. She taught me how to love again."

"That's beautiful, Valerie." Jennifer folded her hands in her lap.

"And the last thing is my mother. I want to get her out of

my head, like I did with Chad. I tried to do it on my own, but I think it will work better with your help."

"Okay, we can do that. Go ahead and get comfortable and close your eyes."

I closed my eyes and put my feet flat on the floor. I rested my hands on my thighs and took a couple deep breaths.

"When you're ready, try to find the first moment you can remember where your mother hurt you."

I pushed past the memory that came back to me the other day. I didn't want to go back to the pain. I wanted to reclaim my power. "I want to go back to my birth."

"Okay, do whatever feels right."

"I want to imagine Norma is my mother. I want to go back in time and hit the reset button."

"You're in control of this, Valerie. Go wherever it takes you."

"In my alternate reality, Norma is my mother. She protected me from all of the people who hurt me. I can see her standing over me and I'm under her cape. She is shielding me from all of the pain." I giggled. "She's like Wonder Woman. She's filling me with love and strength as she becomes smaller. She's leaving me with everything that I need. I can feel the warmth of her love fill my heart." I placed my hands on my chest and felt the tears fall. "I can see Norma cutting the cord that attached my mother to me and she's lighting it with a match." A smile spread across my face. "I see my mother floating away. She looks like a balloon that was released. She's going. Going. Gone. Everything she did to me is over. I'm safe now." I pushed the air out of my lungs and opened my eyes.

"How are you feeling?"

"Free. I feel like I said everything I needed to the last time I saw my mother. I don't want her in my life. I'm not sad that she didn't love me. Everything that she wasn't, Norma more than made up for. No one will ever hurt me again. And, I know no one will hurt my baby. We're free."

Jennifer put her hands to her heart. "I am so happy for you, Valerie. I wished I could have met Norma, she sounds like a very special woman."

"She was."

CHAPTER THIRTY-NINE

The contractions woke me up from a sound sleep. When I caught my breath, I rolled over and tapped Tim. "I think it's time."

"Hmm?" Tim rolled over.

"Tim, I think I need to get to the hospital."

He sat up and fumbled to turn on the lamp. "Now?"

I clenched my teeth as another contraction came on. I gripped the blanket and screamed.

Tim jumped out of bed and pulled a t-shirt over his head. He tripped as he tried to pull on his sock while he was standing.

"Call the doctor and ask her what we should do."

"We need to get to the hospital. We don't have time to talk on the phone."

"You need to tell her we're on the way." I stood up just as another contraction shot through me. I leaned over onto the bed to try to brace myself through the pain. I pushed Tim off of me when he came over to rub my back. "Get off of me." I screamed through gritted teeth. "Call the damn doctor."

Tim grabbed the phone and dropped it before he turned it on. When he picked it back up, he dialed the number and paced the bedroom until it was answered. "My wife's in labor. We have to get there. Tell the doctor." He hung up the phone and tossed it on the bed.

"You didn't tell them my name or her name. You have to call them back." Frustration consumed me as I reached for the phone. "Here, let me do it."

"No, I'll do it. Get ready and we can call on the way."

I pulled on a sweatshirt and handed Tim my overnight bag. When I got to the doorway, I had to brace myself in the doorframe as another surge of pain raced through my body. My scream scared Gabriel, who was now in the hall with the fur on his back standing up. "We have to hurry; I think I have to push."

"No, don't do that. Don't push. We'll get there as fast as we can." Tim put my bag over his shoulder and took my hand. He led me to the car.

"I don't think I can do this." The fear of what was about to happen outweighed the pain, at least in the moment.

"You can. You're going to do great. Why don't you try breathing?" Tim mimicked the breathing from the childbirth classes we took.

"I don't want to. It hurts too bad." I hovered over the seat as the pain kept coming, barely letting up.

Tim put the car in gear and stepped on the gas, peeling out of the driveway. "Buckle up."

"I can't." The tears masked by my screams.

"I'll try to be careful." Tim's foot was to the floor as we raced through the empty streets. Lawrenceville Regional Hospital didn't have a labor and delivery unit so we had to travel to the next town over. On a normal day, it was a thirty-minute drive. Tim was able to cut that time in half.

When we arrived at the hospital, he drove the car to the front door and flew out of the front seat. He rushed into the entrance and returned with a wheelchair. He opened my door and held his hand out for me to take. "Come on, I'll get you inside."

A nurse came outside and helped me get into the wheelchair and wheeled me into the building so Tim could park the car. When the elevator door opened, Tim came running through the hall. "Wait for me."

The nurse held it open with her arm as Tim joined us. "Phew. I think I'm out of shape." He was doubled over on his knees as he tried to catch his breath.

When the door opened, my doctor was waiting for us and led us to an open birthing room. "Someone's in a hurry." Dr. Cannon pulled a gown on over her gloves.

I threw my sweatshirt onto the floor as I got onto the hospital bed. A scream came out as another contraction hit. When she examined me, she told me I was already at nine cementers and I'd be ready to push soon. My legs trembled as they laid out in front of me. I tried to hold them closed, but the pain was too much. "I have to push, now." I grabbed onto the bars on the bed and bared down.

"Okay, Valerie. I want you to focus on your breathing and push when you feel another contraction coming on."

Tim was holding one of my legs and a nurse had the

other. I felt completely violated until the pain took over. "Ahhh." The scream came as I pushed. My head to my chest, pushing as hard as I could.

"Great job. Just a couple more." Dr. Cannon stood between my legs as a light lit the way for Marianne's arrival.

The room went black as I concentrated on my breathing. Everything disappeared as I pulled inside myself and focused on what I needed to do. The screams changed pitch as they went from mine to *hers*. Dr. Cannon placed my baby girl on my chest, and everything came back into focus. My body shook as my legs fell open. "I love you." My tears fell onto the tiny human laying on top of me.

"She's beautiful, Val." Tim's tears matched mine. And in that moment, everything was alright with the world. I loved Marianne more than I had ever loved anyone the second I felt her skin touch mine. Together we were a family. The longest wish I had ever wanted had come true. No one was taking my daughter from me. No one would hurt her. Ever.

CHAPTER FORTY

After Marianne and I were cleaned up and took a few ten-minute naps together, Tim called Gabe and Sonya to tell them the news. I didn't want to let Marianne go when the nurse came in to check her vitals. My arms already felt empty when she was missing from them.

A knock on the door made me jump and a flashback from Gabe's birth settled on my heart. When the door opened, it was Gabe. The memory fell to the floor. Nothing was going to steal him or her from me. We were a family. "Hey, sweetheart, come meet your baby sister." When the softness of my voice hit my ears, I knew I had this mom thing down. These were my babies and no matter how old they got; I would protect them.

"Hi Mom." The smile on his face told me he had his own news to share.

"Do you want to hold your sister?" Tim stood up and let

Gabe have his chair before handing the little bundle of pink to him.

"She's so tiny." He pulled back the corner of the blanket and smiled. "How are you doing?"

"I'm okay, just exhausted."

"I bet. That's a lot of work."

"She's worth it. And so were you." I adjusted the bed so I could get a better look at my two babies. "You know I would have kept you, right?"

"I know that. I'm not upset. I never was. I love you, and I'm so glad I have you in my life now." His smile grew. "I have something to tell you."

"I thought you might."

"You did? How?"

"I'm your mom, I know things." I smiled as I waited for him to continue.

Tim sat on the bed next to me and held my hand as we watched Gabe's excitement grow.

"Carmen and I are getting married."

"Oh my goodness. That was fast." I tried to paste the smile back on my face.

Gabe's attention went to Marianne as she napped in his arms. "And we're moving to California."

"California?" I couldn't fake the smile any longer.

"Yeah, Carmen wants to move back home, and I figured I could get a job out there."

"But California is across the country. Do your parents know yet?"

"Yeah, they're not too happy, but they told me I should

follow my heart. We can call and video chat, and I'm sure we'll be back to visit." Gabe's excitement for his future was stronger than the pain it caused me.

"I'm happy you found love, and I wish you nothing but a life full of happiness."

"Why don't we move, too?" Tim turned to see my reaction.

"To California?"

"Yeah, it's time for us to start over. I've been thinking about giving my notice. I think it would be fun to see another part of the country."

"What about your mom?"

"She can come with us, or we can buy her a ticket whenever she wants to visit. What do you think, Gabe?"

"I think that would be awesome. That way I can watch this little lady grow up, and she'll get to know who her big brother is."

Moving to the other side of the country sounded better and better the more I thought about it. Life changes, people come in and out at all the right times. There was something good on the horizon for us, I could feel it in my bones.

Sonya knocked on the door and slipped in while Gabe said goodbye before he headed to work. He handed her the baby and let her have his seat. "Oh Val, she's gorgeous. She's the perfect combination of you two."

"You think so?" I looked over at Tim and then back to Sonya.

"I do. She's one lucky little girl." Sonya rocked her in her arms. "What's her middle name?"

"Rose."

"So, Marianne is for your gram, where did you get Rose from?"

"Rose was a good friend of mine. She was one of the best people I had the privilege to meet."

"I love it. What a beautiful name." Sonya smiled, her love pouring onto Marianne. "Auntie Sonya loves you little girl. I can't wait for you to meet your cousin, Unity."

I didn't have the heart to tell her yet about the plan that had been set out this morning. It wasn't the time. Maggie had just left. I didn't want to break the news at such a happy time. As we all went our separate ways, I knew we'd always be family. There was nothing that could keep us apart.

Another knock on the door took us all by surprise. Sonya handed the baby back to me and kissed me on the forehead. "I've got to get home to Unity. I'm sure Andrew is pulling his hair out. I love you, Val." She blew a kiss to Marianne. "Love you, too, little lady."

When Sonya left, she let an older woman holding a basket in. "Hey, I got one of these when Unity was born." She pointed to the package as the woman walked past her. "See you all later, try to get some rest."

The woman set the basket on the table before she left the room. "Who is this from?"

"I don't know. It was just delivered to the front desk." She snuck a peek at Marianne before she left the room. "Aww, I just love babies." She smiled and slipped out of the door.

Tim carried the basket to the bed and took the plastic wrap off. A white teddy bear with a pink bow was the focus of the package. When he took the bear out there was an assortment of chocolate and tea. Tim held up a box of rose tea. "Look, for her middle name."

My heart flipped inside my chest as I cradled Marianne close to me. *It couldn't be.* "Is there a card or anything that says who this is from?"

Tim removed all of the items, placing them on the bed around us. "No, I can't find anything. It's a nice surprise."

"I'd say."

"Do you know who it could be from?" Tim squinted his eyes.

"No, I have no clue. Maggie? It must be from her. Sonya said she got the same basket."

When Tim went to the cafeteria to get some lunch, I called Maggie. "Did you get the pictures we sent you?"

"I did. She's precious. I can't wait to snuggle her."

"Did you send us a gift?"

"No, not yet. I have a package ready to mail. It's sitting in my car waiting for me to remember to stop at the post office. Why?"

"Someone sent us, and Sonya, the same gift basket. I thought it was you."

"When I had the girls, the hospital gave us some nice little gifts. Maybe it's from them?"

"Yeah, you're probably right. How is everything in Texas?"

"Jeffrey asked me to marry him." She squealed into the phone.

"Wow, Maggie, that's great. I'm so happy for you. I love you."

"I love you, too, Val. I can't wait to meet your little angel."

Life was happening before my eyes, and my heart was still searching for ghosts. I guess part of me wanted Norma to meet Marianne. She would have loved her. The lack of sleep was getting to me.

CHAPTER FORTY-ONE

Sitting in the rocking chair in Marianne's room, I picked up the white teddy bear off the floor and hugged it close while I rocked. As I rubbed its back a crinkling noise caught my attention. With the bear in my lap I felt around and listened to the rustling of something under the fabric. I held the bear up close to my eyes to look for what could be causing the sound and noticed a different color thread.

I tugged at the thread and watched a small hole form. I pulled at the opening until it was big enough to get my finger inside. I continued to pull it open. A piece of white paper folded into a square filled the exposed space. With the paper out of the bear, I opened it up. An address and a number were the only thing on the paper. My heart wanted me to recognize the handwriting, but I wasn't confident enough to let it be crushed if I were wrong.

I tiptoed out of Marianne's room and picked up my iPad. I entered the address and waited for the results to populate. Lawrenceville Storage Lockers. I had to sit down as I tried to process what was happening. *The key.* I set my iPad down and went to my desk. I pulled open the drawer and moved a few things around before I saw the small copper key.

I swallowed my heart as I picked up the once useless piece of metal. A list of lies started to play on a reel in my head that I was going to tell Tim. I pushed them all out of my mind. I promised Tim no more secrets, and I had to mean it. I had too much to lose if I gave in to the easy way.

I brought the iPad, the note and the key into the bedroom where Tim was taking a nap. I stood over him and pushed him until his eyes opened. "Get up. I need to talk to you."

"What's wrong?" Tim threw the covers off and jumped out of bed.

"I'm not sure. But we have to go for a ride."

Sleep still had a hold of him. "I don't understand. What's going on?" He rubbed his eyes and ran his hand through his hair.

"I found this in Marianne's bear, the one from the hospital." I handed him the note. "I looked it up and it's a storage locker." I held up the key. "And, I found this in Norma's room when Maggie was packing. I didn't know what it went to, but we need to go find out."

"Right now?"

"Yes. We need to go now. I can't wait another minute."

"What about the baby?"

"I'll go get her ready."

"We can't bring her with us."

"It will be okay. I don't think it's anything dangerous. But we need to go, now." My heart danced in my chest as I tried to imagine what we were going to find.

The storage unit was only a ten-minute drive from our house, but it felt twice as long to get there. The anticipation grew with every passing second. I jumped out of the car and raced to the locker number written on the note. I was looking for number four. Once I reached my destination, I looked back to see Tim holding Marianne's car seat. He stood behind me as I put the key into the lock and turned. The lock popped open. I pulled it the rest of the way off and tugged the door up. The sound of the metal gliding up the rollers echoed into the emptiness of the room.

The familiar sting of disappointment clouded my ability to see the plastic tote in the back of the unit. I hung my head as I went to pull the door back down. "What are you doing? Aren't you going to go see what's in there?"

"It's an empty room."

"No, look." Tim led me into the room and pointed to the tote. "Open it." He kept Marianne at the edge of the open door.

I pried off the cover. A black leather purse sat on top of a blanket that was wrapped around the rest of the contents of the tote. I picked up the purse and showed Tim before I unzipped it. I dropped it, the contents spilling on the floor. My mouth dropped with it.

"What is it?"

I got on my hands and knees and cleaned up the spill, stuffing it back into the bag. "It's my mom's."

"Your mom's purse?"

I nodded as I pulled off the blanket. A stack of one hundred-dollar bills rested under an envelope. "Holy shit."

"What is it, Val?"

"Come in, it's safe." I picked up the envelope and opened it. I pulled out the white sheet of paper. The handwriting matched the small square note that led us here. My hands shook as I read the letter to Tim.

Dear Valerie,

I promised you I wouldn't disappear without saying good-bye. Please understand that I had to move on. I love you with every beat of my heart. You are the daughter I always wished I had. Elaine does not deserve that title. She has been taken care of. It was for the best.

There are a lot of pieces I cannot share with you, but know that I am safe. I heard about Chad. I'm glad someone took care of him for us. Remember your promise to me that you will not put yourself in any more dangerous situations. Your baby girl needs you in her life, and I know you will be a great mom.

Thank you for loving me. It was the first time I let myself get close to anyone since I lost Sylvia. You changed my life. I never imagined I'd be able to get the life back I thought I lost so long ago.

Don't forget to drink the rose tea. Everyone needs a little extra love sometimes. With all of my heart. Until we meet again.

Love, Rose

P.S. The money is from Chad's life insurance policy. They wired it to Elaine's bank account. This belongs to you now.

"Wait. Who's Rose?"

I smiled as I folded the note and returned it to the envelope. "That's a story for another day." I winked and giggled. "Marianne got her middle name from a very special woman."

"Okay, I think I understand." He set the car seat on the ground and rocked it to keep Marianne asleep. "Wait... So, she killed your mom?"

"She must have." I turned my head to look at Tim when it hit me. "It was my mom's body in the car. Whoa. She's good." I smiled. "So, Norma really does get to become my mother. This is way better than I expected."

"Really? What were you expecting?"

"I honestly had no idea. I'm just so glad Norma's okay. I couldn't stand the thought that she burned up in her car." I laughed and slapped my hand on my leg. "It was my mother. She's the one who burned up. A fitting ending to an evil witch."

"I'm glad I'm not a detective anymore. I don't think I'd ever be able to wrap my head around any of this." Tim scratched his head. "Norma is one impressive lady."

"Yeah, she really is. Someone I aspire to be." I smirked. "Well, without the murder part of it."

"That's my girl."

And just like that, everything made sense. Norma was okay. And everyone who ever hurt any of Norma's girls was no longer a threat. She picked each and every one of them off until we were safe to roam the Earth without them hurting us, ever again. I hope she keeps her promise and continues to watch over us. Guess I'll have to watch the news to see where she ends up. The one thing I know for certain is there are plenty of other girls who could benefit from having Norma in their life. She is one of a kind.

"What do you want to do with this?" Tim held up the purse.

"Let's take it home and have a bonfire." Uncontrollable laughter echoed in the storage unit. "We can watch it burn, just like she did."

Tim shook his head as he put the cover back on the tote. "I don't know about you."

"What?" My laughter continued. "Can I let you in on a little secret?"

Tim whipped his head around to look at me. "I didn't think there were any more."

"Well, there really isn't. I was trying to find my mom. I left her a message offering her some of Gram's money. I was trying to trick her into meeting me. So I could kill her. She was the last one on my list."

"List?" Tim put his hands on his hips. "You had a hit list?"

"I guess you could call it that. Between you and Norma the items got crossed off rather quickly."

"No more names left on it?"

I shook my head. "Nope. I'm a changed woman." I looked down at my sleeping daughter. "I don't need revenge when I have love. Besides, everyone is already dead."

"Just as they should be. Don't mess with my ladies." Tim came over and wrapped me in a hug. "I love you, killer or no killer."

"Ditto." I squeezed him tight and inhaled the scent of his skin. Wrapped in his arms, I knew I'd always be safe. "Together we make a serial killer."

"What?" He took a step back to look at my face.

"Three murders get you the title. Donald, Jane, and Chad."

"That's not a title I want. How about one of those sweet couple's name? Timorie? Valothy?"

"Um, no. Don't ever refer to us as that. Ever. Just Tim and Val sound great together."

"I agree." He bent down to lift the tote. "What are you going to do with all of this?"

"I have an idea." I smiled as the plan formulated in my head.

CHAPTER FORTY-TWO

It was moving day. All of our belongings were crammed into a twenty-foot U-Haul truck. Gabe and Carmen had already been out there for three weeks. Tim and I found a house online and had Gabe check it out for us. We bought it with plans of starting our lives over. We vowed to leave everything behind us and start fresh. Our days would soon be spent at the beach, or taking Marianne for walks around San Diego. No more snow for us.

Gabe was also cat sitting his namesake. Since they flew out, we figured Gabriel would do better with the shorter trip and without his crying baby sister. We had over forty-six hours on the road ahead of us. There were just two stops we had to make before we left Vermont.

On the way out of Lawrenceville, Tim parked the truck in front of Sonya's place. I unbuckled Marianne and we got out of the U-Haul. Sonya was holding Unity, standing on her front porch. We swapped babies.

"I'm going to miss you so much, Val." Sonya kissed the top of Marianne's head.

"Me, too. This isn't goodbye, though, this is see you later." I squeezed Unity close. "There will be plenty of play dates in the future."

"I don't know what I'm going to do without you." Sonya pulled me into a hug, being careful not to hurt the babies.

"I'm just a plane ride away."

"Yeah, and three-thousand miles."

"We can video chat every day. It won't be that bad." I kissed Unity before we traded babies again. "I love you so much."

"I love you, too. Don't be a stranger."

At the truck, I handed Marianne to Tim and picked up the box off the floor. I ran back over to Sonya. "This is for you. Something to help you reach your dreams." I kissed her and scurried back to the U-Haul. I waved until they were out of sight.

"I hate this part." I pushed the tears off my cheek and gave Marianne my finger.

"I know, but you'll still get to see each other."

The next stop was in Stark County. I asked all of the women to meet me at Cheryl's office. Cheryl agreed to let us borrow her space as long as we were quick. Quick was all we had time for.

The girls from the trial and I hadn't talked much since the last meeting we had. Life was busy for us all, and with the monster out of the equation, many of us had found a way to start healing. Talking about our shared trauma wasn't one of them.

Tim parked the truck in front of the building. We were a few minutes early. It gave me time to bring the nine boxes into Cheryl's office before the others arrived. There were nine boxes wrapped in white paper, each with a red bow waiting for the ladies. I spread the gifts out on the table in the conference room. No name tags needed. They each held the same contents.

The women started to trickle in. I kept my eye on the clock, knowing we would have to get on the road as soon as possible. Emma, Tina, Tonya, Hattie, Beth, Alexa, Melissa, Liz, and Nicole stood around the table. "Thank you ladies for coming here today. I have something I'd like to give you. It's just a little something to help you reach your dreams." It was the same gift and speech I gave to Sonya. "Please, take it home before you open it, but know this is a token of my appreciation for all of your strength. I hope we can stay in contact. I'd love to chat on Facebook." I looked at the clock and saw Tim and Marianne had been waiting in the truck for me for fifteen minutes now. "You're all so brave. I'm honored to have met you."

I walked out the door before anyone could say anything to me. This wasn't a gift from me; not really. There was five hundred thousand dollars in the tote from Chad's life insurance policy. I split it up ten ways. Each woman received fifty-thousand dollars. I gave Sonya my share. Lily and Maggie received life insurance money, and I had my gram's inheritance. It felt like the right thing to do. I didn't want anything connected to Chad, and I didn't tell the ladies where it came from so the money wasn't tainted for them.

I got back in the U-Haul and we were ready to start our

journey. We didn't have a planned route, we were going to let the road lead us to our new life. We had all the time in the world. As the truck crossed the border, leaving Vermont, I blew out all of the air I was holding in my lungs. I had never lived anywhere else. The thought was exhilarating. Goodbye to the toxic memories. Goodbye to the snow. Goodbye.

I saw the sign welcoming us to New York. A twinge of excitement shot through me. "Hey, do you think we can make a detour?"

"Sure." Tim turned the radio up and started singing along to Free Fallin'.

I typed the address into the GPS for the cemetery where Sylvia was laid to rest. We were only twenty minutes from the destination. My heart started to race as I thought about having the chance to say 'hi' to the woman Norma loved. Something told me I *needed* to make this stop before we continued on our trip.

Tim pulled the truck up to the entrance of the cemetery where acres of gravestones covered the rolling hills. "Do you want me come with you?"

"No, it's okay. I think Marianne could use a bottle."

"Who are you going to see?"

"A friend of Norma's."

I hopped out of the truck and made my way to the walkway. I had no idea where I was going, there were so many stones. I closed my eyes as I stood under a tall oak tree and tried to picture where I needed to go. When I opened my eyes I let my feet lead me through the rows of stones. My eyes focused on the ground to make sure I didn't trip. When I looked up, Sylvia Duncan's stone was in front of me.

Chills ran down my spine. "Thanks, Sylvia." I laughed as I bent down to talk to her. "I just wanted to thank you for loving Norma. I mean Rose. You were very special to her, and that makes you special to me." I closed my eyes and placed my hand on the granite slab. "I'm so sorry your life was stolen from you."

"It's a shame, really." The familiar voice made my heart drop.

I stood up and saw *her*. "Norma?" I ran over and threw my arms around her. "Oh my God. Norma. How did you know I'd be here?"

Her arms tightened around me. "I didn't. I was just coming to see Sylvia." She winked.

"Something told me I needed to stop here. I'm so glad I listened."

"See, I told you it's important to trust your gut." She held my hands and looked at me. "You're beautiful, Val. Motherhood looks lovely on you."

"Thank you for the gift."

"Which one?" She smirked.

"All of them. I can't believe you killed *her*."

"She's not dead. You're looking at her."

"Ahh, so you're Elaine Ross?"

"So to speak." She pulled out a cell phone from her purse. "She's still taking calls."

"I can call you?" My hand covered my mouth.

"I think you have a few times." She giggled. "Can you leave the cuss words out of it next time?"

"You bet." I grabbed onto her one last time. "I'm so glad you were here. I love you so much." Unable to pry my arms off of her I kissed her cheek. "You're the best mother I ever had."

"I love you, too, Val. Now, don't you think you better get on your way? It's a long way to California."

"How'd you know?"

"Oh, honey, I'm still watching you."

ACKNOWLEDGMENTS

Many thanks to the people who helped Accountability come to life:

Victoria Cooper for the amazing cover. Her work can be found at Facebook.com/VictoriaCooperArt.

Proofreading by the Page: Samantha Wiley, Rachel Pugh, and Anne Dailey for editing and proofreading.

Jill Nichols, Debbie Russell, Michele Avery, and Caitlyn Page for beta reading.

To the victims of child abuse and domestic violence who become survivors; I believe you. You are stronger than you think. You are not alone. Never stop believing in yourself. You are worth so much more. Take time to love yourself first; you won't regret it.

A special thank you to you. If you have read this far, I want you to know how much I appreciate you. Valerie and the characters in the Scope of Practice trilogy are very close to my heart. Their stories are important and stories many of us have lived ourselves. The more we share, the stronger we become.

Your honest feedback is always appreciated and helps improve my craft. Reviews help other readers as much as they help me. Please consider leaving one.

http://www.amazon.com/review/create-review?&asin=B08FBKGPTJ

If you or someone you know is struggling, please know there is help.

Domestic Violence Hotline

www.thehotline.org

1-800-799-7233

National Suicide Prevention Lifeline

www.suicidepreventionlifeline.org

1-800-273-8255

Child Abuse Hotline

1-800-4-A-CHILD

National Alliance on Mental Illness (NAMI)

www.nami.org

1-800-950-NAMI (6264)

ABOUT THE AUTHOR

Jessica Aiken-Hall, author of her award-winning memoir, *The Monster That Ate My Mommy* lives in New Hampshire with her husband, three children, and three dogs. She is a survivor of child abuse and domestic violence and is a fierce advocate. Her mission is to help others share their story.

She has a master's degree in Mental Health Counseling, with over a decade of experience as a social worker. She is also a Reiki Master and focuses her attention on healing.

When she is not writing, she enjoys listening to Tom Petty, walking along the beach, looking at the moon, and watching murder shows.

To follow what she's doing next check out http://www.jessicaaikenhall.com.